Nelly's Version

By the same author

Fiction

Ghosts

The Seven Ages

Light

Waking

Nonfiction

Patriarchal Attitudes

NELLY'S VERSION

Eva Figes

PANTHEON · BOOKS · NEW · YORK

Library of Congress Cataloging-in-Publication Data
Figes, Eva.
Nelly's Version
I. Title.
PR6056.I46N45   1988   823′.914   88-42615
ISBN 0-679-72035-9 (pbk.)

Manufactured in the United States of America

TO THE MEMORY OF
FAITH LIND

FIRST NOTEBOOK

I

He watched my hand slide across the page as I signed a false name and address in the hotel register. I admired my own coolness: I had seen it done in so many films and now I was doing it myself. Really, it was quite easy. I watched myself standing at the foot of the stairs and admired my own poise, the way I stood there, relaxed and confident, quite unafraid of scrutinising eyes. The porter arrived to show me to my room and I followed him up the carpeted staircase, noting my own progress with approval: head erect, a dignified assurance, and no stumbling. I had obviously been used to far grander hotels than this all my life.

The elderly man in his uniform unlocked a door and stood aside for me to enter before placing the suitcase on the special stand provided. It was a double bedroom, quite spacious, looking out on to the back grounds of the building. I saw lawn and a fringe of high trees through the window. The porter was still standing in the middle of the floor, looking at me. I thought I detected a hint of approval in his ageing, rheumy eyes, in the slight smile that revealed a very false denture. I could hardly blame him, and signified as much by smiling graciously back and placing a tip in his palm. He confirmed the pleasure I felt in my own presence. When the poor old fellow thanked me I felt it was as much for my being there, like a breath of fresh air, a whiff of spring and beauty, as for the coin I had given him.

'When Mr Dean arrives I'll show him up, shall I?'

I stared at him as he stood in the doorway, still trying to ingratiate himself, with his shrinking framework of bone and a head of sparse grey hair. He had developed a permanent stoop, so that putting suitcases down no longer made any difference. What was the fellow talking about? Who on earth was Mr Dean? Lost momentarily, an actress who had forgotten her lines, I covered up my mistake in a manner worthy of a professional leading lady.

'Mr Dean?' I said slowly, thoughtfully, to gain time. Then I remembered. I had given the name Dean when I registered at the desk downstairs. I had also asked for a double room, adding that my husband would be joining me. I volunteered this information on the spur of the moment. My instinct, or the expression on the face of the man behind the desk, told me that my arrival, unaccompanied and without prior booking, ceased to be questionable the moment I ceased being just myself, by myself, and became a married woman in the looming protective shadow of a mythical husband who would shortly arrive to join her. I knew my instinct had been correct when I saw the question dissolve in the dark face of the manager and change to a polite smile. Now, looking into the face of the porter, who was waiting for an answer, I sincerely hoped that the laws of chance did not bring an unsuspecting Mr Dean to my bedroom door. It might prove awkward.

'Thank you,' I said. 'But—' it was the performance of my dreams, every line came pat '—I am not expecting Mr Dean for a day or two. I am expecting a telephone call.'

I was alone, with myself, a stranger. After the door closed behind him I felt an exhilaration, an excitement tinged with fright which in fact heightened the sensation. I felt my pulse thudding a little faster, a singing noise in my ears, and, like a young girl about to undergo her first rape, I could not believe I would be disappointed. For some reason I saw a small boy sitting alone on a railway platform with a packed bag at his feet, and recognised that feeling in the pit of his stomach as my own. But I laughed at the rails shining in distant sunlight, and the feeling dissolved. The hum in my eardrums had become a full orchestra of violins and I imagined myself executing a light-footed dance across the endless carpet. I sang part of a little song to myself, still standing there, though the words made no sense and I do not now remember them, and it occurred to me to marvel, even then, at the richness of imagery, whether recalled or purely imagined, with which my head was crammed. Whatever I was or might once have been, I certainly did not seem to be boring. In fact, I decided, it looked as though I would be good company.

When I took a good look round the room the seductive lilt of strings faded and died. I noticed that my feet had all this time been rooted to the spot, my legs, forgotten in the wild impulse of my imaginings, had never begun to move. Now a deep, uneasy sense of disappointment seeped into my happiness and soon washed it away. It was not so much that the room itself was unsatisfactory: light, clean and spacious, it appeared all that could reasonably be required of a hotel bedroom. No. My elation was extinguished like a guttering candle by the disturbing impression, a conviction I could not dispel, that in spite of everything, and against all reason, I had been in this room before.

I studied the texture of the blue curtains framing the window, the mottled porridge of the white wallpaper, and the pedestrian blue flowers scattered over the bedspread, without being able to find a definite clue. Had I been here before, and if so, had I been drawn back now for a particular reason, by a subconscious force beyond my control? It seemed such an ordinary room, but its very ordinariness, I realised, made it opaque. It gave no hint, told me nothing about itself, or the circumstances which might once have brought me here, or had forced me to come back now. If that were so. Or was it merely a replica of a hundred other bedrooms which I had occupied, or near enough in shape and lay-out to make me think so, to deceive me into thinking I was back where I had started? I could not be sure, but the suspicion dawned on me that escape might not be as easy as I had hoped.

Escape? This word, slipping into my head, gave me something else to think about. From what, or whom? Surely not from anything to do with this comfortable, innocuous room? The fitted carpet muffled my footfalls. I did not have to turn back the flowered bedspread to know how crisply laundered the white sheets would feel, that the mattress would be springy and that I would roll round the bed throughout the night, at sea in a bed too large for one person.

But how did I know all this? Why did I not need to open the drawers of the dressing-table to know that they would be lined with old newspapers, that the wardrobe would have a long mirror on the inside of the door with the key, and that coathangers would rattle on the rail if I confirmed my premonition? Why had I seen the lawn skirted by high trees when the window was hung with white netting through which only a vague blur was visible? I knew even before I walked across the floor and drew back the netting that I would look down on a lawn which had seen better days, patches of brown earth visible from above, that there would be puddles under the trees and shrubs that surrounded it, and that one tree would be much larger and older than the rest, with a thick trunk and heavy spreading branches.

The sky was grey, overcast. It would rain soon.

I let go of the net curtain and turned back into the room. It looked darker now, smaller, with gloom lurking under the furniture. Adequate certainly, for any reasonable purposes, and comfortable enough, but its potential had dwindled. I decided that the odds were against my having been here before. My mind was simply playing one of those tricks to which one would have to get accustomed.

My suitcase lay unopened on the stand near the door. I started to walk across the room, wondering whether it was locked, and if so, whether I had the key. It was then that I experienced another shock. Someone was in the room with me. I swung round sharply and said out loud: 'Who are you, how did you get in?' and found myself staring into a long mirror. She stared back at me, this middle-aged woman, standing near the foot of the double bed, with the wardrobe behind her. Neither of us moved. She looked as startled as I felt, just as aghast. The porter must have made a mistake and put me in the wrong room. I turned round to apologise and the room was empty. The figment of my imagination, this visual error, had vanished as suddenly as it had appeared. I was worried now, still trembling with delayed shock, because this was going a little too far. I was happy to live with an aberrant mind, within limits, but if I was going to start seeing things . . . Unless I believed in ghosts. Did I believe in ghosts? It had certainly behaved like one. I hoped I was not going to be a superstitious type, or clairvoyant, that would be even worse.

This was too much, I thought. I would have to take a firm grip on myself, and start testing these premonitions and apparitions if my mind continued to behave in this curious fashion. I strode purposefully across the room to the wardrobe (I did not, it seemed, lack courage!) and pulled back the door to see whether the interior matched what I had chosen to label a premonition. I heard hangers rattle slightly, but with a hollow sound. And then I saw her again, only very close this time, her eyes just a few inches from mine, so that I could not escape: her accusing stare held mine and dared me to turn my back on her, allow her to vanish into thin air once more.

I released my grip of the wardrobe door and it swung back, taking the image with it. I saw it full length now, the figure as it swung back like an object that had nothing to do with me, no hold on me. But it was obvious that I would have to exercise a firm grip on her. However much I might dislike this appalling, this awful old woman, however distasteful I found her, it was becoming clear that I was not going to get rid of her so easily, if ever. I was stuck with her.

We sized each other up and I had to hand it to her: she was through with evasions, the disappearing trick, and now met my appraising look unwaveringly. She had courage, but then you needed it at her age. When you got to look like that. Because it was possible to make out from the remnants that this had once been an attractive face, more than average, with regular features now partially obscured by skin and tissue which had lost its hold, had loosened and curdled like milk gone sour, then settled in new folds, a bit lumpy; the eyes, large, soft and appealing, still stared out unchanged from the tired skin that surrounded and held them trapped in a web of fine lines, asking for help. But if one took a pace backward they took on a challenging look which defied pity; and with reason, because from a slight distance the general effect was not nearly so good. In fact it was off-putting. Hair streaked with grey, more than a hint of double chin, a lined and sagging neck, and a thickened waistline. The legs, though still fairly shapely, had small patches of blue veins visible through the texture of the nylon stockings; only the slim ankles remained untouched by time.

'Well,' I said out loud, looking at her with a wry expression, slightly askance, as one conspirator might have eyed another if they had not been properly briefed before bumping into each other: 'I wasn't expecting somebody like you. I won't say it hasn't been a shock, because it has. But now that I know, we'll have to get on as best we can – won't we? I'll have to put up with you, won't I? Somehow.'

She did not answer back. I suspected her of being one of those women who had quietly put up with many things without answering back, so that it had become a lifelong habit. Her face wore a resigned expression.

I shut the wardrobe door with a bang, which put paid to any retort she might have been getting ready to make. Slow too, I thought, a hesitant woman, without the art of the quick, bitchy reply. She could so easily have taken the wind out of my sails and put me in my place for good.

Now what? I thought. The skeleton was, for the moment, safely locked in the cupboard, and one could, if necessary, go back to act one, scene one. Bed on the right, exit door left, window to rear through which could be heard the odd birdcall, subdued lighting suggestive of clouds passing and imminent rain. Also dressing-table with mirror. Only that way danger lies, better to avoid it. A certain character who is unfit to be written into any scenario I would wish to take part in or even pay to watch on an idle, rainy Saturday afternoon is liable to make an unscripted entry there and spoil everything.

My eye caught sight of the large blue suitcase resting on the stand near the door, untouched as yet. I went over and tried the locks, which did not give. Then I remembered that I had come in carrying a black leather handbag, rather a conventional one, come to think of it, although the slight but distinctly unpleasant smell betrayed its quality: it was made of real animal skin. I opened this trophy and tipped the contents on to the bed: a wallet, smelling even more strongly of tanned hide, some loose change tucked into a lining pocket, a lipstick and a powder compact, one clean white handkerchief (no initial), and a small key. I examined the wallet and was reassured to find it full of high denomination banknotes (no need to avoid the hotel manager's eye, at least for a while), unscrewed the lipstick and tossed it into the wastepaper basket immediately because it was such a disgusting colour, and noted that the bag contained nothing remotely personal: no diary, no address book or photographs. This fact aroused no emotion in me other than a certain cool relief: I would not have to get involved in disposing of unwelcome evidence.

So I picked up the small key and tried it on the suitcase. It fitted, and I snapped open first one lock, then the other, and lifted the lid. I did it blithely, not knowing that I was in for my next shock.

The suitcase was full of money: bundles upon bundles of banknotes, neatly laid edge to edge, the wads fastened with gummed paper bands. Was it real, this stuff, or some sort of game in which I had become involved as fall-guy or accomplice? How much, if anything, was I supposed to know? Was this the work of some practical joker who liked playing out extravagant fantasies, who sent telegrams to remote acquaintances which read MEET ME HOTEL METROPOLE FOR RETURN MATCH LUDO STOP MARKET RISING STOP SHOULD FACILITATE

ENVISAGED MONOPOLY STOP HAVE ACQUIRED LICENCE TO PRINT MONEY? I picked up one of the bundles: the notes were in mint condition, which was suspicious, and yet the serial numbers followed on convincingly enough. I pulled the first note from under the band and held it against the light from the window, which admittedly was not much: even so the metal strip stood out clearly enough, and the watermark looked convincing. I picked another bundle from the suitcase and withdrew a random note from the middle of the pack, feeling that some invisible conjuror might have led me to choose the only genuine note in a mountain of forgeries, but it looked just as real as the first. Whereupon what was about to become the automatic response of delight was checked in mid-career and became far from pleasurable: I experienced an uncomfortable pumping sensation in the chest and head as it dawned on me that I might be into a very different kind of game, possibly criminal, but certainly dangerous.

A thriller perhaps, with secret assignations in a country hotel, where a woman can prove useful because she is less likely to look suspect: she can check into a hotel, having given a false name, and hang round for days; look unassuming, eat meals, go for little walks, come back, nobody questions her presence, particularly if she is apparently past her first youth, undesirable, the sort rendered unemployed by adult children or defunct relatives and now unemployable, nobody would give her a second glance. My mind went through this scenario very fast: it was both subtle and cunning, particularly the bit about the husband. Of course a member of the gang was liable to show up at any time to make the connection, disguised as Mr Dean, and pick up the loot at this pre-arranged place. In spite of my nervous agitation I had the presence of mind to walk over to the door and lock it before examining the contents of the suitcase more closely.

I began to pile the banknotes on the bedspread. There were four layers of bundled notes, and the bottom layer consisted mainly of used notes, crumpled and soiled, which I somehow found reassuring. Perhaps an inappropriate word, since by this time the situation in which I unexpectedly found myself had sunk in, and I found it necessary to sit down on the bed beside my treasure, feeling distinctly weak at the knees.

There were clothes and toilet articles under the money, but the wardrobe was minimal, and more suitable for a wet weekend than any sort of great adventure imaginable. No clothes which could be used for a magic transformation, and no disguises, unless they were it. A couple of skirts and blouses, a wool dress, some underwear. Whoever she was, she seemed intent on merging into the background, judging from the muted shades of grey and the ordinariness of cut and style. Like a discreet ghost. Only the cloth had a feel of quality about it. Still, there was money enough to scrap all this, change like a chameleon, once I had decided who I was, and what rôle I was supposed to be playing.

In the meantime I would have to make do with this wardrobe. All the garments fitted me very well, including a pair of sensible walking shoes and, being grey, everything seemed to match up with everything else, including the suit I was already wearing. In fact, I decided, the lower contents of the suitcase were just right for someone playing a waiting game, and anxious to remain unnoticed. Having tried the walking shoes for size I kept them on: they were comfortable, and it was obviously necessary to find out the lie of the land at the first opportunity. A walk after lunch was called for.

But first I had to decide what to do about the money. I put one bundle into my handbag, and the rest back into the empty suitcase, which I locked. I managed to stack the suitcase on its side behind the clothes at the back of the wardrobe, which I could also lock. I tucked both keys into my handbag, conscious that my security arrangements were both inadequate and amateurish, but it was all I could do for the moment. I had been taken by surprise. I also became aware, on considering my situation, that I did not know what or whom to fear: as a walking blank, a node of nothingness, I had to choose, for the time being, between a totality of fear, quaking at every shadow, and at least the pretence of a carefree confidence. I would have to be on my guard, obviously, but I came to the conclusion that I might just as well be bold and unafraid since, in my ignorance, I could not avoid taking chances. In that sense I had no choice anyhow.

2

The waitress asked for the number of my room and ushered me to a table near the elongated window. It overlooked a river, separated from the house by a small strip of lawn, the far side fringed by high trees. It all looked peaceful enough. I thought myself lucky to have a table near the window, because the dining room was not large. It was very quiet: nobody talked above a whisper, and the room was dominated by the sound of knives scraping the surface of plates. The room had perhaps not been designed for the discreet formality of separate tables draped with starched cloth, because a certain amount of drawing-in of personal possessions, such as elbows, handbags and bottoms, became necessary as I negotiated my way across the room, and once I almost dragged a tablecloth, complete with four place settings, across the room with me.

Already I felt conspicuous. My table had been set for one, and not only my chair, but an elaborate array of cutlery and glasses, dictated my sitting position in relation to the rest of the room. Had I been a frog or some such weird creature with independently swivelling eyes I could have admired the river scene with one and my fellow humans or frogs with the other. But as it was, I was forced to make an obvious and awkward choice which would eventually become so uncomfortable that I would be reduced to staring straight ahead: an uninviting prospect, consisting only of the opposite wall hung with an ugly mirror framed in wrought iron and flanked by a side-table furnished with sauce bottles and spare cruet sets, and one unoccupied table between me and it.

My situation was, to say the least, uncomfortable. I began by scrutinising the menu, but once I had ordered I felt exposed, particularly on my right flank. I studied my finger nails (cut short and unvarnished), consulted my watch (a gold one of conventional design which I suspected, rightly as it turned out, of being quite tiresomely accurate) and from time to time glanced out at the riverscape beyond the pane as though it were a famous painting with which I had long been familiar: I was doing no more than making sure that it matched up to my memory of it, that the surface had not cracked, that it had not been stolen. Meanwhile I pressed my knees and ankles together and hoped that the bottom half of my body was totally concealed by the draped ends of the table-cloth. I must, I thought, bring in a newspaper or, better still, a book, to appear to give me some sense of purpose, if I go on having to dine alone. Instinct, or some remnant of a previous existence, told me that being an unaccompanied woman in a public place is no joke: it has to be explained. In the absence of more convincing cover I read the menu several times over, as though I might have made a mistake in my choice, and perhaps missed total gratification, which depended on cracking the code, finding the one correct permutation of courses. I frowned till the waitress brought my soup.

Lukewarm, it tasted familiar, like a formula purveyed to a thousand households in as many packages. The sun had come out momentarily and glinted through the grey clouds, the pane of glass. It warmed my left cheek and lit up the water in my carafe, showing up air bubbles and smudges. A waiter leaned solicitously over me and asked if I would like to see the wine list. I said I would. I was not in the mood for alcohol but something told me that an affirmative response was in this case the correct one; it would give me a certain authority. And it would at least pass the time and give me something to do. In the interim I poured myself a glass of water and saw how liquid trapped in light trembled uncertainly, first on the ceiling overhead, then darted across to the opposite wall.

The roast beef was tough, the roast potatoes leathery, and

the peas had been through what is called processing, a mysterious transubstantiation which, no doubt as a result of one small victory in man's endless fight against nature, leaves them, both in taste and appearance, as close to being man-made and artificial as damn it. But the wine was nice, it glowed ruby red in my glass where the sun (still out) caught it, and was impressive both in name and price. I rolled the name on my tongue and tried to catch the precise flavour of its impeccable pedigree on my taste buds, but although I quite enjoyed it, any subtler bouquet it might have had escaped me. If the price of a discriminating palate is always to spit the stuff out I would anyhow prefer to let it go; besides, they do not provide spittoons in high-class dining rooms.

I swallowed a whole glass and thought that perhaps I could pose as an advanced postdoctoral student of something or other, pass the time scribbling complicated equations on my napkin, now and then pausing to frown thoughtfully out of the window. Or I could calculate the movement of light by studying the fairy bobbing up and down on the opposite wall as I nudged the water jug. Would this ultimately prove as constricting as the menu? Perhaps I should go in for abstract philosophy, and prop Kant up against the water jug during meals, as an ultimate defiance of pure reason? I quite liked this last idea.

The head waiter approached my table once more and asked, leaning forward, in a low tone so that we could not be overheard, if everything was satisfactory. I duly smiled back in a conspiratorial manner, and murmured: 'Yes. I think I shall be able to put in a favourable report at head office.' My joking tone and what I hoped was an amused twinkle in my eyes made him, if anything, more serious than before. He became deferential, almost cringing, and I knew that I would no longer have to worry about putting on an act as far as he was concerned. 'We have,' he whispered in my ear, 'some rather special Stilton at the moment. If madam would care to try it.' Madam indicated that she would.

Outside the brief sunshine had been obscured by dark clouds

which threatened rain. The trees on the far bank of the river began to writhe in a sudden gust of wind. The light in the water had died, and with it the dancing, trembling reflection on the wall opposite. It was a rather dreary wall. In the ugly mirror I could see an old lady taking her place at a table for one. She moved slowly and to good effect, if anyone had been watching her, the epitome of all old ladies of stage and screen, with her frail gestures and old-fashioned clothes. Each movement had been carefully rehearsed and even now she was not too sure of herself. I could see that chairs and tables had become part of a daily obstacle course requiring a heroic endurance unknown to climbers scaling Everest, but totally unsung. One false movement, one slip could result in death. And, in spite of the old-fashioned clothes, the white hair, she was real: nobody came to help her.

And yet there was something theatrical about her, the way she paused before easing herself slowly into the chair, looking round the half-empty dining room on a cold and miserable day in – what was it, February perhaps? I did not know, but from the look of the trees outside the year had either died or not yet begun. I felt that she had also noticed me, though I did not turn round. I continued to watch her in the mirror, as though I was safer that way. I could pretend I was not in fact present, in the same room, merely watching a representation, a shadow play.

The waiter had by now arrived, too late to help her into her chair. He pushed ineffectually at the straight back, then decided to move the table forward instead.

'Not a very nice day,' she said. 'It's very cold.'

'Yes,' he agreed. 'It is cold.'

The waiter made as if to withdraw, politely. His hands still rested on the edge of the table, pressing the white cloth against the rim, he leaned forward as though their polite exchange on climate was all that mattered to him, had for the moment obliterated all other thoughts and considerations from his mind, but one foot had already begun to move slyly backward.

'I was hoping there would be a letter from my son today.

That is why I stayed in my room all morning. Or perhaps a telephone message.'

Her voice, perhaps because it was high and clear, carried across the room. But I sensed that her remarks might have been intended for a wider audience.

'I see.' The waiter's impatient foot dropped back into position, like that of a dancer who thought he had heard the music begin too soon.

'He promised to visit me soon. I hoped he could manage this weekend.'

'That would be nice.' The foot was once more poised to *chassé*, but was forced to concede defeat.

'But then he's very busy, you know. He has a very important job. Lots of responsibilities. It's very hard on him, sometimes I think he does too much, and I worry about him. That's why I think a weekend in the country would be so good for him.'

'I'm sure it would.' He had caught the waitress's eye on the far side of the room. She came over, holding her notepad poised.

'Would you like to order?'

'It's too bad of him not to let me know ... What?' She looked uncertainly from the stolid shape of the woman in black standing motionless beside her to the treacherous, smiling face of the waiter, as though she had been asked to leave without disturbing the other guests. Possibly to face discreet extermination of some sort. Her hands had already fluttered in mid-air like startled birds in a cornfield, but only for a moment. They were used to the sound of gunshots, and nestled back in her lap after only the briefest nervous sortie to her throat, the drinking glass, the side of her head.

'I'll have the usual,' she said, without consulting the menu.

I ordered coffee and finished my excellent cheese. A group of businessmen in uniform suits came through from the bar and the waiter went over to settle them at a table. I could hear the pleasantries, yes sir, indeed sir, very good sir, most of which they appeared to ignore in favour of each other's loud conversation, or rather, the waiter was part of the orchestration, background noise, a supporting rôle, but nevertheless vital if their own themes were to have any credence. They lounged in their lounge suits, took their time because he would wait, passed round cigarettes because he lit them, sat because he stood, and talked in loud voices about other things because they knew he could be counted upon to remain dutifully silent. Meanwhile I continued to watch the old woman through the mirror in the opposite wall from time to time. She sipped at her soup, raising the spoon with slow deliberation, superseded and ignored now that the rowdies at the nearby table had arrived, and apparently unaware of my observation. Her pale, watery grey-blue eyes were now fixed on the window, they had widened to take in the whole outside scene which was reflected in them: sad, wintry and cold.

3

In the afternoon I decided to take a walk, partly because there was nothing else to do, and also because I thought I should waste no time in trying to find out where I was geographically. This may sound a little pedantic, and I must admit I had not been particularly disturbed at not knowing where I was. At lunch, for instance, I did not feel an immediate necessity to discover the name, flow and origin of the river outside the window. I was simply surprised to see any river at all, flowing so peacefully between its banks. It would do, I thought, as well as any other river when a river might be required, for the purposes of drowning, boating, or strolling along the banks of, and as a background for a personal drama it was picturesque enough.

But this brings me back to the first reason I gave for going out for a walk: for the moment there was nothing else to do. As yet I had no notion why I was here, and until I received instructions of some kind, telling me what to do, I had not the least idea who I was meant to be, the purpose of my presence in this place, or the exact nature of the action I was supposed to take part in. I was waiting for a cue of some sort, anything which could be regarded as a clue. I lacked definition. Meanwhile, the scenario for life in a small country hotel is notoriously thin, at least in outline. The mood is gentle tedium. Walks were bound to be written into the script.

So I took a walk. Or rather, I decided to take a walk, which is not quite the same thing. It looked unpromising outside, since the grey clouds had perceptibly darkened, grown heavier.

It might start to rain at any moment; on the other hand it might hold off, as it had held off so far, in spite of the outlook. Nobody could say for certain. Because of this uncertainty I had already overheard a variety of opinions over the tinkle of coffee spoons in the lounge. The barometer in the hallway was, I gathered, pessimistic but unreliable, being old-fashioned. I went upstairs to visit the lavatory and assess what my wardrobe had to offer in the way of protection.

There was no umbrella, so I had to make do with an overcoat and headscarf. The absence of an umbrella seemed to me significant, though I could not decide just what the significance was. Perhaps the owner of the suitcase and its contents was not supposed to mind getting wet, or could not be bothered with appendages, or had been bound for a hot climate where it never rained. On the other hand the absent umbrella might have been merely forgotten, or already lost.

The overcoat was almost new, a loose-fitting garment which could be worn over almost anything without looking or feeling odd. The cloth looked and felt expensive, a discreet tweed which may have been shower-proofed, and there was nothing tatty about the lining, which looked almost seamless and felt silky to the touch. I put it on, and gave one or two satisfactory shrugs to enjoy its loosely comfortable fit. Then I put my hands into the two deep pockets.

They were not entirely empty. My fingers touched a thin slip of paper in the left pocket and immediately my blood was pulsating at a rapid and panicky pace. I had expected the usual void, but someone had slipped up. With a feeling of dread I slowly pulled out this unexpected evidence, and at first I hardly dared to glance at it. But I need not have worried: the oversight, if such it was, told me nothing that need disturb me. Merely that someone, somewhere, had on an unknown occasion travelled by public transport. It was a bus ticket, the ink so faint as to be illegible, the only clear markings some numbers which presumably signified fare stages, points of arrival and departure, boarding and alighting, in a code only comprehensible to the bus company.

Nevertheless I took the precaution of screwing it up and throwing it in the wastepaper basket. Then I picked it out again and tore it into tiny shreds. Outside the window the clouds were moving fast now, a swift invasion of uniform grey. The garden below looked deserted and slightly bedraggled, as though it acknowledged defeat. Undaunted, I stepped out of the bedroom, not forgetting to lock the door behind me.

I had already seen the bridge through the dining room window. As it took motor traffic and not merely strollers or pedestrians I decided to take it seriously. It must lead somewhere, constitute a road as well as a bridge. I walked as far as the middle of the bridge and paused to reconnoitre, leaning my elbows on the iron railing. Below me the black water ran fast, disappearing under my feet. Its liquid speed matched the scudding race of the sky above, and one could grow dizzy by looking down and up. But one could also look sideways, and to my left I could see the place from which I had just walked. It was an old inn, conveniently lettered 'The Black Swan' across its whitewashed frontage, since I had no recollection of my arrival, or any events prior to standing at the reception desk inside to register the first (and only) name that came into my head. It gave me a certain comfort, the old inn with its small porch leading on to the strip of neatly cropped lawn along the river's edge: it not only did not move, but it appeared to have been there for some considerable time, at least a couple of centuries. It was not an elegant building, had no pretensions, a once humble inn which had expanded so slowly over the decades that the addition of a new outhouse in one century, and a small annexe in the hundred years that followed, had passed almost unnoticed.

Had I walked through that porch only a few hours ago? I could not trace the faintest recollection of the event in my mind, although I remembered coming out a few minutes ago clearly enough. I had been worried in case the desk clerk had noticed the fact that I had not handed in my key as I passed through the hall and considered it suspicious, when I suddenly found my exit blocked by a group of rowdy young men, one of whom bumped into me without apologising, since I apparently remained invisible to him even then. Their noisy good spirits gave way to loud expressions of disappointment when they found that they were too late: that the bar had closed a few minutes before. Their howls of disgruntled disgust in the hallway behind me sounded much like a pack of young dogs deprived of chase and quarry; then they began arguing about the time, found that none of their watches told the same time, and that one had stopped more than an hour ago.

Now I stood in the centre of the bridge and allowed my mind to wander off in musings of a rather philosophical kind. The river flowed under my feet. I did not know its name. But could it, anyhow, be right to name a river, which was liquid in continuous motion, and could not really be called the same river for two minutes together? I had doubts even about putting two minutes together, but I let that pass, as I was forced to let the water pass under my feet, watching the whirling pattern it made round the boulder below. The pattern repeated itself again and again, but it was different water, not the same at all. Could it be said that the woman who walked through that porch on the left bank some time before lunch this morning was the same woman who had come out just now? I knew nothing at all about her, and I could not put a name to her either, but perhaps that did not matter. Any name would do, and the signs which had traced her previous existence officially were as misleading and inadequate as the thin line wandering across an ordnance survey map was to describe this rush of black, turbulent water living and dying under my feet.

I found a certain consolation in these meditations, in spite of the traffic at my back which occasionally deafened me. They seemed to promise a new dimension, a potential which had nothing to do with the person who had hidden all that money in the wardrobe, a deeper, less frenetic excitement, and also something approaching inner peace. It may sound corny, but I could have stood on that bridge all day, watching the water

28

move under its own momentum, or being moved, trying to decide which it was; admiring the whorls of water round the boulder and the bridge supports. I forgot all about the walk I had intended to take, my exploratory survey to see how the land lay. It lay on water, that was enough, or rather, its folds had brought this mass of water together to flow under my feet at this point. The rest was rubbish. I kicked a used matchstick under the railing and watched it disappear.

As I say, I could have stood on that bridge all day, or what was left of it, still an abnormally long time. If I did not do so, I was not moved to proceed up the road by a sudden brisk sense of purpose, or a consciousness of the oddity of my behaviour, or of the precariousness of my hold on reality, or the potential danger of my situation insofar as I understood it. No. The heavens opened, and I was attacked by a sudden squall of rain so vicious in its fury that cold wet discomfort drove me back to the hotel in a hurry. I suppose I had a choice between going on and turning back, but I did not see it as such.

4

The shower did not in fact last long, although it was so heavy, and by the time I got to the porch of the hotel it was almost over. I sheltered there and watched the trees on the opposite bank writhing about, wondering where and when I had watched such trees before.

I stood in the porch because I was reluctant to go back into the hallway, where I might be seen by the desk clerk who, I felt, must by now regard me with a suspicious eye, or at least think my behaviour odd enough to store in his memory bank for future reference: as a woman who was inconsistent, apparently did not know whether she was coming or going. Who had not handed in her key. Troubled by these thoughts, as I watched water dripping from the porch gable, I began to wonder whether my foolish remark about head office over lunch had been passed on to the entire staff. It had been a foolhardy thing to say, since I did not even know if there was such a place, and in either event my impromptu joke could have unfortunate consequences. Would they bother to check the false entry in the register? If they did so, they would indubitably go on to search my room, using a pass key in my absence.

So when the rain finally stopped I sniffed the air and set forth again, this time at a cracking pace, a totally different woman, one of action and purpose, aware that she had no time to lose, certainly not for the melancholic musings whilst leaning against a parapet gazing into deep water, on which too much time had already been lost, to be made up for now.

The important thing was to get to the other side. All other considerations were irrelevant, though I did glance down just long enough to notice that the river, now swollen with the recent rain, was moving much faster now, and that its purpose appeared to be to wash away the bridge supports. I hurried on.

My first reaction on reaching the other side was one of disappointment. It had not been worth it. My motive for crossing the bridge in the first place was a distinct impression, unsupported by any concrete evidence, that the hub and centre of the town or village in which I found myself lay on the bank opposite to the one on which I found myself, and on which the hotel stood. This supposition arose, not from anything I could make out beyond the fringe of trees on the far side, but from the nondescript character and a curious sense of deadness on the side of the river from which I had started out.

However, the houses on the far side of the bridge looked equally nondescript, although there were a few small shops. Feeling somewhat exhausted already, I wondered why I had bothered to come, but then, that is not a question I am as yet able to answer. Had I deliberately chosen this dull little place, for reasons now lost to me, or was it an accidental stop-off on a route from nowhere to nowhere? I hoped that time would tell, but I could not be sure even of that: how would I know whether any drama that did unfold against this modest and somehow unlikely background was planned, and not a mere accident?

There seemed to be very few people about, though I did not know whether this was explicable in terms of the day of the week, which I did not know, or the total population, of which I was ignorant, or merely the unpredictable weather. Apart from one man unloading a delivery van outside a shop I saw nobody. The first shop I came to on my side of the road was a newsagent's and tobacconist, one of those all-purpose shops which provide an entire neighbourhood with everything from sweets to minor items of stationery. No district, I thought, standing outside, could function without it, and for the first time I had an inkling of recognition. On the pavement under the window full of dummy cigarette packets and dusty sweet jars a rusted metal plate advertising ice cream creaked in the wind. I forgot my situation and mentally began to count out small coins in a dusty pocket to discover whether I had enough. The apparition in the bedroom, the stash of banknotes locked in the wardrobe, even the biting-cold wind on my face might never have existed, compared to the promise of a vanilla cornet which might never be purchased, the lick of remembered ice round my mouth as it melted, and the crisp nibble of a diminishing cone.

I looked at the old metal sign rusting in the wind with its garish image, a device that looked about ready for the scrap heap, and wondered what it was about the interim that it could have failed so abysmally to match up to a trivial childhood experience; unlike the creaking sign, it had left nothing behind, no memory, no feeling.

I stood on the pavement and considered my next existential choice: whether to enter the shop. I would, of course, have to purchase something. But that was not important: anything would do, and I did not have to worry about paying for it. I stood in a state of indecision for some time, glancing at the ice cream sign, the dusty windows which had not been refurbished for some time, as though they offered some sort of threat. My indecision might have seemed odd, even absurd, to an outsider, but then most people have never experienced what it is like to function in a vacuum where one course of action might be just as meaningless or pregnant as any other, and where total freedom can become an intolerable weight pressing on one's shoulders. If I went into that shop, I thought, any number of things might happen. And the sense of familiarity made me uneasy: I wanted to fill the vacuum with elements of my own choice, not to be invaded by those which I preferred to forget. Even if I did not know what they were. Or because I did not know.

But in this world to do nothing is also not possible. While I stood on the pavement considering the possible consequences of entering the shop, the door suddenly opened with the ping of a distant bell. A woman of uncertain but fairly advanced years stood on the threshold, looking straight at me, holding the door ajar with one hand. She stared at me with hostile and suspicious eyes out of a plump puddingy face which had begun to lose its shape, to clot and run at the edges with the passage of time, as milk puddings are liable to do. Her skirt and sweater bulged like a sack stuffed with unmentionable things.

We stared at each other for what seemed a long moment. Her eyes did not waver. 'Can I help you?' she asked finally, but her voice did not sound helpful. It had a distinctly sharp edge.

'I doubt it,' I said. Cold wind blew in the space between us. I tucked my overcoat more closely round me, seeking comfort in its huddled warmth.

She waited on the doorstep for me to make a move, her face slowly going a mottled mauve with cold. Her suspicion suggested a total lack of recognition, which reassured me. I wondered whether I should offer to go in and buy something, whether she was merely lacking customers and had emerged out of boredom, having spied me through the window. I stepped forward, reducing the gap between us.

'You sell ices?' The words were hardly out of my mouth when I realised their absurdity. It was definitely the wrong time of year for ice cream.

She nodded, beginning to shiver slightly in the doorway. The hand holding the door ajar had gone deathly white at the tips, the flesh bluish; it shook, so that the cardboard which showed her to be in business swung on its cord behind the glass, still saying OPEN. She looked as though she might bang the door shut at any moment. I ventured to take another step forward.

'That sign,' I said, pointing to the rusting metal image still creaking in the wind. 'Has it been here a long time?'

She took a step backward. 'How should I know,' she snapped. 'I only work here.'

33

She slammed the door closed between us and faded into the dim interior. The OPEN sign swung even more energetically, negating itself, whilst I remained outside in a somewhat bewildered state of mind, considering the words *How should I know —I only work here* from all possible angles without being able to reach an understanding. I began to feel that I had lost touch, not only with places and events, but with human language also, since her last words had been flung down with all the assurance of a token that would be picked up and utilised. And yet I did not know what to do with it. *How should I know—I only work here.* The more I thought about it, the more obscure this message became. Was she too suffering from some form of selective amnesia peculiar to employment, or did the total statement signify something other than itself, so that one heard between the words, rather than the words themselves? This latter possibility, that whole groups of words could not be taken at face value, deeply disturbed me: if I had to find my bearings without even a common language to guide me, I was in a mess. I had managed quite well so far, I thought, but I now realised I had taken this common factor for granted, presumed that I was dealing with at least one known quantity in an algebraic puzzle bristling with unqualified symbols whose relationship to each other also remained unexplained. But if my knowledge of the ground rules was imperfect, if you needed access to special tables or slide rules to find the solution, how could I ever hope to find some answer to my problem? If I had to find my way round an alien country with an incomplete vocabulary, how could I know for certain that I was even on the right track, let alone pick up coded messages that really might be meant for me? It was not beyond the bounds of possibility that the words of the saleslady were of that order. It would explain the odd way she had come to the door to speak to me, an apparent stranger, and perhaps the fixity of her gaze.

Should I follow her into the shop? I stood on the pavement in something of a dilemma, now not in the least tempted to go inside that faded and rather shabby interior, with its dead flies lying wings down under the shelves of dummy cigarette packets, chewing gum and old comics. But I had already found out that it was not safe to loiter without intent, and the alternative was no more tempting: to go on walking down that bleak little High Street in the cold wind, looking – for what?

I decided to go inside the shop. I could always buy something.

The bell rang somewhere in the interior behind the shop, which was empty. The dark, old-fashioned fittings, the counter with its glass frontage, suggested that nothing had changed in half a century except the stock. The woman emerged from a door at the back behind the counter.

'Oh,' she said, 'it's you. What do you want?'

There were crumbs round the edge of her mouth, and judging from this and the sounds which had come from beyond the doorway she had been having afternoon tea and a snack. Perhaps the tone of hostility in her voice was due to my having interrupted her. But there was another possibility, which now occurred to me. *It's you* she had said as though stating a fact, an indisputable fact, and the alarming possibility now entered my head that she might know me, might have recognised me for whoever I was. Should I pretend she had made a mistake, and ignore the implications? Whatever she knew, it was more than I did, and this would put me at a distinct disadvantage.

One thing was certain: whether or not she had known me before, she disliked me. I had not been mistaken about the hostility in her voice, which was confirmed by the cold grey eyes which now met mine across the counter. I had to think of something fast. My eyes wandered round the stacked tins of tobacco, the displays of multi-coloured sweets and magazines, the children's comics which looked familiar, the crude printing with its air of antiquity fresh from the press, old blocks, old jokes on thin cheap paper with a frayed look at the edges.

'I'd like a notebook,' I said.

I had not thought about it before I said it. I simply knew that if I wanted anything in this shop it would have to be a notebook.

'What kind?' she asked, standing her ground, not moving. She seemed determined to be as unhelpful as possible, make me do all the running on my own.

35

'Oh,' I said vaguely. 'I don't mind. Anything.'

She produced a handful of very small pocket books in a variety of bindings. 'This is the cheapest,' she said, without attempting to hide the contempt in her voice. She held out a tiny book in stiffened red paper with the word MEMOS stamped in black across the front.

'No,' I said, 'that won't do. I want something much larger.'

'Larger,' she repeated.

'Yes,' I went on, 'one I could write in as much as I wanted. I don't know how much yet, but it's got to have a lot of blank pages.'

'A lot of blank pages,' she murmured to herself, ducking down behind the counter. Her head reappeared. 'Do you object to lines?' I shook my head. 'Then this is the best.' She got up and placed a thick pad with a wire spiral back on the counter. 'The advantage of these is that you can tear pages out if you make a mistake.'

'I see.' I flipped through the thick wad of empty pages, marked only with pale blue lines.

'In a school exercise book, if you tear a page out at the front you lose one at the back, and vice versa. Because of the way they are stapled. If you are more than halfway through you can't tear out and start again.' Amazingly, she giggled nervously. 'The teacher would be liable to notice missing pages. I think they take a delight in seeing your mistakes, what you have crossed out. And suppose the page that came away ruined the continuity, or was part of something you really thought good?'

'I see what you mean,' I said. And laid the palm of my hand lightly on the spiralled pad. 'I think this will do very nicely.'

She put the notebook in a paper bag for me. 'Anything else?'

I thought, then said: 'I suppose I ought to have a pen.'

She indicated a container of ballpoint pens on the counter. From a wide choice of shrill synthetic colours I picked out the only black one.

'You'd better try it,' she said, and pushed forward a scribbling pad. The top page was already half covered with a multiplicity of meaningless lines in various colours. I turned over a new leaf and signed a fictitious name while she watched my hand. It came easily enough.

'Fine,' I said. 'I'll take it.' And she dropped it into the bag beside the notebook.

I glanced round the shop with a sense of minor achievement, of having got somewhere. I also felt the tension between us had eased a good deal. 'Do you sell newspapers?' I asked curiously.

'Yes,' she said, 'but it's a bit late in the day. Most people buy their newspapers in the morning on their way to work. They've all gone by now.' She dived under the counter. 'You could have this one. It was reserved for Mrs Glossop but she won't be in now. I was going to throw it out. She's very old, often poorly. Could have died. In which case she won't be wanting it now.'

She laid the folded newspaper on the counter between us, and my eye caught the words DISASTER, FAILURE and CRASH. It was also apparently a Tuesday, though date, month and year were concealed on the other side of the fold.

'I don't think I'll bother,' I said, cautiously pushing the newspaper away from me. 'I was only asking in a general kind of way. In case I decide to stay.'

'You haven't been here for some time.' It was more a statement than a question. At least, that was how it sounded.

'No,' I said, watching her pale flat thumb with its larger and paler moon cover Tuesday and dispose of this day's record of human mishaps under the counter.

'Your memory's going,' she said. 'We've always sold news-papers.' Her tone was still brusque, but now had a hint of familiarity.

'You're right,' I said, and forced a little dry laugh, 'it is bad.' I looked round the shop: the children's colouring books on a shelf nearby, the revolving rack of picture postcards, the old re-frigerator, ice cream posters pasted to its sides, purring away in the far corner. I looked into the face of the woman standing opposite, watching me, and recognised a face which was be-ginning to fall apart, in spite of panic registered in the eyes, in the centre of the pupils, two small black points travelling backwards at the speed of light; the skin had lost its elasticity and could no

37

longer hold the curdling flesh in position. There was nothing the eyes, or those hands, could do about it. I stood there, looking back at her with a growing warmth. Until I realised that she was waiting for me to pay her.

Hastily I opened my handbag on the counter and took out my purse. She placed the change in my palm with the till still open, and again I noticed those pale half-moons. Her hands were very clean, the skin very white, an unnatural underground white, of roots and live things which never come above ground. There was something unused about her, in the face also, a baby softness in the sagging texture of her skin.

Our fingertips touched briefly as my hands closed over the change. I dropped it into the open purse. Our commerce seemed at an end. She banged the till drawer shut, but something made me inclined to linger. Out of nowhere I heard myself saying:

'Do you still sell pen nibs?'

She shook her head. 'Not for years now. There's no demand for them. The children all use the kind of thing you've just bought. Even bottles of ink have become an item for the specialist shop. We don't stock them.'

I realised that this woman had been lying to me when she declared *I only work here*. She was rooted in this dark place, had probably not once seen daylight. *Not for years now*, she had answered much too quickly. Its dust was engrained in her skin, not face powder, giving it that chalky look. And if her face looked unused it was for this reason, that all she could remember was the shame of crossing out in her exercise book, blots that the scratchy nib made, and the terror of telltale frayed edges if she tried to remove her guilt by ripping the page out.

But I bet, I thought, she knows to this day how many bushels make a peck, and the respective lengths of rods, poles and perches, even if she has never used any of them. If I asked her how many gills in a gallon she would tell me straight off. Some people's memories are made of this.

She had begun to drum her fingers on the counter, nervously, probably waiting for me to leave. I saw white marks on the dark wood where the stain had been worn away by her fingertips over the years. She was trapped behind the counter like a tamed animal that had forgotten how to run, fly, jump, fight, roll in the earth and breed. All she could now do was fidget in her cage and pretend it was an underground burrow, sleep, though uneasily, not only through the winter months but for years on end.

'You should have left years ago,' I said. 'What kept you? I presume this town has a railway station?'

She blinked and nodded. 'Turn left as you leave the shop, then first right.'

'There you are then—what kept you? Were you afraid of getting lost in another town, that you wouldn't be able to find your way around? It's always possible to buy a map, you know, or ask someone. But then you were always afraid of asking, weren't you? When your father wanted help in the shop it never occurred to you to object, did it? Or refuse and tell him to hire someone? In fact I don't suppose it even occurred to you that you had a choice, or that given an alternative you could have taken it, because you never consciously wanted anything. You gave in all along the line, didn't you? The good girl, afraid of blotting her copy book, irritating the teacher. You were always resigned, obedient, terrified of being noticed. And you mistook it all for duty.'

A pink flush had gradually risen up her neck and flooded her unaccustomed cheeks. Now it reached her startled, slightly protruding eyes.

'How dare you speak to me like that?' she whispered. 'Who do you think you are?'

She had got me there: I could not answer. After a pause she seemed to simmer down a little, and her tone changed to one of sly curiosity.

'Do I know you?' Getting no response, she went on to insist: 'I do know you, don't I?' She leaned across the counter and whispered confidentially: 'My father married again. After all I did for him. Less than six months after she died, and she took some nursing towards the end, I can tell you. I hardly got a night's sleep, and my nerves were all on edge. My health has

39

never been the same since. Of course I moved out. He didn't try to stop me, in fact I think he rather expected it. But I certainly wasn't going to stay under the same roof with her, not after all I'd had to put up with. Doreen emigrated to Australia. Trust her to do that. She was always good at getting out of things, even when we were at school. It was always me who ended up doing the shopping or the washing up. You remember Doreen, she was two years lower down the school, blonde, fairer than me, good at sport. Of course she had to go because of her husband's job—they were going out together even then. Mother encouraged her, let her go out as much as she wanted. She approved of her because she was going to get engaged. Bought her clothes, made a fuss of her. Most of the people I grew up with have moved away, and I don't see much of the rest. One grows apart, doesn't one? People have their own lives to lead.'

She had leaned further forward. Now her hand gripped my arm firmly just above the wrist. I could feel her breath on my face as she spoke. She had a slight tendency to spit at specific points in speech.

'But we mustn't think it has all been wasted, must we? We must remember the good times, mustn't we? And there were good times. I think about them a lot, in here, when there isn't much to do. And at nights. I go over them more and more, now that everybody's gone. I have so much time on my hands, you see.' Her face took on an entirely new shape as she smiled, hinting at unsuspected possibilities in the corners of eyes and mouth. 'Do you remember the annual Christmas dance, and the time we spent dressing for it? How self-conscious we were in our finery?'

'Somebody played a gramophone and all the boys lined up at one end of the hall, eyeing the girls at the other end of the hall—who laughed and giggled amongst themselves, pretending not to notice. As though they weren't waiting to be asked to dance.'

'Alice Blue Gown,' she said, and began to hum rather tunelessly, with a tremor at the back of her throat.

'And when one of them did take the initiative and walk across the dance floor,' I went on, 'he was usually ridiculous, spotty, with big feet. So that most of the girls would look the other way or turn to the wall, hoping to discourage him. On the other hand it was just as bad if the boy you fancied walked over and asked someone else. Not just as bad, worse—much, much worse. You, I think, suffered a hopeless crush on someone called—'

'Charles Wilson,' she said immediately, interrupting her waltz-time hum and opening her eyes which had closed dreamily as her body swayed slightly from side to side, and now looked at me in startled shock. 'How did you know that? I was so humiliated, but I was sure nobody knew about it.'

'It wasn't hard to guess,' I said lightly. 'It was the way your eyes followed him round the room. And the one time he actually did ask you to dance, you blushed a violent scarlet.'

Her face confirmed this, flushing a darker shade, but she modified this exhibition with a giggle. 'I was so nervous, I kept stepping on his feet and having to apologise. He never said a word, but I lived off that moment for weeks.'

'Years,' I said, 'even after he started going out with that other girl.'

'I thought he'd get over it,' she explained, 'she was such a silly, uninteresting girl. All she had was looks.'

'Rather like your sister,' I ventured.

'I never told her,' she answered hotly, defensively. 'I wouldn't want you to think that I ever held it against her. Or that I tried to make trouble between them. I'm not like that. Anyway by that time...' she trailed off, at a loss for an explanation.

'By that time you tried to pretend it had never happened,' I prompted, 'that you had never suffered on account of him, or had those feelings.'

She admitted it, but without apology. 'One has to find a way of living,' she said, 'as best one can.'

I tucked my purchases under one arm, slung the handbag over the other forearm. 'Well...' I said uncertainly, not quite knowing how to break away, glancing towards the street door with its sign, which from here read CLOSED. By this time I had had enough, and was longing to break away and breathe fresh air. The fact that I had no known objective was a bit of a hindrance.

'Must you go?' she asked anxiously, thus making it not simply a hindrance but an insuperable obstacle, a chasm without linking bridge. 'I haven't seen you for so long. To tell you the truth I didn't recognise you when I first saw you, though I thought I knew your face from somewhere. It struck a chord, if you know what I mean. I'm sorry if I was rude. Only you can't be too careful nowadays, people can be very odd. And to tell you the truth—' she had come out from behind the counter and gripped my forearm '—I thought you were a bit gone in the head when I first saw you standing out on the pavement.' The girlish giggle was back. She put her other hand to her mouth to stifle it.

I tried to draw back, out of her grasp, but she held on tight. 'You're mistaken,' I said, still trying to withdraw from her clutch.

'Of course,' she said, pulling me gently by degrees to the back of the shop. 'I know,' she said, still pulling, 'I realise now it must have been a very moving moment for you, coming back after all this time.'

'No,' I protested. 'I mean you're mistaken—I've never been here before. You don't know me.'

She laughed. 'Come come now. You can't fool me. No doubt you have your reasons for saying that—who hasn't? But like I said, I never forget a face. Come into the back of the shop and I'll show you.'

There was nothing for me to do but follow. The room behind the shop was comparatively dark, stacked with cardboard boxes almost to the ceiling, from which one light bulb dangled and feebly illuminated the room, its filament clearly visible through the pear-shaped glass. A teapot, cup and saucer, and a half-empty bottle of milk stood on a small deal table, beside a magazine open at a page illustrating a knitting pattern for

42

a woman's jacket. The model wearing the finished garment, made up in an ugly shade of forceful pink, smiled out of the picture with a sense of achievement, no doubt more than smug at having managed to decipher the printed code on the page opposite. There was some tea left in the cup, which had gone cold since my arrival, and turned a light shade of purple.

The woman, whose name I still did not know, had been bending down to pull out a cardboard box from the lowest shelf behind the table, exposing a couple of knobbly vertebrae at the back of her neck. Below the edge of her skirt her upper thighs were fat and fleshy, with blue veins visible at the back of her knees through the texture of her stockings. She put the box, covered in dust which came away on her fingers, on top of the open magazine, covering all but the smiling eyes of the artificial lady, and the matted top of her groomed head. When the lid was taken off even that was obscured.

Out of the box fell misty photographs of girls grouped against brick walls, or distant playing fields fringed with trees. They wore identical uniforms, gymslips, shirts and striped ties, and the identical milky smile on an unlined face.

'Don't you recognise yourself?' she asked, picking out one of the photographs.

'No,' I said.

'That one,' she went on, her half-mooned thumbnail pressed on another image, 'was taken on the last day of the summer term.' Several faces squinted into bright sunlight, in distortions somewhere between grins and grimaces. 'Most of us would not be coming back the following term.'

'What has all this to do with me?' I protested. 'Why do you keep all this trash?'

'It's important,' she answered without heat, riffling through the remaining photographs and spreading some of them out on the table before me. 'If you don't hold on to something, all these bits of the distant past ... Oh, I know they may not mean much to you, you've got other things on your mind—but it's different for me. If you don't keep a hold on these things, how do you know who you are?'

43

'I don't know,' I said, resigned and honest.

She sighed, leaning over the photograph she had pointed out to me. Her body warmth was uncomfortably close. 'Such a sad day,' she commented, 'and yet most of us were happy too. Sorry in a way, but excited. The way ahead looked so full of promise. Oh dear, I could cry even now when I think of it. Even more, now.'

'Don't,' I said, trying to remove myself from the proximity of her body, but now hopelessly trapped as she leaned over me. 'I don't think it would help—in fact I'm sure it wouldn't.' Her body exuded an odd, sweetish odour which seemed to come from her untouched, untapped bosom. Although it was not strictly speaking unpleasant, I found myself reluctant to inhale it. 'In fact I should throw it all out. Get rid of it, once and for all.' I started to shuffle all the photographs into a heap and, alarmed, she hastily put her hands on the pile, rescued them, and put them back in the cardboard box.

'I think you're cruel,' she said accusingly, with a plaintive edge to her voice. 'Maliciously and wantonly cruel. What's got into you? You didn't used to be like that. I still read one of the essays you wrote.' She bent down and picked up a small pile of faded school magazines, yellow, with a brown crest on the cover. She leafed through the top one and read out: 'The sky weeps for the death of a bird. The trees drip melancholy. God's tears run down my window pane. Tomorrow the sun will shine, making the drops of water sparkle like diamonds, each one a rainbow.'

'How utterly appalling,' I almost shouted, trying to push back my chair, extricate myself from the nearness of her embracing arms, from this whole ludicrous situation. 'I never heard such tripe. How could anyone have been so naïve, so foolish?'

She looked at me accusingly. 'You wrote it.'

I managed to get up from the chair, which toppled backwards on to the floor under the impetus of my jerky movement. 'I deny it. You've got me confused with someone else.'

'You always were a liar,' she said in a slow, hostile tone,

44

staring at me, clutching the thin magazine to her bosom like a threatened infant.

'If you say so,' I retorted coldly, backing towards the door. She made no move to stop me, just stood there watching me, with an accusing look in her eyes. I turned round and lurched forward as my heel caught in the frayed carpet, stumbled, nearly fell, but managed to regain my balance. I was almost at the outer door to the street when she called me back. I turned round and saw her framed in the doorway to her inner sanctum.

'You forgot your purchases,' she said, holding out the paper package.

I went back for the notepad and pen, avoiding her eyes. But I have failed to forget the hard accusing look in those slightly protruding eyes.

5

I stood outside the shop feeling bewildered and out of breath: for the moment I had forgotten where I was, and from which direction I had come. Even in my flustered state I was struck by the absurdity of the situation—one could not even walk down an unknown street in an unknown town without being molested, one's senses assaulted by undesired encounters. I felt like going back to the hotel, changing all my clothes, and making a fresh start on square one: in family games one is allowed a false start if one is a learner and has not played the game before. But this, I knew, was no cardboard game; I also realised that if I did go back to the hotel fear would induce me to confine my movements to the other side of the river, and who knows what unpleasant experiences would lie in wait for me there. It was even possible that my mad shopkeeper would close her premises on a Sunday and take a stroll on the other side of the river, thus finding me by chance or even design. The prospect was not encouraging.

There was only one thing for it: to pack my things, take a train, and get out.

I stood on the pavement, thinking all this, and then felt obliged to move, disturbed by the notion that my peculiar shopkeeper might still be watching me from behind the window. Conscious of the fact that above all else it was necessary to move purposefully, I moved too soon, to the right, withdrew the foot, thought, I had better make inquiries, turned left, dithered, what had she said: turn left and then right? I set out for the station.

Only to find out about services, timetables etcetera, I told myself. It would not take me long to go back to the hotel and collect my things afterwards. After I had decided which train to take, and how far to go. I began to cross the road, wondering whether I was not taking too much of a risk in not going back to the hotel first since, if the number of trains turned out to be limited, I might miss any number or, indeed, all my chances and choices by going back to the hotel later for my luggage. It was, I told myself, a risk I had to take: life was full of such risks, particularly for a person in my situation, particularly if one was in a hurry, as I was now. There was always tomorrow, but that already looked like a defeat. It had to be today. But my rushing stream of consciousness was abruptly stopped by a wild screech of brakes, followed by silence.

'Can't you look where you are going?' The man had opened his car door to make sure I heard him as he yelled at me, his face scarlet with rage.

'That's just what I was doing, unfortunately,' I said as mildly as I could. I was, fleetingly, quite concerned on his behalf: he looked as though he might give himself a heart attack at any moment, and I would not have liked to have felt myself the occasion, if not the cause, of such an eventuality.

The man slammed the car door and I saw his lips moving beyond the glass of his windscreen, though I could not hear the words. Apparently still angry, he stalled twice, jerked forward, almost banging his head against the front of the car, and finally drove off much too fast. A few moments later I heard an alarmed hooting of various horns and more brakes screeching. The sounds came from behind me, no doubt from the approach to the bridge, where I knew that the road narrowed. I did not turn round: the sounds were too noisy to indicate anything more serious than impatience and pent-up emotion. It could have been worse.

I came to a road junction, beyond which the main road formed a hump, like a cake beginning to rise in the oven. I surmised that this was where the road ran over the railway tracks and, looking to my right, I could indeed see the railway station. I stood poised at what appeared to be the dead centre of the town or village in which I found myself, with four imposing if ugly buildings placed at the four corners of the crossroads, four buildings somewhat larger in stature and heavier in construction than the modest frontages that the High Street had so far offered. Directly opposite me, and close enough to the railway station to catch unwary, no doubt weary travellers, stood a public house with 'The Railway Tavern' blazoned in gold across its flushed frontage which, unlike the others, was not built of grey stone but of deep red brick, now slightly subdued by old soot. But what it might have lacked in classy, structural dignity it made up for in sprawling size: on its convenient site, unhemmed in by immediate neighbours, it looked ready to swallow all comers in its scruffy portals.

The buildings on the remaining three corners stood in relation to the public house as three respectably established professional men might do to the local floosy or prostitute: publicly aloof, if no doubt aware. They might know of its existence, pay the occasional visit for a quick one, but one had only to look at their uniform frontages, the solid grey stone expensively trimmed and cut with a look of high-class finish, to know that they regarded themselves as superior and apart. On the other side of the road an estate agent and a bank stood opposite each other, looking for all the world as though they were in the habit of conferring almost daily on matters of mutual interest and concern. Judging by the expensively produced auction notices complete with photographs of desirable houses, to say nothing of the small and more discreet notices, the entire town was up for sale to the highest bidder. Always depending, of course, on the approving scrutiny of the bank opposite.

It came as something of a shock, when I took a longer look at the building immediately behind me, to find that it was not another bank, as I had first supposed, since it looked like its architectural twin and had certainly been put up during the same period, to find that it undertook, not investments, but FUNERALS & CREMATIONS, 24 HOUR SERVICE. Forms of reassurance bolstering up the four corners of the imagined earth. Blow your trumpets, angels, and arise, arise, you numberless infinities.

Where on earth, I thought, did that voice come from? Did it come from behind me, or did it stray into my head out of a black, dead past? I looked suspiciously at a salesman carrying a heavy suitcase who had just emerged from the station forecourt and was now walking towards me. Would he try to sell me something, or was he putting words into my head by remote control? Perhaps I was the victim of a brain operation which made me a walking receiver of curious messages, and I would take no conscious part in any mission, other than to wait, and be used, as it suited someone else's purpose?

He walked towards me and stopped, a slight smile on his lips. He had ginger freckles scattered under his eyes, and reddish hair which curled round his pink ears.

'Are you the angel of death?' I asked, because they were the first words that came into my head and I could say no other, even if it was not the code.

He looked at me oddly for a protracted moment, as though considering his answer, or me. 'No,' he said finally, 'I'm a brush salesman. Do I look so bad this morning? My stomach is playing me up again.'

'I'm sorry. I must have mistaken you for somebody else. Perhaps you should have stayed in bed.'

'Can't afford to. Got to keep on the move. Perhaps you could direct me to Maiden Lane?'

I shook my head. 'I'm sorry,' I answered slowly, and as I answered, listened to the words coming out of my mouth: 'I'm a stranger here myself.' The words sounded suspiciously like a formula, they rolled out of me like a string of beads. Perhaps this was the code after all. But he only said: 'Oh well, I expect I'll get there in the end. We all do, don't we?' And turned down the High Street, having invited me to laugh with him, briefly, before moving off.

Leaving me to my own devices. Any sense of assurance and freedom which had so far carried me through this first day had suddenly dissipated. I was on my own—but was I? I had thought of myself as a free agent, but how could I account for such oddities coming into my head, out of nothingness, so to speak? The idea that I might have been programmed had to be considered: it would certainly be one way of accounting for the large amount of ready money in the suitcase, for the lack of past, for my calm assurance in fact, given such odd circumstances. Perhaps I had not panicked or even worried because I did not need to, somebody else had planned it all, and was perhaps even now controlling my movements.

I stood at the corner facing the Railway Tavern with the station forecourt just visible to my right and found it difficult to remember why I had come this far. What I was doing here, or anywhere else, come to that. Then I remembered: I had come to find out about trains, about getting away from this area. I looked at the station frontage and saw for the first time that it had a name, though it was meaningless and recalled nothing. But I did not move at once, because I then had to consider whether someone had triggered me off to behave in just this way. I listened to my head but heard nothing, no voice, no words coming out of beyond. And then my eye caught sight of the stonemason's yard round the back of the undertaker's premises. I laughed out loud, because there stood the stone model of an angel, head bowed in pious sorrow. I must have noticed it before.

A small van and a couple of cars stood in the station forecourt, but there was no sign of life. The dark grey building looked as though it had seen better days, when railway travel still evoked excitement, as the modern way of going further and faster than anybody had ever done before. Now the brickwork was impregnated with decades of grime and soot, corners had been chipped off and the damage ignored until more dirt healed it over. The light above the entrance had a cracked glass shade.

There seemed to be nobody about inside the main booking hall, either, whom I could ask. The barrier to the platforms had been left unguarded, nor could I see anybody behind the small window of the ticket office. A railway timetable on one wall was almost illegible in the gloom, and anyhow I found the numerous columns of numbers and names impossible to decipher: I did not know at what point to start looking, or how to go on from there.

I walked through the barrier on to the platform, and found myself facing another platform with a roof like the one under which I was standing, supported by iron columns and struts. Between this and the opposite platform two lines of track stretched from left to right and right to left, depending on where you stood. To my left a footbridge allowed passengers wishing to go in the opposite direction (to whatever the first one was) to get to the other side after climbing high above the track. But uniformed personnel were allowed to cut straight across the track at ground level, I saw evidence of that right away. I also saw that the signal lights glowed red in both directions, to my left and to my right.

I sat down on a nearby bench and looked around me. The newspaper kiosk near the bottom steps of the footbridge had its rolled shutters down, while the door marked REFRESHMENTS was locked. A sudden gust of wind blew an empty cigarette packet past my feet: it made a hollow rattling sound on the hard concrete. I felt cold as the wind went through my clothes. To my right, at the far end of the platform which sloped off to join the track in a mess of nettles and other weeds, an old porter suddenly appeared with a hand trolley. He must have heard me approach, because he answered my presumed but unspoken question without bothering to look up. 'There's no train for another twenty minutes.'

'Oh,' I said somewhat at a loss, since he seemed intent on watching his trolley, which was empty anyhow. Then I added: 'What train is that?'

'The up train. The down train comes in twenty-eight minutes.'

I looked from left to right and from right to left, but the land looked equally flat in both directions.

'Where does it go ... the up train?' I asked, feeling some-what foolish, and more so when he answered, banging his hand trolley about in a dark doorway: 'Depends where you want to go, doesn't it? It'll take you anywhere, provided you know when to get off and change. It's all a matter of connections.'

He disappeared inside and I was made to feel that he had no further use for me. I was conscious of the fact that he had not once looked me in the face during our brief exchange. Now he kicked the door, which was marked PRIVATE, shut behind him with one booted foot.

I was left to myself again, to my own devices. The wind blew in another sudden gust, penetrating my clothes. I shivered, wondering whether it was an up or a down wind. To my right, beyond the weeds and stinging nettles, a line of poplars along the track writhed and twisted in the rushing air. The track curved slightly, but only very slightly, beyond the poplars and out of sight, flat tracks disappearing into the flat land. They merged into each other. Did the line vanish into a tunnel on the far horizon? I could not be sure. But the signal lights glowed red. I looked to my left but my vision was partially obscured by the footbridge, so I could only see metal track fixed to wooden sleepers.

I walked along the platform, past several bundles of old newspapers stacked along the wall, the shuttered kiosk with its magazines and road maps displayed in a side window, and climbed up the worn stone steps. The bridge itself was floored only with wooden planks, so that my footsteps thudded in a curiously hollow way in the enclosed space, making me aware of the empty air beneath my feet, and the drop on to an elec-trified track.

Platform two offered me a view of platform one, still un-peopled, with its door marked PRIVATE, the bench on which I had sat, and the closed refreshment room. Several large posters became noticeable at this distance, including a huge billboard promoting alcohol just above the weeds. I noticed that each roof was exactly the same height as the other and had the same fretwork border. Looking under the footbridge I now saw that my vision was still obscured by a bridge carrying the road a little further along the track. I could make out small bits of tree, oak perhaps, or elm, just beyond, but not much more. Was that dark patch the mouth of a tunnel? I could not be sure. Even if I had known, there was no knowing how long, how dark and deep it would have turned out to be, or what, if anything, might emerge on the far side.

The porter came out of the door marked PRIVATE and walked along the platform towards the exit. He whistled to himself, scuffing his boots along the concrete surface. He had bent, slightly bandy legs, and his back looked crooked too. Behind me an empty railway carriage stood on a siding, with a silent timber-merchant's yard beyond it. Platform two had a slot machine, a door marked WAITING ROOM, and different lavatories for men and women, or rather, LADIES and GENTS.

I decided to go into the waiting room, not so much to wait, but to consider my total situation. This was likely to take some time, and it was now very cold outside. It was certainly warmer inside, in fact the fug of warm air which hit me had begun to steam up the windows and this, together with the steady hiss of the heater now using up the remaining oxygen induced a soporific stupor only counteracted by the cold stone floor and the draught coming under the door. Where was I going, I asked myself, and why? Had I intended to go anywhere, and if not, why not? Was it a bad thing and if not, had I in fact arrived? Was it better to travel hopefully, and if so, would I be worse off? Should I be resigned to this, or would I have to blame myself for lack of something? While these thoughts were being inconclusively sifted through my mind the day was visibly ebbing into night outside, and darkness falling. Also the door had opened once, twice, letting in an icy blast, as passengers began to arrive for the expected train.

An elderly couple sat down on the bench opposite. Both broader than they were long, perhaps because of the layers of old worn clothes, they carried several carrier bags, one bulging fit to split, which they deposited round them with heavy sighs. Most of the time they just stared straight ahead, saying little or nothing. He fidgeted with his hands, backs flecked brown and joints distorted. She gave him little instructions, told him to mind the bags, where to put them. He did not answer, perhaps because his dentures fitted so badly. Besides, they were used to each other's tiresome little ways, like two pebbles grating against each other through half a century of ebb and flow.

A woman who had reproduced within the decade entered with her two young children, worrying at them like a snappish sheepdog. They were noisy and would not sit still. The old woman opposite turned her head to watch with mild curiosity, assessing their behaviour. Looking at the mother's heavy over-blown features, the crude make-up and the sullen expression, it was forgivable to wonder why and how she had ever reproduced at all. Watching her trying to keep the children under control one could see that she had her own (quite different) motives for harbouring the same thought. She slapped them when they tried to climb up on the bench, and slapped one of them harder when he screamed with rage at being stopped. The little girl began playing on the floor and got her hands wiped for picking up bits of rubbish and, on being scolded, began to whimper. Whereupon she was banged firmly on the bottom and told to shut her mouth.

I stood up to leave, having got nowhere by meditation, and carefully closed the waiting room door behind me to keep in what little warmth remained inside. I felt responsible for, or rather, protective towards the little group of people left inside, because they still had a long way to go and were not enviable. I walked back towards the footbridge: a few electric lights had been switched on and now burned a feeble yellow, darkening the evening sky further.

At the exit I had an altercation with the ticket collector, now back at his post, who, when I did not produce a valid ticket, told me that it was an offence to travel without one. I told him that I believed him, but that I had not been travelling. He looked first incredulous, then a false light dawned on his face: 'You've been seeing somebody off. Well,' he added indulgently, 'you should by rights have bought a platform ticket at that machine over there but...'

I suppose I should have left it at that and been thankful for small mercies, but a streak of obstinacy, of meticulous pedantry, made me say firmly: 'No, I have not been seeing anybody off. I simply came to the booking hall to make some enquiries, but there did not seem to be anyone about, so I wandered through.'

This riled him. 'Madam,' he said, 'there is a timetable over there, as you will observe. In addition there is always someone on duty at the ticket window. And this barrier is never left unattended. It would be strictly against regulations to do so. I'm afraid I must ask for your name and address.'

He produced a small notebook and a stub of pencil. I gave my false name easily enough and watched as his hand laboriously formed the letters on the dog-eared page, but the hand stopped moving when I gave the name of the hotel.

'I'm afraid we shall need your permanent address.'

I hesitated, conscious of walking into a possible quagmire. Then I said, in what I hoped was a tone of quiet authority: 'I have no other address at present.'

'I see. And how long have you been staying at the Black Swan?'

'Look here,' I said, getting annoyed. 'What is this? I booked in this morning, but I really don't see...'

'Travelling without a ticket is a very serious offence,' he interrupted firmly. 'If you have only been staying at the Swan since this morning I am afraid I must ask you for your previous address ... where you came from.'

I stared at him. He stared back. 'I'm afraid I can't tell you that,' I said with more truth than he realised. 'Look, if you'll only ask the porter, I spoke to him ... he'll remember me.'

'That won't be necessary. If you'll just sign here. Purely a formality, you understand.' He held out the notebook and watched as my hand signed the false name with his blunt pencil.

Several people had been waiting to get through the barrier during this exchange. They stared at me with cold curiosity as I moved out of their way, and I found myself, to my own shame, flushing a hot embarrassed red. I walked quickly through the booking hall and out into the forecourt. Behind me I could hear the train approaching.

6

I got back to the hotel feeling cold, tired and confused. My first venture into the unknown had not been encouraging: it seemed that I could not put a foot outside the door without putting it wrong. I could feel myself getting depressed, and tried to struggle against the rising tide before it engulfed me: I told myself that I would forget all about the stupid incident at the railway station, the dreadful waiting room, the fact that I had barely escaped getting knocked down and possibly killed by a passing car, all within the relatively short period of about an hour. When I thought back I recalled that my outing had begun with the weird woman in the shop, and that she had almost slipped my mind since. Which proves how pointless it is even to try to hold on to the immediate past, let alone brood about it.

My mood was not improved when I entered the hotel lobby and the desk clerk stopped me, not just with a 'Good evening', which I acknowledged, though I could not concur, but with the addendum, pronounced just as I reached the foot of the stairs: 'There's a gentleman waiting to see you.'

I was shocked into sudden immobility, one foot on the bottom step of the staircase leading to my room and the privacy I craved. But I knew I had to take this seriously, in spite of my wild, panicky urge to run up the flight of stairs to my room and lock myself in.

'Are you sure?' I asked, to gain time. And added foolishly:

'There must be some mistake.' I could hardly go on to voice what was going through my mind: how could anyone have asked for me by the false name I had adopted only hours before?

'I'm quite sure, madam,' he answered, staring at me as though I was behaving oddly, and I knew that the one person most likely to make mistakes now or in the next half-hour was myself. Could anybody who knew me have caught up with my whereabouts so quickly? Or was this some pre-arranged assignation? In either case I would have to play it blind.

'Did he give his name?' I asked, as though that could possibly help me.

'No, madam. But he is waiting in the bar. I told him you were out, but he said he would wait.'

I still stood hesitating, my outdoor clothes getting too warm in the hotel lobby, clutching my new notebook in its paper bag. My new-found freedom had palled quickly, perhaps now it was already over. I did not know what to do.

The desk clerk, seeing me still standing there, explained: 'I know you were expecting Mr Dean, but since he did not give his name I thought it better to ask him to wait in the public rooms, and did not divulge your room number.'

I nodded in appreciation of his discretion and considered whether, if there was a back staircase, I should make a quick exit with my suitcase.

'Anyhow, he seemed quite happy to wait in the bar.'

I dismissed the idea as impracticable, and wildly foolish. All I could do was procrastinate, since escape seemed out of the question.

'In that case I think I'll go up to my room, take off my things, and freshen up a bit. I'll be down directly.'

Once I had locked the door of my bedroom behind me I flopped down on the bed, handbag and package in my lap, and found myself beginning to shake. Where, I asked myself, was the heroine of the morning who had waited so hopefully for what she hoped would be her cue, for the scenario to start and the film to unroll? Now that things appeared to have started moving I found myself unprepared, I did not have a clue about my own rôle, how I could possibly handle the situation waiting for me downstairs, since I did not know what it would be. Had I been waiting for him, or had he succeeded in tracking me down? Were we allies, or had I been foolish enough to make a break for it and run away with a stack of money large enough to provoke retaliation? In either event, what kind of business had I, or we, been involved in? Was it legitimate? Did I look like a gangster's moll? I got up to have a look at myself in the dressing-table mirror, and could reach no conclusion, only that I looked a mess. I began to comb my wind-blown locks, dabbed some facepowder on my nose and cheeks to cover the blemishes, and returned, for a brief moment, the look of alarm in the startled eyes with their unnaturally dilated pupils, before getting up to confront whatever was coming to me.

I locked the bedroom door behind me and walked down the stairs with considerable poise and at least the semblance of calm. I could hear the sound of voices coming from the bar even before I entered it, since the smallish room, decorated in a sombre shade of dark red, was already beginning to fill up for the pre-dinner drinking hour. I hesitated in the doorway, hastily scanned the room but saw no one looking directly at me, and went over to the bar. I made a show of trying to catch the barman's eye, and whilst he was busy serving a group of noisy middle-aged men I manoeuvred one thigh on to a high bar stool which left me dangling uncomfortably with one foot off the ground. I committed my entire bottom to the false and slippery leather, and thus perched with no more hold on the floor, I allowed myself a surreptitious glance at the faces near me: engrossed faces, preoccupied or tired faces, all engulfed in fumes of one sort or another in the smoky atmosphere. Nobody took any notice of me. The men all appeared to be standing in groups, though one or two sat with their women in the far corner, and I reckoned I could count them out anyway.

The barman took my order and I had just begun to sip at the drink when a voice behind me, quite close to my ear, said

quietly: 'Mrs ... um ... Dean? Could I have a word with you?'
I almost choked on the pungent, bitter liquid: the way he had
spoken my assumed name made me feel as though somebody
had seen right through me; as though I had forgotten to put
pants on under my clothes, or something shameful was going
on down there, and this man knew all about it.

I took a large gulp of my drink before I turned round. The
man was standing uncomfortably close to me, his face on a
level with mine because of the high stool. I could feel my
cheeks flushing with what I hoped could not be mistaken for
anything but the effects of the alcohol, but I immediately
sensed that such physical manifestations were of no interest to
him. He would also be indifferent to the lure of possible charm.
His dark eyes were looking straight at me with an expression
which was unamused and devoid of complicity. I could make
nothing of it.

'Yes?' I said as lightly as I could. He stood there calmly
with both hands in the pockets of his loose raincoat. I felt sure,
but knew I could not be sure, that I did not know him; had
never seen him before. He had bushy black eyebrows, and a
fold of skin made a vertical furrow between them, above the
nose, which was average and unremarkable. What I did notice
was his complexion, which was coarse and pitted, with stubble
showing through like printer's shadow.

'Could we go somewhere more private, a bit quieter?' he
asked, glancing round at the increasingly noisy crush of customers now trying to push their way up to the bar.

'Why?' I asked, trying to sound cool and neutral.

He looked embarrassed, as though anxious not to be overheard, so I became more courageous. I also felt safe while we
were both in a crowd. I took a chance.

'I don't think I know you ... do I?'

'No,' he said mildly, to my surprise and relief, 'you don't.
I'm sorry, I should have introduced myself. Smith is the name
– Detective Inspector Smith.' I spilt some of the drink down
my skirt. 'Now you understand why I wanted to go somewhere
quiet, where we can't be overheard,' he added, without re-

proach. I nodded dumbly. Put down the emptied glass and slid off the stool.

My heart had begun to thud uncomfortably. Of course I was thinking of the money locked away in my room. He had come to get it, and to get me. Then it suddenly occurred to me that Smith sounded like an implausible pseudonym invented on the spur of the moment, anyone could call himself a police officer in plain clothes, and in an embarrassing public place like this he was likely to get away with it. It was a favourite ploy in numerous films where, the victim once got out of the public bar, he was driven off in a screeching car with several guns stuck into his ribs, or left for dead in a back alley.

I slid back on to the stool, leaned my elbows on the bar behind in what was supposed to be a nonchalant attitude but felt far from it, and decided to make a scene. Or rather, to act it out.

'Really,' I said in a loud voice which I hoped could be heard above the hubbub: 'How interesting. I've never met a detective inspector before. Do tell me, have you come to arrest me? What fun!' My theatrically frivolous voice appeared to have projected across a wide area with rather more success than I had anticipated. The hubbub of confused talk subsided audibly, and the bystanders turned into an audience.

This was awkward, because I had no idea how to go on. I swung one leg and raised both eyebrows to fill in the vacuum, thinking: one really needed a prepared script for this sort of thing. But my interlocutor had no such doubts. Without hesitation, and without once flinching under the gaze of those now watching us, he said steadily: 'This is no joking matter, madam.' I began to think it was not, and that I had been quite wrong. At any rate, he had obviously put in a lot more practice. 'I am here on a serious inquiry. We expect responsible members of the public to assist us, and when you hear the nature of the inquiry I am sure you would wish to do so.' To my added embarrassment he fished out official identification from an inner pocket and held it under my nose.

My face now a deeper shade of red, I pushed it away without looking at it properly. 'I'm sorry,' I mumbled, 'I thought it was some sort of practical joke.' And, in a slightly louder voice, hoping to save face: 'Of course I'll be only too glad to help.'

I slid off the stool a second time, without a hope, now, of doing it unobtrusively. An ungainly movement at best, for a woman of my years and clumsy build, not blessed with the legs of a giraffe. Now I twisted an ankle, and had to be stopped in mid-fall and assisted to the door.

'Are you all right?' my captor asked quite solicitously, as I lowered myself into an armchair in the television lounge, which we had found empty, and began to rub my ankle.

'I think so,' I answered lamely, conscious of the feeble resistance I had put up. He was still standing over me, watching me nurse my ankle. 'Do you have a warrant?' I asked, because I felt it was expected of me: not that I would have known one if I saw it.

'No, of course not.' He had sat down beside me and was now taking a notebook from an inner pocket of his raincoat. 'If I could just ask you...'

'So you haven't come to arrest me?'

He began to laugh, perhaps at my wide-eyed expression. 'I don't think that will be necessary,' he said in a relaxed tone. And added: 'In any case, I'm sure a nice respectable lady like yourself would come down to the station without giving any trouble.'

I was not sure whether I was supposed to take this last remark as a joke, or if it was a hint that I would do well to cooperate. In other words, a veiled threat. I looked into his face and saw that he was smiling at me, but in a curious way, as though humour came hard to him.

'I wouldn't be so sure, if I were you,' I said coquettishly, having decided to fend the whole thing off as a joke. Meanwhile the inspector was fidgeting with the spring of a ballpoint pen which he held poised above the blank page.

'I understand you arrived today?' I did not answer, allowing him to draw his own conclusion. Silence was non-committal, I felt. Whilst I was not denying anything. He started to doodle on the corner of the page: the ballpoint went round and round, like a snail's house. 'Did you come by train?'

'Why do you ask?' I said, and whilst I was saying the words I thought I already knew the answer. I remembered the absurd incident at the railway station and wanted to laugh with relief, then less with relief and more at the idiocy of this possible entanglement.

'No particular reason,' he said absently, still convoluting the shell, which had grown darker. 'I just wondered. You may have noticed something—or somebody—out of the ordinary. A detail which could prove an important lead.' He suddenly sat up straight and stopped doodling. 'I'll tell you why I'm here, Mrs Dean. A certain Miss Wyckham, who runs a newsagent's shop in the High Street, was brutally assaulted this afternoon. She is now in the local hospital with severe head injuries, but she was able to give us a statement. At the moment she is rather confused, you understand, and she has no recollection of her assailant. But she does remember your visit. I understand you are an old friend of hers, and that she had not seen you for many years. Which is probably why it is the only clear memory she has, just now, of the past few hours.'

I was bewildered before I was shocked. It took me a while to realise whom he was talking about, and that I did not interest him. I had totally miscalculated in my performance, got lost and ended up by overacting in somebody else's story.

I made sympathetic noises: 'How awful. How dreadful. I'm *so* sorry. You must have thought me ... Is she badly hurt?'

'I'm afraid so. She's at St Quentin's, Ward Five, when you go to visit her. But I should leave it for a day or two—she's in no fit state to see anybody at the moment.'

'You misunderstand me, Inspector. I hardly know her. She seemed to take it into her head that we were old friends ... or perhaps she took me for somebody else. I don't know. It was very odd. I went into the shop by pure chance, and to the best of my recollection I'd never seen her in my life before.'

The inspector looked me in the face without saying anything, his eyebrows just slightly lifted. I looked back at him: it was an exercise in sincerity. 'Frankly,' I said, trying to sound frank, and helpful, 'I don't see how I can help you.'

'The attack seems to have taken place very shortly after you left the shop. Probably within the next half hour. I want to know if you noticed anything in particular. Anybody. Not necessarily suspicious. Anything you can bring to mind.'

'I nearly got run over just afterwards, I do remember that. The man was very angry—but I think it was my fault.' I tried to remember the scene outside the shop and got snapshot fragments: a delivery van with the rear doors open, a stray dog sniffing in the doorway who jumped back nervously as I came hurriedly out. 'There was a young couple looking into a shop window opposite. I think it was an antique shop or something. They were holding hands, I noticed. And when I got to the corner opposite the public house a man asked me the way to Maiden Lane.'

'Could you describe him?'

'We had an odd conversation. Youngish. Fairish. With freckles. He said he was a brush salesman.'

'Odd.'

'What—being a brush salesman?'

'Could be. It's an outdated profession. And then Miss Wyckham lives in Maiden Lane.'

'I couldn't tell him the way anyhow. He just said he'd find it in the end.'

'Would you know this man if you saw him again?'

'I expect so. But I thought you said she was attacked in the shop?'

He got up from the chair and tucked the notebook in his coat pocket. The previously blank page had nothing on it other than two words surrounded by centrifugal spirals, cross-hatched. I took the words to be *brush salesman*. 'I am not saying there is necessarily a connection. Not at this stage. Though there may be. Which is why it is important to try to remember anything and everything. Perhaps you'd be kind enough to get in touch if anything else comes back to you.'

'Of course.'

We shook hands and I accompanied him to the door. He stopped and, before opening it, said he would probably be in touch again anyhow. I nodded. Then, instead of turning the knob, he asked how long I was intending to stay? I hesitated, watching his hand inert on the doorknob, conscious of his body placed between myself and the possible exit, and finally confessed that I had not yet made up my mind, and was not sure. He said he quite understood, which I doubted, pulled open the door and stood back to allow me to go through first. Would I, he asked, be so good as to leave a forwarding address where I could be contacted, should I decide to go. That might be a bit difficult, I told him, but I supposed I would have to think of some way round the problem.

Did people always know where they were going next? I wondered, as I watched the inspector walk across the lobby and out through the main door. Was it normal to leave a forwarding address, and how odd that he should assume that I had somewhere to go. But perhaps the man only thought in this fashion because he was a policeman, and had a tidy mind for whom 'no fixed abode' was synonymous with 'criminal'?

Feeling in need of a drink, I went back to the bar. I had already forgotten the scene I had created here only half an hour before, until an odd look from the barman reminded me. Several other people turned round to stare. I brazened it out by asking for a double in a loud voice and hoisted myself back on to a high stool.

With the drink in front of me I forgot my surroundings and began to brood, both on my own situation and the new information I had just been given. I was conscious that I had just had a narrow escape, but poor Miss Wyckham had not. I wished now, that I had told the policeman that the brush salesman had seemed both likeable and harmless. I hoped the poor man would not find himself enmeshed in a crime he knew nothing about on account of me. I imagined the woman lying on the floor with blood on her face, and I hoped she was not going to die. But how odd that our three fates should have coincided, and that I should have heard those words going through my head.

7

I slept badly last night, having gone to bed in an alcoholic haze. I suppose the number of drinks I had swallowed should have ensured a good night's sleep, but instead I felt that my head was moving through space, swimming in shifting shadows of liquid air, and that I had no control over it. Towards morning I had a dream: I was standing on the platform of a railway station; it was dark and cold and I was quite alone. The place was deserted. I knew that the last train had left several hours ago, but for some reason that was not clear to me I kept pacing up and down the dimly lit platform. Sometimes I paused and stared down at the tracks, or my eye followed them into the dark. It was impossible to see more than a few yards. Even the signals had been switched off in the impenetrable night.

I have decided that, if I cannot control my sleeping hours, I must at least try to establish a workable shape and pattern in my waking ones. To that end, I have begun to keep a systematic record in my new notebook. It will help to pass the time while I wait for my true situation to become clearer; but, more important, it will provide indisputable evidence in case I become the victim of further mental aberrations. I can refer back to it, if my memory continues to be unreliable in future.

So I spent the early part of the morning in my room, catching up on yesterday. Already I cannot be sure that it is entirely accurate, but at least I have begun at the beginning.

When I woke I had an impression of unnaturally prolonged gloom. I drew back the curtains and found drops of water running down the window pane, beyond it the sky a dirty shade of grey. The lawn below was waterlogged, brown puddles merging into marsh. The bushes dripped. I went back to bed and began to make my notes about yesterday in last night's electric artificial light, which cast a yellow glow and kept the grim grey of today at a distance, for the time being. Once I switched on the radio next to the bedhead, to hear that 'a depression is moving eastward, southern areas will be mainly cloudy with prolonged outbreaks of rain which are expected to clear in the afternoon'. I switched it off.

I have decided that from now on I will take things at a much more leisurely pace, and cultivate personal comfort if nothing else. Yesterday I was in too much of a hurry, I could not wait to begin, without a notion of what I might be rushing into. As a result I got myself unnecessarily agitated, put every foot wrong, and was extremely fortunate not to land up in serious trouble. I might still have to extricate myself from the mistakes I made in my first panicky euphoria.

I telephoned room service and asked for breakfast to be brought up to me. So much cosier, and I do not see why I should bother to put up a public performance at this uneasy hour. Added to which I am far from sure what my rôle ought to be, or how to go about it. I do not want to continue yesterday's series of blunders: on the contrary, I am anxious to put them out of my mind as soon as possible.

There was a knock at the door. On command a frilled maid brought in a tray loaded with all the appurtenances of a luxury breakfast, hot coffee in a silvery-looking coffeepot, toast in a toast rack, boiled egg in an eggcup, marmalade in a marmalade dish, and butter not merely in a butter dish but arranged in icy twirls like buttery seashells.

'Good morning, madam,' she said, sliding the tray under the glow of the lamp. And added, as though the first remark had nothing to do with the second, and did not contradict it: 'Not a very nice morning.'

'Awful,' I said, admiring the variegated and crested display.

She walked over to the window and pushed the curtains as far back as they would go. 'It's been a terrible winter,' she said, staring out. 'I don't know, it must be all these satellites and rockets we keep sending up. The weather never used to be like this in the old days.'

'The element of fire is quite put out,' I recited, cracking the top of my egg and watching the yolk break like sunrise on the spoon. 'The sun is lost, and the earth, and no man's wit, can well direct him where to look for it.' I waved the spoon in the air, having savoured my first mouthful.

The maid turned round near the door and gawped at me with her mouth open. 'Beg pardon?'

'Nothing,' I said airily, rather surprised myself at this sudden gift of tongues. 'I was just agreeing with you, that's all. It could of course have been the atom bomb. Or aerosol hair-sprays destroying the earth's ozone layer—or does that strike you as too unlikely?'

'I don't know, madam, I'm sure.' She stood with her back to the door, uncertain whether she could consider herself dismissed, free to go, superfluous. Was I simply filling the air with inconsequential nothings, or was I trying to have a conversation which it would be rude to ignore?

'Tell me,' I said, 'what was it like in the old days—before it was like this?'

I watched the growing uncertainty on her face, mingled with the appalled suspicion that I was going to keep her from her duties, and that the drift of the conversation might be beyond her, if not mad. But she thought hard, making a visibly conscientious effort.

'I don't know,' she said at last, frowning inwardly, 'but it was different—better. Really cold in winter and blazing hot all summer. You knew where you were. Not this half-way misery all through the year we seem to get now. We had lovely times when we were kids—picnics out-of-doors with the grass all smelling of dry hot sun. And the winter was just as nice in a way, with snow coming down, and snowball fights, and sliding on the ice on the way home from school.'

'Are you sure?' I asked dubiously, watching her face, which was smiling now from within.

'Of course,' she answered. 'Seems like yesterday. Everybody remembers what it was like when they were young—don't you?'

'No,' I said quite sadly. 'I'm not sure that I do.'

After she had gone I lay snugly in bed, eating buttered toast and considering the chambermaid's childhood. It sounded very enviable, like something read in a storybook. I scraped the remains of the egg out of its shell and found myself murmuring once more the words about the sun being lost, and the earth, and thought perhaps some scrap of childhood doggerel, a nursery rhyme or words used for bouncing a ball or skipping through a rope had after all forced its way through my obdurate brain to consciousness. Who knows? I lay back with a second cup of coffee, wondering what else I could dredge up from my hidden store, if it existed.

I stared at the wall opposite, but the door in it reminded me of the chambermaid who had just gone; it was not quite blank enough, so I shifted my attention to the ceiling which had nothing to offer except shadows. Eeny meeny miny mo, catch a nigger—oh dear, I thought, not very nice, before the words took me on to 'toe'. Surely the chambermaid's head did not store such vulgarities? Try again. One potato, two potato, three potato, *four*, five potato, six potato, seven potato, *more*. Now what was one supposed to make of that? It rhymed of course. Had I spent my early childhood counting vegetables? And did this indicate a farming background where offspring became numerate with a primary abacus of peas and beans? Anything was possible.

It was then that I heard the distant notes of a piano sounding quite clearly out of what might have been a church hall or some such bare place. The notes of the simple melody sounded hollow, echoing and reverberating in what was clearly the wrong sort of space for a piano. When a straggle of high piping voices joined in I knew the words they were singing, possibly because I recognised the tune:

Glad that I live am I . . .

70

'That the sky is blue,' I chipped in, and jumped out of bed to find out where the sound was coming from. I looked out of the window: it had stopped raining, but the sky was still overcast with a thick blanket of low grey clouds.

Glad for the country rains...

'And the fall of dew,' I chirruped, happy at knowing the next line. The sound seemed to be coming from beyond the line of dripping trees. I lifted the sash window, shivered somewhat as the cold air hit me, smelt the damp earth in the garden below, and heard rainwater drip from the trees. Now the infant choir could be heard quite clearly:

> *After the sun the rain*
> *After the rain the sun*
> *And the fall o-of night*
> *When the day is done.*

I banged the window shut as a gust of cold air hit me. The bedraggled trees began to writhe, scattering what was left of last year's dead leaves and this year's promise.

Once out of bed, I decided there was nothing for it but to get dressed. I switched the radio on again and, impatient of the inane jollity of orchestrated sound, twiddled the nob till I heard what sounded like a sane voice talking calmly: 'Areas of high pressure are called an-ti-cy-clones,' it said slowly. 'In these an-ti-cy-clones the pressure is highest at the centre, and so the winds tend to blow towards where the pressure is lower. But, because the earth is spinning round, is ro-tating, all winds in the northern half of the globe, what we call the northern hemisphere, are deflected to the right, whilst in the south they are deflected to the left. So that in the northern hemisphere the winds round an anticyclone blow in a clockwise direction, and in the southern hemisphere they blow anti-clockwise.' I glanced out of the window and tried to establish whether the trees looked as though they were writhing about in a clockwise motion, but they just seemed to be swaying to and fro any old how, in what could have been taken for the throes of utter desperation. 'The approach of a body of warm air,' the voice went on, and sounded optimistic and full of soothing promise, so I stopped to listen attentively, 'is signified by a freshening of the wind from the southerly direction.' I glanced out at the scudding clouds beyond the window, but had no notion in what direction they were moving, other than towards me. I knew that the sun rose in the east but it had not been glimpsed so far this morning. But the voice went on: 'Then the sky becomes covered with a thin film of cloud which increases in thickness until heavier rain clouds appear, and a steady downpour begins, usually accompanied by a strong wind.' I switched the radio off, thinking that I could do without further education at this time of morning, then blamed myself for lack of patience and switched it on again. The voice had not given up: 'When the warm front has passed, there is often a clearance of cloud and there may be a fine spell; but as the cold front at the rear of the depression approaches, heavy downpours are frequent.'

This time I turned him off for good, banged my hair with a hairbrush, pulling even worse faces at myself in the mirror, and decided I had better purchase an umbrella at once. But on second thoughts I concluded that an umbrella would be unlikely to withstand the wind, would either blow inside out or become an uncontrollable parachute.

I left the breakfast tray outside my door, and walked down to the lobby. Once having got that far, however, I found myself in an uneasy quandary, having nothing to do. The weather was too bad to think of going out, and I could hardly eat a second breakfast to pass the time. In any case, they had probably stopped serving. An old gentleman was tapping the barometer which hung near the door to the dining room. He shook his head gloomily. 'Still falling,' he muttered.

'We've got a nice fire going in the lounge, madam.' The desk clerk had been watching me, my indecision. My awareness of him watching had been putting pressure on me to do something, now, decisively, and at the same time increased my indecision. I turned round when I heard his voice.

'Any letters for me?' I asked coolly, avoiding his eyes to study the pigeon holes behind him. I could see at once that mine was empty. He shook his head.

'Not a very nice day,' he remarked, adding: 'What's more, it looks set for the day.'

'You think so?'

He nodded: 'Can't be sure, of course. But I wouldn't bank on it clearing up. Certainly not before lunch.'

'Then I think I'll go and ...' The desk telephone had begun ringing and my answer went unheeded. There was something, I thought, to be said for an occupation, however futile. And strolled unnoticed into the empty room, where a fire was indeed blazing, crackling and spitting sparks, long yellow tongues licking at logs which burned to ashes in the grate for no one in particular.

I sat down in an armchair and gazed into the red heat, hoping that no one would come in and see me. I wished that I had a book in which I could at least pretend to be absorbed. The trouble with staying in a hotel, I thought un-easily, was that one had to be ready to play a rôle at all hours, and my lack of one that was even half-way defined made this more than usually difficult. So far I had dithered between possibilities, and succeeded only in over-acting each time.

I considered finding a newspaper and hiding behind it, pick-ing my way through the chaos of world affairs. I thought about going back up to my room, but realised I would be inter-rupted by somebody coming in to clean up and make the bed. For some time I stared out of the window: drops of water trickled down the pane, dispersed and were as soon replaced, running in competition down random tracks. Impossible to know where so much water could come from; yet there seemed no reason why it should ever stop.

I heard a sound behind me and turned my head to the door. The old woman whom I had seen yesterday in the dining-room was moving slowly towards the focal glow of the fireplace. She used a stick, and her body was slightly bent at the neck like a flower with a damaged stem, so that the head dangled forward. She lowered herself with some difficulty into an arm-

73

chair close to the fire. The stick slid forward. A burning log shifted, and wood below erupted in a shower of sparks and finally disintegrated to grey ash.

'What a dreadful morning,' she said, either to herself or to me, since she was staring into the fire. Her hands, blue-veined, bones prominent under the skin, kept touching each other nervously as though to make sure they were still there, like an old blind couple. The tongues in the grate licked hungrily now, and I fed them a fresh log from the basket by the polished fender. I did not know what, if anything, to say, and she continued to gaze into the fireplace, though her lower jaw ruminated over inarticulate thoughts of some kind.

'I get tired,' she said, 'waiting for it to stop. Nothing to do. And this damp is bad for my rheumatism.'

From beyond the door came the unexpected sound of running feet and the high excited voice of a child laughing. The disturbance seemed to bring her round.

'No manners,' she muttered, glancing at me to indicate that she expected my support and approval. 'No discipline nowadays. Young people. Everything falling apart. I don't know where it will end.'

'Really?' I tried to make it sound polite.

The door behind us was opened with some difficulty. I saw the knob turn this way and that before a child's face peered through the doorway into the room. Not finding whom she was looking for, she ran away. The flames guttered in the cold draught.

'You see what I mean: no control, none whatever. Would you mind closing the door? I feel the cold so.'

'Well,' I said indulgently, as I got up and walked towards the door, 'we were all young once ... I suppose.'

I looked out into the hallway to catch another glimpse of the child before I closed it, but she had vanished. Impossible to know where she had gone, or what had become of her. Sadly I returned to my chair near the old lady, who was fumbling nervously with an old-fashioned engraved locket she wore at her throat.

'Childhood is not what it was,' she maintained vehemently. 'Too much freedom nowadays. No values. It can't be good for them.' She picked up her walking stick and rapped the tip against the floor several times. 'I'm glad I won't live to see it, but they'll suffer for it later on, all of them.'

'In what way?'

She stared into the fire for a while; her lips moved, formed what could have become a grimace, trembled.

'There's no framework any more,' she said slowly, still staring into the glowing heart of the fire now falling to ashes through the iron grate. Another log shifted and crumbled. 'In my day, nobody allowed us to run about like wild things. And it never did us any harm—we were better for it. They have to know what's what.'

'Which is?'

She turned to me with raised eyebrows, a look of inquiry on her face.

'I'm sorry,' I tried to explain, 'but I'm not sure I know ... I mean, what *is* what?'

'In my day,' she said with emphasis, an edge of disapproval in her voice, 'children knew their place. Everybody did. One knew who one was.'

'Really?' I asked, and added warmly: 'That must have been nice. I wish I did.'

'There you are. That's just it. Nobody does nowadays. It can only end badly.' She rubbed her white hands together as though this might restore circulation, bring back warm blood. 'All this so-called freedom, I don't hold with it. What's the good of being left to think for yourself, if you don't even know who you are?'

'You have a point,' I admitted.

'And you don't know who you are until you've been told. Nobody does. If people are left to decide for themselves it just wastes a lot of time and messes things up.'

'Is that so bad?' I asked humbly. 'I mean, what things? I'm only asking. Is time really that valuable?'

'The only thing to be done with life,' she said, her voice

tremulous with age, not lack of conviction, 'is to get on and live it. And if you were my age you wouldn't need to ask whether time was valuable.' There was a silence: she appeared to be listening to the crackling sounds of the fire, the odd hiss and spit as the burning tongues continued to consume wood, but perhaps not, perhaps she was hearing quite other things. 'It was hard,' she said slowly, 'but it will become harder. We did not expect much, and got less. But if we were sometimes unhappy, it was nothing to what will come now, when people demand and expect so much.' She stroked the worn gold ring on her left hand, below the swollen knuckle which held it prisoner. In the distance, far away in the lobby, we heard a human shriek.

'The child,' I said, 'is playing exciting games,' and smiled across at her. She looked at me, then turned her head back to the fire, to the private images that breathed and glowed in the embers.

'The child,' she said, 'is collecting bruises.'

The old woman now stared into the fire, her dark pupils strangely enlarged. I could see the heat reflected in them. She began to rock rhythmically to and fro, forward and back, never taking her eyes from the fire in the grate. 'I did a good job for my son,' she murmured, and sighed heavily. I tried to imagine what she saw in the fire, images of domestic bliss long past perhaps. I saw only another log slip, crumble and curl into greywhite ash. She sighed again. 'But now...' her voice had taken on an odd chanting tone, '... now I see only ruin. Fire and brimstone, death and decay.' The fire gleamed in her eyes as she went on, totally absorbed now, in her own thoughts: 'Son shall rise against father, brother's hand be set against brother, and the country will become ungovernable. It will not be safe for young women or old men to walk the streets at nights, and no one will sleep easy in his own bed. The baby will cry with hunger and no one will comfort it, and the old will freeze to death in unsanitary and forgotten rooms. Cities will burn, once peaceful streets become a battleground, and the gutters run with blood. Harvests will fail, and dust storms sweep over the dry land. Cattle will die, and the parched mouths of the helpless will cry for help without hope of answer. The fish in the sea will die, poisoned by human plague, and all the oceans become dead, stinking swamps of corruption. Thus the sins of the father fall upon the children, even to the third generation, and all will be ill.'

'Oh dear,' I said. There was a long pause: it was difficult to know what, if anything, to say. The fire had died down and I found myself shivering a little, so I stooped forward to take another log from the basket. A shower of sparks blew up the dark chimney as the tenuous glowing structure collapsed under its fresh weight. The old lady had stopped swaying, but was still stroking her wedding ring with her right thumb, as though for comfort, as though the gold might spark something off. Now she turned to me with the most ordinary expression in the world and said mildly: 'You mustn't mind me, my dear. I've always tended to look on the gloomy side. As my poor husband used to say: "Sybil," he'd say, "you may well be right, but you must try and remember that people don't want to hear about it."'

'He sounds like a wise man,' I said, only partly to flatter her.

'He was a fool,' she said firmly, 'a born optimist. Why, only the day he died he said to me: "Sybil, I'm getting better. I'll be home in a few days." I'd hardly got back from the hospital when they rang to tell me he'd gone. It was a terrible shock.' I made an indeterminate noise intended to express sympathy. She leaned forward confidentially: 'You see, I'd been brought up to think that men knew best, and that it was only right for a wife to defer to her husband. I suddenly realised I'd spent the best part of fifty years with someone who had been wrong, not only about this, but about everything. I felt cheated, to tell you the truth. Particularly so because I felt I had guessed it all along. And now it was too late. I couldn't even tell him.'

'Never mind,' I said. 'You mustn't hold it against him. Bearing grudges makes for unnecessary luggage.'

I had become aware of a subtle change in the room, a sense

77

of lightness, as of spirits lifting. I glanced towards the window and saw that it had stopped raining: a gentle silence spread across the sky, now calm and luminous through thin white cloud.

'How about a little walk?' I prompted, getting out of my chair. Stretching. Yawning.

But she shook her head gloomily, not without a certain self-pity. 'There's nowhere left to go,' she said, 'and anyhow, I can't get far.' She indicated her stick with a touch of contempt, as though it was another inadequate husband to whom she was wedded. I stood, undecided about how to make my escape, when she suddenly smiled at me. 'I think I'll just sit here and wait for my son. He may call at any time now, and I wouldn't like him to miss me. He's such a comfort—I don't know what I'd do without him. But please don't let me keep you.' She was now in command of the gracious dignity of age and good breeding. I retreated towards the door, though her smile was not unmixed with pathos; she had an aura of the forgotten idol about her, of resigned self-righteousness.

'I think I'll just go out for a breath of fresh air,' I murmured. 'Work up an appetite for lunch.'

'I eat very little nowadays.' It sounded like a reproach. 'And I hardly sleep at all.' I had already closed the door behind me, but the voice came through the wood with plaintive persistence.

8

For my second walk I started off in the opposite direction:
along a rather dull road lined with residential houses leading
away from the river and the bridge, which must, I felt, have
been constructed to enable those stuck on this side to get across
to the other side, rather than vice versa. Never, by any standards, had these houses had any pretensions whatsoever, even
in the decade when they were new. Huddled together, the
ground sites were mere tokens of privacy and ownership, with
narrow front yards, mean windows, and grudging footpaths to
obscure entrances all overshadowed and further diminished by
an unnecessary clutter of dividing walls and fences in a state
of some decay. But it was from this direction that I had heard
the sound of childish voices singing in chorus first thing in
the morning.

The road led into one which meandered gently along the
base of a green hillslope, and here I found an old squat building made of discoloured brick, set well back from the road in an
empty expanse of blackish asphalt behind a high wire fence.
I looked through at the empty space but could hear no sound,
detect no signs of activity in the silence. But drops of water
hung like precious beads on the wire, catching light in their
clear roundness before they fell in a shower as the fence
trembled under my hand. And one small puddle showed a
patch of blue sky where the grey asphalt dipped to collect
water, or the ground beneath had subsided.

But the silence did not last. I heard a bell sound within the
building and a few seconds afterwards a murmur, followed by

the sound of wood shifting on concrete, feet scuffling and stamping, shrieks and yells as a horde of small figures ran out of the building and invaded the playground, fanning out over the flat grey spaces. There were secret patterns behind their apparent disorder and lack of purpose, as they ran and milled about, jumping, hopping, skipping, kicking, all with deadly purpose and passionate intent. Several boys tried to push each other over to gain possession of a large white ball marked with black hexagons, a girl threw a small ball high in the air and cupped her hands, gazing eagerly skyward, to catch it on its downward path, a steep parabola. She missed, and the ball bounced and rolled away out of sight and reach beyond the moving legs of too many moving, struggling beings. The sounds of chanting came from the far end of the playground, though I could not make out any words, only the emphatic rhythm, and six small bodies in a variety of coloured pullovers had now lined up nearby with their backs against the wire fence, all watching the movements and gestures of a fair-haired girl who stood some yards in front. They appeared to be watching and waiting for her to falter, put a foot wrong or make some other error, and when this did indeed occur, judging by the reaction, the yelps of triumph which broke the attentive silence, the jumping and pointing where before there had been a rigid stance observable from the back as several small hands gripped the wire, one of the group ran forward to take her place and the fair-haired child, looking subdued and sheepish, came and stood by the fence with the rest. But it only needed the rapid downfall of her successor for her face to be laughing again.

Suddenly a large bright blue ball flew over the fence, narrowly missed hitting me on the head, and made its first bounce nearby. It was already rolling across the road as a chorus of pleading prisoners hung on the wire, calling 'Hey, miss, please could you get our ball back?' and 'Can you get it?' and more 'Hey missus, please missus, our ball...' But already I could feel that the initial shock of loss had been replaced by curiosity as to the speed at which I could move to retrieve the ball now rolling in the gutter opposite, no longer pushed by its own momentum but helped by the downward slope of the road, which continued all the way to the river. Now I was on trial, and I could feel it, in the eyes at my back, the solitary voice egging me on in the sudden hush, in my large clumsy body and slow legs. So I stepped into the road and ignored the sound of a car approaching until it came to a halt with a screech of brakes only yards from me. 'Not you again!' A man had lowered the side window and now poked his head out. 'Next time, choose somebody else, would you? It's not that I mind killing you, but the police would never believe it wasn't an accident. Why don't you jump off the bridge and have done with it? That way you don't get other people into trouble.' I started to open my mouth by way of an apology or explanation, not yet sure what it would be, when he turned the ignition key and drove off at full throttle. The sound of his irate engine faded into the distance.

Meanwhile the blue plastic ball had come to a halt further down the road by settling in the iron grill of a drain. Having picked up a fair amount of mud on the way it now nestled comfortably in an accumulation of soggy dead leaves which the recent rain had washed this far and no further. This time I looked carefully to right and left of the empty road before going across, but although I picked it up gingerly some of the muck came off on my hands, and a further film splattered on to my clothes when the ball failed to clear the fence at the first attempt and bounced back on to the pavement. This final proof of my ineptitude, together with the mounting impatience generated by a long wait, meant that the waiting mob forgot to thank me before running after the ball as it finally lobbed over the top of the fence and bounced away on the playground.

I took a clean handkerchief out of my pocket and wiped the mud on my fingers into it, then tried to remove the marks on my coat. An elderly man had been watching me for some time, no doubt for want of anything better to do; hands deep in his shabby coat pockets, he was muffled up to his frail chin and pink protruding ears in the folds of a thick woollen scarf. Above it his eyes seemed about to dissolve in their own liquid, to swim like pale oysters in wrinkled shells, concaves from which a salty trickle overflowed on to cheeks now almost transparent.

'Kids,' he said. 'That ball hit me on the head once. Laughed, that's what they did. Laughed. Catch me giving them their ball back. You nearly had an accident.'

'Yes,' I said, and added: 'But I should have looked where I was going. It was my own fault.'

'It's not safe,' he went on, his quavering voice indignant. 'You want to mind out,' moving his head slightly within the folds of protective clothing, the tip of a bald spindle wrapped thick with yarn. 'It's not safe to go out on the streets nowadays. A lot of thugs about. Nobody's doing anything about it. You want to mind out,' he repeated, and began to walk on slowly, moving his feet forward with caution, as though wary of uneven paving stones.

The road sloped down towards the river, and I allowed the old man time to put some distance between us. A bell had rung inside the school building and now the playground was as empty as before, a silent space, the patterns dispersed. The hillside on my left looked steep and impassable, the grass slippery and sodden with rain, and I could see no footpath. Resignedly I continued on the course I had started, following the old man on his downward slope. The pavement really was uneven: once I nearly stumbled on the protruding edge of a cracked slab, and further down my heel caught in a sudden dip which had possibly been caused by a falling meteorite, to judge from the multiple radiating fractures. Below I could just make out a small cross-section of the continuing river, cold, slate-grey and uninviting.

The first building past the school was a small and ugly chapel, elaborately built of utilitarian brick, perhaps left over from a large factory, mill, or some such industrial enterprise of the period. *'Enter in the Name of the Lord'* was carved into the stonework of the portal, but the wooden door had obviously been locked up firmly for some considerable time. I read more inscriptions: the building had an air about it, as though it had begun by waiting for the last trumpet which would herald the rising of souls, but was now merely marking time until the right moment came to sell at optimum land value.

But beyond the chapel stood a public library. I do not know why I stopped, found myself lingering outside, instead of walking on. Perhaps the fact that, unlike the school and the chapel, it did not exclude me, one with frenetic new life and the other with a rusted padlock and dead windows, was enough. The other boards had stipulated that one had to be young enough for primary education or old enough for prayer, burial and communion, but this notice simply read *Open to the Public*, and I saw no reason to suppose that this did not include me. Moreover, judging by the warm electric glow coming through the windows, it actually was open. *Monday to Saturday*, it read, *from 9.30 a.m. to 6 p.m.* which, allowing for eating and several hours' sleep, just about catered for any time available, however much. It had begun to dawn on me that nothing was necessarily going to happen in a hurry, that I might have to wait some time for my new life to begin, for the necessary cue, contact or clarification which would set the whole machine in motion. I recalled the tedium of sitting in my bedroom waiting for the rain to stop, and even in my newborn state of mind I already suspected there would be more to it than hoping for fine weather. So it would not be a bad thing to have something to do, to ward off the creeping boredom of which I was already becoming aware. I went inside.

I pushed open the door rather timidly, conscious of trespassing on alien territory. After the bleak day outside I was at first quite overcome by the warm atmosphere, the bright lights overhead, the dark shelves crowded with bound volumes, and a palpable hush made audible by the sound of a newspaper rustling in the far corner as an old man read, the dull thud of one book being stacked on another by a librarian, and my own discreet footsteps. I could hear my own breathing, the old man sniff and then cough, the librarian's heels squeak oddly as she walked across to the shelves to replace several books, and a consistent hum coming from the lights above. I heard somebody, hidden in the aisles of bookcases, turn a page.

I tiptoed across the floor and began running my eyes along the rows and rows of books, each spine with its own author and title, though some had worn down with age and were scarcely legible. The base of each spine also had numbers and letters which, since they were not otherwise comprehensible, must have been part of a code which I did not understand. This was a pity, since I simply had no idea where to start looking, which volume to pull out first: none of the names or titles meant a thing to me, and each was as meaningless or, put another way, as potentially meaningful as any other. They all seemed to have a claim on my attention, something about the mysterious phrase of a title or the portentous ring of a name included in that title was, I felt, intended to suggest that bound within these pages, and these pages alone, the secret of life lay concealed. And who knows, I thought, perhaps it was so: I was the last person, with a blank past and at present an equally blank future, to ignore the wisdom which might indeed lie between these thousands of pages. Who knows what riddle any one of these books might answer? The problem was in knowing which one, or at the very least, given a maximum of time and patience, what system to employ in working methodically through most of them, since it was clearly impossible to read them all.

I did the only possible thing, and pulled out a book at random. It fell open at a crack in the binding and I read the first lines of a paragraph which began near the top of the right-hand page:

He watched my hand slide across the page as I signed a false name and address in the hotel register. Really, it was quite easy. The porter arrived to show me to my room and I followed him up the carpeted staircase. He unlocked a door and stood aside for me to enter.

Nothing new here. I closed the book, put it back on the shelf, and had a look at the one adjacent to it. The style of this was rather different, the words more densely packed together, so one had to concentrate hard to get the meaning. This time I tried the opening page:

Cold. Wintry. Grey sky, grey buildings. A sudden gust of wind set the trees shivering, blew through my coat. A discarded cigarette packet rattled on the concrete by my feet. Finally a porter appeared. 'There's no train for another twenty minutes,' he told me. I said nothing. What could I say? The bare trees along the railway track bent under the force of the wind. I had forgotten where I was going, or why. Finally I forced myself to ask him: 'Is that the up train or the down train?' He looked at me as though I was slightly mad, and perhaps I was. Behind his head I saw the sky crack into shards of broken china blue beyond the rainclouds. He seemed to be weighing his words as he answered, watching me shrewdly. 'It all depends how you look at it, doesn't it? Where do you want to go?' I considered the question, which I had not asked myself before. It suddenly assumed a new dimension, as I realised how important it was. This simple old man had unwittingly probed to the heart of the problem. I did not know.

I pushed the book back in its place with a distinct feeling that I was getting nowhere. Nothing new about any of this. I walked to the end of the aisle and found that this section of the library was categorised as fiction, which slightly surprised me, since the passages I had just read struck me as having the ring of mundane truth. But I nevertheless crossed the room to a group of bookcases clearly marked BIOGRAPHY, and had a look at the spines. Judging by a certain lack of variety about the titles, one life must have been very much like another; also, it was not always possible to ascertain quickly whether the name most prominent on the volume was that of subject or author, a distinction I somehow found much easier to make in the fiction section. When an author had chosen to write an autobiography this confusion was happily avoided. There was something reassuring about these books, I thought, as I pulled out one or two volumes at random. Of course, I could not know who the people concerned were, but on the pages, printed in black and white, were dates, whole letters written by somebody to someone else, the names of places, and even photographs to substantiate the reality and essential veracity of the contents. It was only when I began to study these pictures more closely that I began to have doubts, a suspicion that quickly turned to certainty: all the figures were posed in make-up and costumes, and one could only gasp at the crude deception—the waxed moustaches, the fulsome beards and bosoms, the artificial interiors and flat backdrops of streets and scenery that could never have existed. In some of the more amateurish photographs those who posed themselves stared back in disbelief, not quite knowing how to stand, or who they were supposed to be. Blurred definition, too much light or not enough, was part of the deception.

I decided to read only books without pictures. Finally I found one, and skimmed through the opening pages. I read: *I had a very happy childhood*, and further down the page:

I adored my father, who took me on his knee and told me improbable tales which he made up as the mood took him, and which by turns excited and terrified me.

Her mother, it seemed, would try to stop these goings on, but without success. She claimed it was bad for the child. A page or two further on the author recreated her childhood in more detail:

The weather, like much else, has changed since I was a girl. The seasons were more clearly defined, with crisp cold winters and long hot summers. I remember seemingly endless days passed playing in the meadows under a cloudless blue sky, days of blazing sunshine when we picnicked by the river in the shade of a spreading oak, the drone of insects and drunk bumble bees in the rosebushes and later, towards autumn, the smell of new-mown hay drying in the sun, which tickled our nostrils as we tumbled about in it and made us sneeze. I do not think it ever rained, though I recall a thunderstorm once, at the end of a hot afternoon, which was very dramatic.

I replaced the book and pulled out the one next to it. *When I got back to the hotel*, read the start of the first paragraph to catch my eye,

I was told in the lobby that there was a man waiting to see me, information which made me distinctly uneasy. I went up to my room on the pretext of having a wash, but really to slip a revolver into an inner pocket. I was ordering my first drink at the bar when a man approached me, identified himself as a plainclothes police detective, and told me that Elizabeth had been found brutally assaulted at five o'clock that afternoon, and was still unconscious in the local hospital. He asked me to account for my movements. Badly shaken, I ordered another drink. The police were waiting at her bedside for a statement, but it was always on the cards that she would not survive to name her attacker, or clear my name.

By this time I was distinctly uncomfortable, not to say badly shaken. I did not wish to read on, so I flipped back a few pages.

Needless to say I signed a false name in the hotel register, then waited for my contact to arrive. I had been instructed to do nothing on my own initiative, but after a prolonged period of waiting boredom began to make me restive, although I knew the dangers. The only diversion in a tedious succession of days was constructing an identity for myself. I told myself I did this to allay any possible suspicions in the minds of the other guests and the hotel staff, but it was probably unnecessary. They were a dull lot, with no particular interest in me. If the truth were known I was probably the only person who thought my behaviour and very presence odd enough to warrant explanation, and what amounted to an act, a continuous performance.

At this point I stopped reading and made an unsuccessful attempt to check, by looking at the preliminary pages, whether the book had not been placed in the wrong category by mistake. But, having not heard of the author or anybody else in my limited existence, and being unfamiliar with the library code, I could not be sure. I considered consulting the young librarian on duty, but realised that I did not know what to ask her.

I sat down at a nearby table and looked around me, by now somewhat dispirited and confused. Such a variety of names and titles, so many books, categorised aisles of laden shelves, and yet, judging by the quality of what I had so far picked out at random, nothing special. I was disheartened by a certain sameness, even here. It had looked so promising, but it was no different from what I had so far found outside.

The old gentleman scraped back his chair and walked slowly towards the main door, which swung shut behind him. The librarian, her shoes still squeaking along the floor, crossed the room to replace the newspaper in the appropriate rack. It was very quiet. I slipped off my shoes under the table to ease my aching feet and stared out of the blank grey window. A bird flew past. Suddenly a man with a very black face and negroid features came out from behind a bookcase. He must have been hidden there all the time, unnoticed. He walked out, carrying a notebook. From where I was sitting I could see that there were several sections I had not yet sampled, because they were clearly marked out in white letters on a black ground, and I saw that there must be lots of information stored in the various sections, if you had any use for it. But I doubted whether I would know what to do with it, or how to start. I slipped my feet back into my shoes and wandered rather despondently over to the history section, thinking it was time I filled in some of my missing background, but I was discouraged by the gulfs of time left unaccounted for between the volumes, all of which seemed to deal in great detail with people and places I knew nothing whatsoever about and cared about even less: I was finally deterred when I turned the corner of a bookcase to proceed from the Dark and Middle Ages to Renaissance and Enlightenment and found a man in a dirty raincoat holding a limp penis in his hand, looking at me meanwhile.

I beat a hasty retreat and scanned my eye over the poetry section which had the advantage of lining the back wall of the room, thus open to public view and the supervision of the librarian. It was also small in scope, with a certain uniformity which I found consoling: most of the volumes were unassumingly entitled *Poems*, or *Shorter Poems*, *Early Poems*, and so on; a few had titles obviously intended to convey simply a poetic image, leaves, trees, clouds and the like, which I found refreshingly direct after tomes about Merovingian dynasties and Councils of Trent: and some had a directness of utter certainty which appealed to me most of all, being labelled *Collected Works*. There were a lot of *Collected Works*, plainly lettered, respectably bound in sober shades of dark blue or brown. I picked one of these out at random and the page fell open. I read the first lines that caught my eye:

> *At the round earths imagin'd corners, blow*
> *Your trumpets, Angells, and arise, arise*
> *From death, you numberless infinities*

and my heart beat faster, I could hear the blood drumming in my ears because for the first time I had found a link between these last two days and the blotted out past. I did not know what it meant, or what the connection was. I did not know whether I had found this volume and opened this particular page by chance, or whether it was meant from the start, planned down to the last detail. I did not know whether the intersection of two roads at the Railway Tavern, the brush salesman walking towards me from the station forecourt, and the man showing me his penis in the history section, had anything to do with it, or everything. But I not only recognised the words with my eyes, because of the message which had run through my head: my pulsing blood acknowledged them.

I walked across the room to the librarian's desk and put the book down.

'I'll take this one please.'

She smiled at me, opening the front cover. 'Can I see your ticket please.'

I told her I had not got one. She told me that it was strictly against regulations to issue books without a membership ticket. I felt I had heard this rigmarole before. I told her I was staying at the Black Swan Hotel, and she said it would be all right for me to have a temporary membership ticket. But they would also need my permanent home address. She placed a form on the counter and watched my hand forming the letters as I filled in a false name and address. I had already developed a certain consistency: it was always the same false name and fictitious address. I watched her laboriously copying the details on to a small cardboard ticket, which she handed to me, and I walked off with the book under my arm.

9

It began to rain again and I spent most of what was left of the day in my room, recording my experiences in my notebook and turning over the pages of my library book. Studying antique words which had an almost unbearably familiar ring. I was excited but puzzled by them.

Dinner was much the same as lunch. The business of eating has already become a tedious process of mastication and swallowing, and the boredom is not really relieved by studying the other diners doing the same thing. Old Sybil was sitting at her usual table, but I could not catch her eye: she spent most of the time staring into space or fiddling with a bread roll which she did not eat. I caught up with her on our way to the coffee lounge.

'How are you?' I asked. 'Have you heard from your son?'

She appeared to have gone deaf since I saw her in the morning. 'It's been a nice day,' she said tremulously, with a wan childish smile. This remark was so wildly inaccurate that I began to have suspicions about her mental health.

'Have you heard from your son?' I repeated, raising my voice, and watched anxiously as she lowered herself into an armchair.

'What?' asked Sybil. A middle-aged woman, holding a tray loaded with coffee cups was standing nearby. I noticed her looking at me with the meaningful expression of eyes which had bad news to impart, news which must at all costs be kept from the third party whom it concerned.

'She hasn't got a son,' the woman murmured in a low voice,

whilst Sybil was busy propping her walking stick against the side of the chair.

I found it difficult to start a convincing conversation after that and anyhow, Sybil did not appear to want one. I drank my coffee, she stared into the fire. For want of anything better to do I wandered into the television lounge, where several people were engrossed in an old film, made in black and white, about a couple who arrange to elope because he already has a wife. He was, as far as I could gather, also wanted by the police, whether for something he had or had not done was still far from clear to anyone but the heroine, who was sufficiently blinded or, if you like, illuminated by love, to be convinced of his innocence. Or perhaps she was an accomplice now, who had put herself beyond the law. I do not know. Anyhow, one saw her arriving at the hotel and walking through the lobby in curiously outdated clothes, obviously conscious of herself as the epitome of elegance and good taste. She signed a false name and address in the hotel register and one saw by just the shade of a flicker of her curled eyelashes, shown in closeup, that she was doing so. Otherwise her face was a smooth expanse of blank flawless beauty. In spite of all this the film had an unhappy ending. The man was caught by the police, his wife, or both, and never even arrived. Or perhaps he had become trapped in a series of unforeseen mishaps. Whatever the reason, regardless of the protagonists' innocence or guilt, the result was unsatisfactory. Two luminous tears rolled slowly down the flawless cheeks of the beautiful young woman, who believed herself a uniquely tragic figure, and would never know the real reason for anything.

'How sad,' said a grey-haired woman who was knitting steadily, after the final gush of background music had died away. Her husband got up to switch off the news broadcast.

An elderly gentleman grunted and got up from his chair. 'I've just remembered,' he said in disgust, in the tone of someone who had been cheated. 'I've seen this film before.'

He closed the door behind him.

I O

The weather was mild and soft today, with what could have been mistaken for a promise of spring in the air. When I emerged for my morning walk I could hear birds celebrating noisily and I felt it, prematurely, in the bare trees overhead, and the air was soft as a mother's hand on my face. It offered no resistance, only the illusion of moving freely through a friendly element. Even the river passing under the bridge seemed to have slackened its liquid fury just a little. Stones and bridge-work had perhaps won a respite, small though it might be.

The shop in which I had met Miss Wyckham was closed, and the blinds were drawn firmly down over the impenetrable glass. It reminded me that I had a duty to perform: to visit the poor woman in her hospital bed. The idea was not inviting, and I dreaded the distinct possibility that her ravings, those rambling ideas, might have become worse as a result of the unfortunate event which had overtaken her, and that I would become the focus of her mania. Nevertheless, I feel that I must go. I am told that the hospital is situated on the other side of the railway track. I am also curious.

But I did not go this morning. Instead I turned left at the road junction on the High Street, past the bank on the corner, and found myself strolling, in a somewhat bemused state, down a quiet residential road, unlike any road I had found until now. The houses were all large, set well back from the road in care-fully tended grounds. Several of the houses had more than one gate, with a wide sweep of gravel drive forming an arc between the two. They had their exits and their entrances, and trades-men were relegated to those at the side or rear.

In spite of lavish pretensions, including porches, gables, several stone lions and even one medieval turret, the houses were uniform in their lack of authenticity. They looked as though they had been put up in a hurry by a contractor intent on getting rich and getting out, before something collapsed. Quality had been replaced by a false flavour of the past, and no amount of variation could disguise the fact that they were a job lot. The houses tried too hard to look different: one had two gables instead of three, or brickwork instead of false lathe and plaster; several had porches with a flight of steps, and one had the main door off-centre. Such minor details only emphasised their underlying uniformity.

One house had a FOR SALE notice posted at the gate, and on an inexplicable impulse I walked back to the estate agent's office at the corner of the High Street, opposite the bank, and asked for the key. I was drawn to its several blank windows and look of abandoned solitude with the pull of a floating leaf into a whirlpool, though I told myself it was merely one way of passing the time, and at the moment one was as good as any other. And then I told myself it would be quite interesting to see what kind of people lived in these houses, the lay-out of their lives, what colour they painted their walls. As I walked back from the estate agent's office I was struck by the fact that so far I had seen no one: the road was deserted, no face appeared at a curtained window, no sounds of music or a baby crying, no one walked the pavement or worked amongst the dark glossy evergreens or wintry footpaths. I saw just one stray dog of uncertain but distinctive breeding trot along the pavement, stopping at each gatepost. Having lifted his leg and established his claim by the smallest of symbolic dribbles, he passed on.

'The house has been on the market for some time,' the young man at the estate agent's office had told me reassuringly, after he had named a price, to which I did not react, since I had not asked for it. In the confidential tones of a double agent trying not to lose a customer he went on: 'I think they are open to offers.'

He went on to murmur something about 'family circumstances' which I did not quite follow, though I got the feeling that something had gone wrong in the house. Walking back towards it I tried to imagine what circumstances could have made such owner-occupiers not only open to, but obviously vulnerable to offers, circumstances which had not been taken into account when the lay-out of the road and the houses in it was planned. The road, I noticed, had diminished, grown shorter, walking along it a second time.

At first I thought the door had jammed or I had been given the wrong key, since it would not turn in the lock. Then I found that by pushing the key home and then withdrawing it slightly I could get the door open without further difficulty. It gave way under my hand and I heard my own footfalls echo in the hallway and up the hollow stairwell to the empty rooms above. White paintwork had turned yellow, bare floorboards and an area of unpainted wood down the centre of the staircase showed where carpets had been removed. The air was cold and musty from disuse, so damp that I shivered slightly, before I pulled myself together. Dust had settled above old radiators, wafted towards the ceiling by currents of circulating air, and now marked the faded floral wallpaper. Pictures had been removed, leaving unnaturally blank patches. I tried to imagine what possible circumstances could have created such an appalling emptiness. I tried to imagine myself, or anyone else, for that matter, inhabiting this space, walking from room to room, and failed.

The kitchen door stood ajar and I could see light at the far end of the house: a window overlooking an unkempt and deserted garden.

I do not know why I walked from room to room, looking for something. For what? Anyhow, everything had been removed. Apart from the odd picture hook and a few old curtain rails nothing remained of a family history now demolished, crated up, auctioned, given away for jumble, distributed somehow, to somewhere. Perhaps it had all been taken away and re-assembled under another roof, just like the old days, or almost, a little better, a little worse, but otherwise much the same. It could be. But the smell of decay was unmistakable.

I walked up the stairs and looked down at the road below from the windows of the front bedroom. One would, I suppose, get accustomed to any view, but it looked like a dismal prospect to wake up to in the morning hours. False façades, anonymous windows, dreary privet hedges and evergreens, no traffic to speak of, apart from the milk float rattling past once a day. That was something to listen for. And the sound of the radiator ticking quietly as it continued to send more dust up the walls. It was a circumstance in itself, that. One which could send a person round the bend.

What did people do in houses? I asked myself, and found that I did not know. I suppose I must have known once. Perhaps they moved from room to room trying to stop the dust settling on the wallpaper, adjusting the one picture that had always hung crooked, in spite of numerous attempts to get it straight, until somebody had finally given up trying. Or had been forced to stop.

I went back downstairs and found a kitchen door which opened on to the back garden. It was jammed, the wood swollen with damp and beginning to rot under the peeling paintwork. I put my shoulder to it and the pane of mottled glass gave way instead, tinkling on to the concrete step outside. A blast of cold fresh air came through the hole. I tried kicking the door with my foot and it finally gave way. The house, the place, everything looked better from the back: neglected, private, slightly overgrown. Instead of a forbidding row of frontages only a distant row of houses, shrouded in old trees and undergrowth, with fences in between. I walked down the length of the gravel path which ran alongside the damp uncut lawn beside a strip of dark earth which might once have been bright with flowers for every season, but which was now bare, apart from a few stunted shrubs, and turned to look at the house from the back. Two attic windows in the sloping roof betrayed rooms which had escaped my notice whilst I was indoors. I could not remember whether I had seen the staircase turn to a further floor, and why, after standing so long brooding at the window of the first-floor bedroom, I had not bothered to climb up and explore the rooms under the roof. Now, quite suddenly and oddly, in a curious way I could not explain, I had a suspicion that the house was not entirely un-occupied. Somebody lived in those top rooms, or room, for perhaps both windows belonged to one room. I thought I had seen the outline of a face looking down at me, fleetingly, but it happened so fast and was over so quickly that I could not be sure it was not a trick of the light, or my own imagination, misled possibly by something moving outside, the shadow of a cloud moving on the window pane and thrown back.

I began to get cold feet, standing there in the damp earth. I lit a cigarette and trod the match into the ground, watching. I saw that the back of the house bore no relation to the style of the front. Simple windows, cheap brickwork, a welcome lack of ornamentation. Downright shoddy, like the back of neigh-bouring houses. I went on watching those two small windows under the roof for some time, but saw nothing. Meanwhile, someone was watching me.

An elderly woman, a scarf wrapped over her grey hair and knotted under her chin, stood quite motionless in the middle of her back garden next door, eyeing me across the top of the wooden fence which divided the two territories. The expression on her face was not much, a sleepwalker made wary, a grizzled old house dog roused by an intruder, the old bitch now watched me with a mixture of suspicion and curiosity. I got the impression that if she had once had any purpose in coming out of doors other than to find out what I was doing, she had long forgotten it.

'Good morning,' I said loudly, deliberate and polite. She blinked, slowly, but said nothing. She seemed to be considering what reply, if any, was appropriate. Meanwhile I had turned my attention back to the attic windows. This time I was sure I had seen something move, the dark outline of a face surfaced behind the glass only to submerge a moment later.

I heard a snuffling sound. My neighbour had moved closer

to the wooden fence, an animal caught long ago in the wild and for years a tamed resident in a zoo enclosure, whose instinctive wariness and initial timidity was soon overcome by a greed for titbits. She just managed to poke her chin over the top of the fence.

'Can I help you?'

Her voice sounded cracked, as though it had not been used for several years. I considered the question, studying her white pinched face, and glanced up at the attic windows just once more, briefly.

'I don't know,' I said. I ground the cigarette stub into the gravel with my foot. She watched it, the deliberate twisting action, as though I might have been squashing an insect or burning a hole in a carpet. I decided to try her:

'Is there anybody up there?' I asked frankly, nodding towards the roof with its two attic windows. 'Do you think?'

She stared at me, wide-eyed, the eyes faded; looked up at the roof, then back at me.

'We were very sorry to hear of the old man's death,' she said finally. I watched her face, and she looked back at me: I was not sure whether her look held sympathy or accusation. 'He often talked about you,' she went on, weighing her words now, sizing me up. I took a pace back and my heels sank into the earth heavy with moisture. 'Poor old soul'—her voice had gained momentum now, ran smoothly, oiled and spittled, a loose wheel running downhill—'nobody came to see him, he hardly had any visitors. No doubt you all have your own life to lead, but I know what it feels like. Because I'm alone also. But at least I've got my health. He was always poorly these past few years. Still, it comes as a shock, even when you expect it.'

I said nothing, but saw an old man stretched out with finality under a white sheet: eyes closed, sharp nose, worn feet laid side by side. Once the funeral was over everything had to be disposed of: underwear, several pairs of walking shoes, worn clothes, drawers full of old receipts, correspondence, and his ageing dog, now almost blind. Perhaps even now the attic was full of mementoes which no one had found the courage to get rid of, or the time: silly souvenirs of outgrown childhoods, clumsily inscribed 'With love to grandpa', postcards sent from abroad long ago in the first flush of freedom after leaving home, his old razor, a pair of reading glasses with a cracked lens.

'Are you going to live here now?'

The question was unexpected, nor did I see what business it was of hers.

'Why?' I asked coolly.

'It has been standing empty far too long,' she went on in an aggrieved tone. 'It makes me nervous, living next door. Sometimes, at night, I begin to imagine I can hear things. Noises, as though somebody was creeping about. It scares me. We might all be murdered in our beds. And it's not good for the neighbourhood. People will think there is something wrong with the district. Which is not true.'

'No?'

'Of course not. This has always been considered a highly desirable area.'

I began to feel that I had offended, and that she felt herself attacked. I hit back. 'Are you sure? I get the impression ... I understand that the house has been on the market for some time.'

'That's how rumours start,' she went on, openly accusing now, 'and before you know where you are property values have fallen, and nobody wants to buy. It's high time the house was occupied, not allowed to go to rack and ruin.'

'What do you want me to do about it?' I asked, studying the determined set of her chin above the wooden fence, the hardening corneas of her veined and yellowed eyes.

'That's for you to decide,' she said shortly. 'But it's high time the house was occupied by somebody. I mean, of course, the right kind of person. Even if at some personal sacrifice, financial or otherwise. One has a duty.'

'Duty?'

'To maintain standards.'

'I don't see,' I said, trying to sound friendly, to ward off

99

her obvious and mounting hostility, 'what I can do about it. In any case,' I went on reassuringly, 'I'm sure somebody must be looking for a home, once the price is right.'

'That's just it,' she snapped, 'the riff-raff will start to move in.'

I tried to think of some suitable answer, but thought that nothing could possibly penetrate that dense head.

She said: 'A coloured family was seen walking down the road a month ago.'

I retorted: 'I don't think this district is so desirable. I would not like you as a neighbour.'

'I was always very good to your father,' she snapped. 'More so than some, who should have been. His next of kin.' She levered herself up slightly by holding on to the top of the fence with both hands, the joints enlarged and distorted with an arthritic complaint. The fence shook somewhat under her weight, but she gained little height by this attempt. My feet were getting cold: if I stood my ground it was because I was interested in her; and I remembered that she had heard strange noises in the night, which might have been other than fearful imaginings in the dark.

'To tell you the truth,' she went on, and the fence rattled with her emphasis, one slat slipped loose, 'your father was not all that he should have been in the last few years. As a neighbour and resident, I mean. Of course, he was old, I know that. But all the same—he let the guttering go, and he refused to repair the fence. It would have fallen down if we had not got a lawyer.'

'You are fortunate to have a lawyer who is handy with a hammer,' I said. 'Do you think there is anything, anybody up there?' I repeated, nodding towards the sloping roof, the two attic windows. 'What kind of noises do you hear at night?'

She looked at me, the roof, back at me, as though she did not understand the question. A look of wary suspicion entered her eyes, like the holes carved in stone faces which give an illusion of sight: that is how she looked at, saw me now. 'What kind of game are you playing? I'm not saying any more. You don't catch me that way. Want to get rid of me, don't you? Prove an old woman is mad, don't you? That would just suit your little game. But you don't catch me that way. I'm not saying anything.'

I approached the fence. My shoes sank into the soft mud of the bare flowerbed as the surface gave way under my feet. She let go of the fence, which juddered, and retreated, walking backwards unsteadily towards her house.

'You misunderstand me,' I said as gently as I knew how. But it was no good. She was riddled with fear, ossified rigid with it.

'I'm not talking to you,' she called out. Then added, across the growing space between us: 'But I will say this—people are moving in. Dark people, strange people. And it's all your fault.' I wanted to ask her not to be afraid, but I did not know how to begin. 'I'll get the police,' she warned shrilly. 'What's more, she used to stink, that old dog your father insisted on keeping. Filthy old bitch. Used to come through the hole and foul my rosebed.'

She had got up the concrete step now and opened her back door, her hands unsteady with a tremor compounded of age and outrage, a nervous lack of control. She slammed the door shut behind her, and there was nothing I could do about it.

I stood for a moment, looking round at the desolate winter gardens, the bare trees, mournful and scruffy shrubs pruned back to a knotty cluster of fingery dry sticks for the raw season, before walking slowly back down the gravel path to the kitchen door. I slammed it shut, and remembered to push the bolt home. As I walked back into the entrance hall I heard my own footsteps echo from the bare wooden boards with their obvious gaps and flaws, round the stained walls and up through the empty living spaces which had once been occupied. Only how? Had they once been fully inhabited, every nook and corner fully used, or was that also a lie?

Also? I found myself asking why I had used the word. What had made it enter my head? I stood for a few more moments in the hallway, wondering why I had come here, wasted so much time. It was, after all, only an empty house, no doubt much like any other. I lit another cigarette and dropped the flared match on to the stripped and dusty floor, where it fell into a dark crack between the mouldering boards. I inhaled deeply just once before leaving, blowing a cloud of blue smoke up the silent stairwell. Are you, is anyone up there, I asked myself, but I did not say it out loud. There would, I felt, not have been much point, and I was not sure I any longer cared. Nor did I expect a reply.

I slammed the front door shut behind me and returned the key to the house agent on the High Street with a polite, non-committal smile.

This evening I had another visit from Detective Inspector Smith, who arrived to see me after dinner. I had spent the latter half of the day pleasantly enough, recording my impressions of the morning, doing a little reading from the collected works. His arrival reminded me of the unhappy incident which he had reported on his previous call, and I assured the detective inspector that I would visit Miss Wyckham in a day or two. How was the poor woman? I hoped his visit did not mean that her condition had deteriorated?

The detective inspector's face looked blank, as though he did not understand what I was talking about. I gave him time to recollect, but got a distinct impression that he had quite forgotten poor Miss Wyckham and her misfortune. Obviously Miss Wyckham was old business. Much had happened in the interim, a mere forty-eight in my book, only two days, but light years away as far as he was concerned.

He had, he said, come on quite another matter. It seems that the empty house I viewed this morning has since been gutted by fire. It was as yet too early to say whether it had been started deliberately, but it was odd, since the house had been standing empty for some time. The possibility of arson could not be ruled out, there would undoubtedly be an insurance claim, but meanwhile there was the question of hooliganism, tramps or vagabonds drunk on methylated spirits, even squatters. Had I noticed anything suspicious whilst I was there? I shook my head slowly. Why had I gone to inspect the house? I told him I was thinking of buying a place in the district.

He seemed satisfied with my answer, and did not pursue the question. Had I gone over the whole house? No, I told him, I had not bothered to go up to the attic rooms, which I only noticed from the garden. As a matter of fact, I went on, then hesitated ... he pressed me to say what was on my mind, and I told him that I had spoken with a neighbour, an old lady who struck me as distinctly odd. In what way, odd? he asked. I don't know I said vaguely, searching for words. I got the impression she was not quite right in the head. She seemed very resentful, somehow, about the place being empty. And yet, on the other hand, she did not seem to think the house was empty, suggested that she had heard things, especially at night. And she was obviously watching the place day and night: the moment she saw me appear in the back garden she was out of her back door to find out what I was doing. I shrugged.

'I don't know,' I said. 'She was probably just a bit cracked. But you might have a word with her.'

He wrote down a description of the old bitch, and the fact that her house had been the one to the right-hand side, coming from the main road.

'Is the house badly damaged?' I asked, whilst he was still jotting in his notebook.

'I think so. In fact, it will probably be written off as a total loss.'

'Really? That's bad—for the owners, I mean.'

'On the contrary,' he said drily, closing his notebook and clicking at his ballpoint pen. 'According to the agent it has been on the market for several months, and there has obviously been some difficulty in getting rid of it. At an acceptable price, of course. Since it was fully insured at the asking price I don't suppose any tears will be shed.'

He tucked away his notebook and pen into the breast pocket of his jacket and got up to go. For the first time I saw, the edge of sarcasm in his voice drawing it to my notice, that he was a man who had worked hard to reach a class and style of life he still could not quite afford. The asking price was one he had not been able to find. And he resented it, oh how he hated them for turning down a not unreasonable offer. But it was not quite enough, and perhaps now it would never be enough. He felt undervalued, cheated. I suppose the fact that he had so far stayed honest made him that much more bitter.

12

As yet there has been no attempt at contact, no sign of any sort, to my knowledge. I must admit this is beginning to worry me just a little, for several reasons. And then I do find this place somewhat tiresome. My days are hardly very eventful, and I am easily bored during the long intervals between meals; even more so during the meals, when I sit at a table by myself, surreptitiously watching the other guests, and hoping I am myself not being watched; masticating steadily and casually, as if, though knowing myself to be watched, I am quite unconcerned about my lonely situation. And then the food is so boring, with the menu displaying only sameness dressed up as variety, ringing the changes of monotony.

My situation is made more difficult by the awkward fact that I do not know which individuals, if any, I should encourage and possibly cultivate in overtures of civility and budding acquaintance, and the persons I should avoid. And at this stage I cannot entirely exclude the possibility that I am now ignorant of some vital link, an important clue, whether a word or a face, and have thus already missed my cue for entry into the intended action. My record so far has not been encouraging, with two visits from the local police in the first three days.

At breakfast this morning I did see a man who interested me, who for some reason looked familiar, though I could not of course say why. He was dark, going grey, assured: he moved casually, his big-boned limbs encased in clothes of quality, as though he did not belong in this place, but did not care who saw him. He flipped quizzically at his morning paper, scarcely glanced at the waitress who took his order, and used a lot of salt. His elbows covered the table, his legs sprawled out from under the draped tablecloth, now and then he glanced at a gold watch as though the world was waiting for him, but would have to do so a little longer, until it suited him to go. I waited for him to catch my eye, thinking, this is it: I got quite flustered over my grapefruit, felt my face going uncomfortably dark red and hot, my pulse quicken, the muscle in my chest thumping, as I tried to go on looking cool, casual, and unconcerned. Once he did look in my direction, without a sign of recognition. I did not know how to take this, or what it might mean. Then he got up and left the dining room, without a second glance in my direction. Later, in the lobby, I saw him checking out.

I am also getting nervous about the money in the suitcase. It is an exceedingly large amount, and the hotel wardrobe is hardly a safe place for it if I am to remain in this state of limbo much longer. The possibility that someone, knowing about the money, is at this moment playing a game of wait and see, a war of nerves which I am expected to lose, has also occurred to me. I decided to take no chances.

With this thought uppermost in my mind, I got ready to pay a call at the bank. I unlocked the wardrobe, took enough bundles of notes out of the suitcase to cater for my present needs and possible future ones, and hid the money under piles of clothes and underwear in drawers which could be locked. The rest I locked up again in the suitcase, and started off for the High Street.

Perhaps I am beginning to get hypersensitive to the impression I make on strangers, but I thought the cashier behind the heavy iron grille looked distinctly startled, almost alarmed, when I entered the bank and heaved the large suitcase on to the counter. The case blocked out most of the view not already obscured by the security bars, but from what I could make out of his face one might have thought I had escaped from a zoo, or that he knew my face for some reason, had heard of my reputation and had been hoping, unreasonably, that I would not come.

'I want to put this money in the bank,' I said loudly and clearly, patting the suitcase. I felt that it was necessary to spell it out. The young man behind the bars looked even more confused.

'Have you got an account with us?' he stammered.

'Not so far as I know,' I said truthfully. 'Is that necessary?'

Further along the counter a higher primate in a shabby raincoat, who had been collecting peanuts from under the grille, was staring at me. The iron bars curved high above our heads to stop a persistent climber swinging his way over the top.

'Just a moment,' mumbled the young man, slipped off his stool, and disappeared through a door marked PRIVATE. A moment later he was back.

'Would you go through that door,' he said softly, indicating a door near the entrance marked MANAGER. It was made of solid mahogany, finished in a rich dark veneer. I knocked timidly and a voice said 'Enter'. It seemed there was a way round the ostentatious protective bars, into, or out of, this particular zoo.

The manager looked like an older, greying version of the young cashier, one who had put on substance. He could have been his father, I thought, as he got heavily out of his chair and leaned forward to shake my hand across the ornate, leather-topped desk.

'So you wish to open an account?'

I said yes, I did. He said that normally the bank required references, simply as a safeguard.

'A pure formality, you understand,' he added, flashing me a bored, false smile.

Well, I said, that was a bit awkward, since I was anxious to deposit some money for safe keeping right away. It was not as though I was asking for credit, or anything like that.

'How much money, may I ask?' he enquired, rather condescendingly, I thought, leaning his folded hands on the many papers strewn on his desk.

I opened the suitcase.

Half an hour later (it took some time to count out all the notes) I walked out of the bank with my first cheque book, duly inscribed with my false name, which I now sign quite naturally. During the interim a total metamorphosis had occurred. The last vestige of the bank manager's bland condescension had disappeared. He seemed to be suffering from shock. When I gave my name as Mrs Dean, produced no identification, and told him I was looking for somewhere to live and was temporarily staying at the Black Swan Hotel, he asked no further questions, simply took down this sparse information.

'You'll find this a nice spot,' he said, apropros of nothing, bringing his pen to an unnecessary halt, as though he had forgotten what he was supposed to be doing. 'We are spared most of the sordid side of life, what one might call the horrors of the big city.' He smiled, and this time the smile was not so broad, or so false: it was slight, wan, and unconscious. 'No slums, no heavy industry, no influx of undesirable immigrants. I hope you'll be very happy here. May I welcome you on behalf of the whole community.' He insisted on shaking my hand again, adding, 'The cashier will sort out the details,' and crossed the room to see me out of the door, holding it open to allow me to pass through.

The young man behind the counter had obviously tried to pull himself together during the interim, but without much success. His cleancut, forgettable face looked distinctly flustered whilst he counted the notes, the frown between his tidy eyebrows, his slightly flushed complexion, all suggested some kind of disturbance which looked like anger. My own predominant emotion, meanwhile, was simply relief that the authenticity of the notes was not called in question. Not being an expert on counterfeiting, at least so far as I know, the possibility that they might yet prove forgeries had not escaped me. The cashier had finally finished counting, added up his sums, and filled out some sort of receipt which he asked me to sign. He watched through the bars as my hand slipped easily across the sheet of paper, signing my false name almost without hesitation. What in banking terms is referred to as a normal signature, to guard against abuses such as impersonation and cheque frauds.

I had to wait a while for my cheque book to be prepared. Business was slack, with only one other customer further along the counter.

'Do you also like living there?' I asked the young cashier, who had nothing to do, remembering the words of his boss, the manager, who could also have been his father. He shrugged neatly tailored shoulders, which immediately fell back into place.

'I suppose it depends what you want,' he said sulkily. 'It's very peaceful, quiet, clean, that sort of thing. But nothing ever happens here.'

'Really?' I said. 'I heard there was a fire, only yesterday.'

'I mean, it's no place to be if you want to get on in the business world. It's just a dormitory for the big city, where the real action is. But women like it,' he added bitterly, 'and I suppose you can't blame them. Nice clean air, a good place for bringing up children, peaceful. That sort of thing.'

'Are you sure?' I asked, thinking of the women I had met so far, including myself. I remembered poor Miss Wyckham. 'I heard that a woman nearly got murdered a few days ago, just down the road from here.'

'It's all too slow,' he muttered, as though he had not heard a word I said. 'Mortgage, annual increments, pension scheme. My wife wants both the girls put down for private schools in the area. I'm committed up to the hilt for the next twenty years.'

A young woman appeared from an inner sanctum and handed him a cheque book, which he slipped across the counter and under the metal grille towards me. 'Have fun,' he said sourly, as though he had quite forgotten his position.

'I'll do my best,' I said.

13

I decided it was about time I paid a charitable call on Miss Wyckham, whose misfortunes I had by no means forgotten, in spite of my own dilemma, or perhaps because of it. A mission of mercy would at least give me something to do. On making enquiries at the hotel desk I learnt that St Quentin's Hospital is within walking distance, just over the railway bridge at the far end of the High Street.

It was the first time I had walked over the hump across the railway track, and I found the few buildings on the other side much smaller and shabbier, a forgotten tail-end of tiny shops and workshops. In a shoe repair shop a man in a long apron worked amid a brownish black stack of worn leather moulds, scuffed, down-at-heel, redolent of old sweat, bulging and misshapen with a history of corns and aching feet, whose owners had not yet finished with them. Small mice in small cages nested in the straw and sawdust of a pet shop, whilst an unwanted puppy barked and wagged its tail in hopeful eagerness through the glass and an old bedraggled parrot sulked on its perch, looking as though it had seen better days and knew it. Finally a junk shop where all the flotsam of the past seemed to have been washed up. So much, it spilled out on to the pavement, ugly tables with scratched surfaces, soiled armchairs spewing their guts out, old-fashioned dressers with no mirror, a loose mirror which belonged nowhere propped against the wall, another cracked, a lame chair with its back support broken, a whatnot without a function, a tatty and rusted perambulator, a harmonium which had been silent for years and would be incapable of producing a sound, some cracked china ornaments of dogs and women, and a broken rocking chair with nowhere to go.

There were almost no houses or buildings beyond this point, open ground fringed with nettles, the road winding, as I had been told, to the right. And there it stood, a huge modern hospital complex, set back from the road in an expanse of asphalt with special ambulance approaches and a car park marked out in white paint, a forest of signs for different departments which all seemed to be pointing the same way, and a few miserable flowerbeds with nothing but brown earth in them. It looked capable of swallowing up the entire community it was intended to serve without any inconvenience, and with more than room to spare; the glass surfaces of the central tower block threw back a reflection of sky and moving clouds, as though it was not really there, or had assumed the surrounding atmosphere as camouflage, insubstantial as wind and weather.

An unseen eye had seen me coming and the glass doors opened of their own accord to swallow me up. Once inside the mood was quite different, not at all suggestive of airy palaces in the clouds. It was distinctly down-to-earth. Male porters and young women in starched white overalls walked briskly through the main concourse and down a variety of white passages, pushing chairs or trolleys laden with bodies in various stages of decrepitude, limbs stiff in plaster or huddled despondently in striped dressing-gowns. Other uniformed young women carried armfuls of files and X-rays to and fro, whilst in the main concourse several more sat behind a barricade of reception desks and ordered a motley collection of bewildered civilians to their posts. Many of these badly educated visitors, whose ordinary clothes stood out as downright shabby in these uniformly hygienic surroundings, looked bewildered, and had to be given instructions several times in a language they did not quite understand, like an indigenous population invaded by an alien and undoubtedly superior civilisation. Meanwhile names were called over the intercom system, bleepers bleeped in the white lapels of important personnel, red and green lights blinked, and lifts opened their stainless steel doors at regular intervals to carry human bodies to upper or lower regions.

There were several rows of benches between the lifts and the reception desks. Every place was occupied. I had not expected there to be so many, men and women, young, old and middle-aged, all patient, not speaking much, just waiting for their turn. In most cases it was not possible to see what was wrong with them, but you could see that most of them had been sitting there for several hours, and had done so before. The great majority had grown used to it, their faces looked resigned.

I was directed to the fourth floor by a girl behind the enquiry desk, and once the almost noiseless lift had whirred me to it I found myself in surroundings just as cleanly hygienic but subtly different. The atmosphere was more relaxed, the unusual had taken on a mood of everyday. An old lady sat in a wheelchair propelled by a young nurse beside the doors to the lift, waiting to be carted off somewhere. Meanwhile she was having a joking conversation with the nurse, plucking at the blanket tucked round her legs. A few yards further down a young man lay on a trolley, apparently forgotten: by the way he raised himself on his elbow as I came through the lift doors to look at me I guessed that he had been awaiting collection for some time.

Inside the ward I asked a nurse, and found Miss Wyckham lying in the fourth bed on the left-hand side, her bandaged head propped up with pillows. Her face looked a dirty shade of yellow. Under the bedclothes her body made a shallow mound, with her arms lying slack and listless alongside on the bedspread, as though they had been placed there. She seemed to be staring at some point on the ceiling.

'My dear,' I said, leaning over her in an attitude of concern I was not far from feeling. 'How are you?'

Her eyes widened, looked suddenly startled, as though she had seen a ghost. She seemed to shrink back into the pillows, or tried to, without success.

'Who are you?' she whispered, gasping for breath, and then

113

louder: 'Why have you come to persecute me? What harm have I ever done you?' She put her two shaky hands to her bandaged head, as though to shield it. 'I shall call a nurse,' she said threateningly, glaring at me. 'Nurse,' she said feebly, trying with some difficulty to look round for one, and then, in a stronger and almost peremptory tone of voice: 'Nurse! Come here immediately.'

Embarrassed and somewhat at a loss I stood at her bedside, uncertain what to do, and acutely conscious of the fact that the attention of those patients in the ward who were conscious enough to have any to bestow was now focused on myself. A young nurse walked briskly towards us and automatically felt for Miss Wyckham's pulse as soon as she reached the bedside.

'Now then,' she said firmly, as though speaking to a recalcitrant child. 'What's all this?'

Miss Wyckham panted for breath. 'Get rid of this person,' she said between gasps. 'I will not be upset. Call the police.'

The nurse met my eyes across the bed, and her look was almost conspiratorial with an unspoken assessment, a shared misgiving. 'She has been like this with several visitors,' she told me, drawing me away from the bed. 'You mustn't mind. If you'll wait outside for a few minutes I'll see what we can do.' She went back to Miss Wyckham and leaned over her, patting her hand. 'Now then,' she said again in a loud voice, as though the recumbent figure might be slightly deaf, 'we can't have this, can we? When this lady has come all this way, just to see you. I think it's time for one of your shots.'

Rather reluctantly, I allowed myself to be guided to the main swing doors of the ward by the nurse, who told me reassuringly: 'I'll call you when she has calmed down. I'm afraid she has been like this ever since she regained consciousness. But it's quite normal. Nothing to worry about.'

I sat down on a bench in the corridor, near a large expanse of plate glass through which a moving cloudscape of overcast sky could be observed. An old lady sat nearby in a wheelchair, watching two young men dressed as hospital porters, who had just begun to move the man lying on the trolley. A robust first-year nurse with a striped uniform, plump bare arms and a round face rich in freckles popped her head round the swing door of the ward.

'All right, Mrs Baxter?'

The old lady looked dubious. 'How long do I have to wait like this?' she asked querulously. The joints of her deformed hands were swollen. Her head shook uncontrollably.

'Not long now, dearie,' the young girl answered with un-mitigated cheerfulness. 'But we're very busy today.'

'I thought you'd forgotten me,' the old woman complained. To nobody, since the nurse had once more vanished behind the ward door. I could hear her voice on the telephone, coming from the small office just inside the ward.

The door was pushed open once more and the senior nurse who had attended Miss Wyckham leaned towards me.

'You can come in now,' she said.

I followed her through the ward to Miss Wyckham's bed rather tentatively, and with some misgiving. I felt now that it was a mistake to have come. But this time Miss Wyckham did not react at all to my reappearance. She just lay there, slack, relaxed. I pulled out the visitor's seat from under the bed and sat down.

'How do you feel?' I asked at last, feeling foolish, and for want of anything else to say. She moved her head slightly in my direction, as though she had heard something, but was not sure what. She looked at me as though she saw something, but possibly not me. Her eyes, bleary and unfocused, showed no signs of recognition, but neither did they darken with fear.

'Everyone is very kind,' she said in a slurred voice. 'So kind. I don't want to be a bother. You shouldn't have come,' she added, but this time her voice was not accusing, but self-deprecatingly grateful.

'You must get well,' I said, gently stroking the slack hand close by me on the bedspread. I half expected it to react like a wild animal, jerk back nervously, but it did no such thing. Simply lay there and permitted the contact, allowed me to do whatever I took it into my head to do. 'And then,' I went on in the same soothing voice, 'you must put it all behind you. Treat it like a bad dream. The past is best forgotten, that's what I think.'

She gazed into my face as though it floated in a dream from which she could not wake. 'We used to be so happy,' she said slowly, in a voice so low I could hardly catch the words. Her eyelids drooped.

'Yes,' I said. 'We used to be so happy,' and forgave myself the lie because she was past hearing me anyhow. Her eyes were closed, her bony, barren ribcage with its slack and meagre breasts hardly moved as she breathed slowly, though I could see the eyeballs stir uneasily under the closed lids. I watched her for a while, thinking it was time I slipped quietly away, but anxious about her condition. The nurse who had taken care of me before saw me look round uncertainly and came over.

'That's better,' she said, glancing into Miss Wyckham's face. Her mouth had fallen slightly open. She began to snore. 'Stay if you want to, but she'll be out for the next hour or two.'

'Are you sure?' I asked. 'Is she going to be all right? How long has this been going on?'

'Don't worry,' the nurse said coolly, testing the unconscious Miss Wyckham's pulse yet again, this time with a watch: 'It's quite normal. It's not good for her to get excited. We have to sedate her for her own sake, and for the other patients, who would get no peace otherwise. But once her delusions go she'll probably be right as rain. With luck she won't even remember what happened. Of course,' she added bitterly, 'the police haven't exactly helped, coming here at all hours, disturbing our routine. It's our job to get her better, theirs is only to find out who did it, and the two functions conflict. She goes berserk each time they ask her questions, and they get nowhere.'

I took a last look at Miss Wyckham before turning to go. Her mouth had closed again. The bandaged head sank heavily into the high pillows. Under the closed lids fringed with short pale lashes the eyeballs had begun to move with increasing restlessness. Her lips moved, appearing to murmur unintelligible words then, to my amazement, they curved into a secret smile.

14

A young man came to see me today. He claims to be my son.
It would not, normally, have been an incident I would have
thought worthy of recording in my notebook, but he was very
persistent. I was engrossed at the time in my library book, and
much struck by a passage in which the author describes human
logic as a net of meridians and parallels thrown across the universe to make it captive. The more I thought about these lines,
the more convinced I became that this insight had something
to do with my own condition at present. I had escaped the
net, just as, the author points out, the sun and stars had not
conformed to the pattern established by man. A shadow came
between me and the reading light in the quiet hotel lounge,
falling on the pages of my library book.

'Hello, mother,' he said.

I looked up and saw this rather conventional young man
standing by my chair in neat clothes, with a dark tie precisely
knotted under the white collar of a freshly laundered shirt and
a suit only recently pressed. Nothing about his features was
in any way remarkable. It was not the sort of face that sticks
in the memory: young and unlined, with no distinguishing
marks (I calculated he was probably in his mid or late
twenties), good-looking enough, I suppose, in a bland sort of
way, though I noticed that his dark brown eyes had a look
of uncertainty, a tendency to shift and lose ground under
scrutiny.

'Good afternoon,' I said sharply, to show my annoyance at

being disturbed. 'Who are you? I don't think we have been introduced.'

His smooth young face flushed somewhat, and his dark brown eyes became a marshy bog in which he floundered. But, far from removing himself with an apology, he continued to stand there.

'But, mother,' he said, in a tone which I would have called ingratiating if it had been used, for instance, by a hotel waiter, but sounded odd coming from him, 'surely you know your own son?'

I put down the book with a sigh, careful to mark the page I had been reading. I could not imagine what he wanted of me. 'I know no such thing,' I told him. 'You don't remind me of anybody. And even if you did, it must be a long time since you resembled a baby. Women give birth to babies, you know, not grown men. Besides, what do you want? Why are you going round looking for a mother? Surely you have been weaned?'

Then I realised that perhaps I had been too hard on him. Perhaps he genuinely had a problem: he certainly looked put out. He tried to stammer something, his colour darkened even further, and his eyes now had the look of a drowning man who could not even call for help.

'Well anyhow,' I said kindly, 'now you're here you'd better sit down and have some coffee.' It had also occurred to me that the young man, in spite of his appearance, was possibly a little unbalanced, and it might be wise to humour him. After all, it would not do to instigate a scene in public.

I ordered coffee and the waiter brought a tray within minutes. I must say I find the service here very good.

The young man continued to stand, awkwardly. He looked suspicious, as though he was not sure whether somebody was not playing a game with him, or whether he ought not to stand on his dignity, since he might have been humiliated. I saw him glance round in an embarrassed fashion at neighbouring tables, where more coffee-drinking was going on. I patted the seat of an adjacent chair as though he really had been a small and possibly sulky boy, and he finally allowed himself to sit down.

'How do you like your coffee, Mr...?'

'Oh,' he said hastily, 'black, with just a dash of milk. No sugar.' But he still had not introduced himself. He sat uncomfortably on the edge of his seat, watching me pouring the coffee. Afterwards he leaned forward and began drinking, still without telling me his name, or, for that matter, saying anything. The young man seemed singularly lacking in small talk.

'The weather,' I remarked finally, 'was quite good this morning, don't you think? For the time of year.'

He did not answer, apparently engrossed in his coffee.

'I hope it is to your liking,' I said, leaning forward.

'What?' He had obviously not heard a word.

'The coffee.'

'Oh ... oh, yes. It's fine.' He put the empty cup back into its saucer jerkily, with too loud a bang. The people at the neighbouring table got up and left the room. I heard them say something about walking along the river. A sudden ray of pale sunlight broke through the cloud beyond the window. I had an urge to go for a walk too, and take in some fresh air.

'Don't let me keep you,' I finally said, gently but somewhat pointedly. The young man's behaviour was positively unsociable, one could almost have called it surly. 'I'm sure you must have a job to go to.'

If I had reminded him, he seemed undisturbed by his obligations. Perhaps he had taken the day off. He simply shook his head slowly, then suddenly said, abruptly and with a distinct note of accusation:

'We've all been very worried about you.'

I withdrew into the wings of my armchair to escape the sudden glint of anger in his sharpening, tight little pupils, and the aggressive set of his jaw. He seemed to think an apology was called for.

'That's very nice of you,' I answered in a level tone, to humour him, 'but I can't think why. There is absolutely no reason. And even if there was, why should it worry you?'

He seemed at a loss for words. Trying to put him at his ease, I said: 'By the way, you haven't told me anything about yourself—your name, for instance. And what kind of work do you do?'

'Don't play games with me, mother. This is serious, what you've done.'

'Oh, but I'm not,' I said, anxious to pour oil on troubled waters, since he sounded irritable and annoyed. 'I would genuinely like to know.' But even as I said the words I knew them to be a lie, or perhaps just one of those lifelong reflex actions of meaningless but polite conversation which had come back: I was not in the least interested in anything this young man might do or say.

'I'm an executive,' he said sulkily, examining his fingernails to avoid looking in my direction. 'As you very well know.'

I felt I was somehow dealing with a small boy who had come home from school and been denied the attention to which he believed himself to be entitled. As though I had failed to be suitably impressed by his prowess in the football team. If only to avoid unnecessary trouble or aggravation I was anxious to make up for any past neglect, whether real or imagined. So I said encouragingly:

'Really? Is that interesting? What—or should I say whom?—do you execute? And are you happy in your work?'

He had stopped pushing back the skin of his cuticles and was now fiddling with the coffee spoon in his saucer. 'That's not the point,' he said, making a nervous attempt to bend the poor spoon, which resisted. 'The point is to get on, a rung up the ladder. One can't expect much at this stage, but I'm still under thirty and the sky's the limit if you've got what it takes. But I didn't come here to talk about my career prospects. What's the big idea, mother?'

He had put down the coffee spoon and now, leaning forward, stared me straight in the eyes. I stared back, returning the challenge. He blinked first. I thought he had rather nasty eyes, a mean look, with pupils like small hard stones, shrivelled black pips which would not grow.

'I find you rather rude, if not downright offensive, young man,' I told him coldly. 'I don't know what claim you imagine you could possibly have on me, or why you think you have a right to speak to me at all, let alone in such a tone. But I think you'd better leave.'

There was a long silence. I really felt like taking a walk before it began to rain again, and I was about to excuse myself and leave the room when he suddenly said, in a much more gentle voice: 'I'm sorry, mother. But we've all been very worried about you. You should have told somebody.'

I got up, firmly and with some dignity, to make it clear that as far as I was concerned the encounter was at an end. Then—I hardly know what made me say it, perhaps the daily pathos of old Sybil waiting for a son who had long forgotten her—I said quite sharply: 'When did you last get in touch with *your* mother? Or even bother to telephone her? Do you let her know what *you* are doing?'

He got up too, to face me before he spoke, but he could not look me in the eyes. Instead he tried rather nervously to touch my arm, but gave up the attempt half way.

'I suppose I have been neglecting you,' he said slowly. 'I should have made sure you were all right. But I've been a bit preoccupied lately, what with one thing and another. The office. The new house. And things have been a bit difficult with Susan lately.'

'Susan?'

Now he did lift his head to look me in the eyes. 'Susan is my wife, mother,' he said slowly and reproachfully.

'Oh.' I picked up my handbag and the book. 'Well, if you'll excuse me, I think I'll take a little walk. It gets dark so early these days.'

He stood in front of me, blocking my path to the door. 'I hadn't realised,' he began, while I tried to get past him without being too obviously rude. 'I suppose I should have understood that you have been under a great strain recently. I didn't think. Too preoccupied with my own problems, I suppose. How are you feeling now?'

'Impatient,' I said. 'I want some fresh air.'

He let me move forward now, which was just as well, since I had begun to make small side-stepping movements like a bird performing a courtship dance in my attempts to get away. But he held on to my elbow.

'You're looking very well,' he said solicitously. Then added, as I marched through the lounge door into the hallway: 'But don't you think you should see a doctor?'

This time I really turned on him, throwing politeness to the winds. 'Look here, young man,' I said loudly, 'I've just about had enough of you. I don't know who you are and I don't care. Just kindly go away and stop interfering in what is none of your business.'

He looked alarmed, tried to pat my shoulder to placate me, but I moved back. When he saw that the lobby was empty, and that we had not been overheard, he seemed relieved. Moving towards the staircase I got the impression that he had nothing left to say, also that his mind was now elsewhere and preoccupied. I started up the stairs to fetch my overcoat, when his voice followed me up.

'It looks very comfortable here.'

I turned round to see him at the foot of the staircase, looking up at me with a disingenuous expression. It seemed an odd remark, I thought.

'It is,' I answered, looking down at him. And waited.

'It must be quite expensive,' he went on. 'How are you managing for money, mother?'

So that was it. I might have known. His face had assumed a guileless expression full of guile. The concern in his voice was not for me, however he intended it to sound.

'Get out,' I said.

He refused to be insulted. 'Goodbye,' he said. 'I'll come to see you again soon. Enjoy your walk.'

I did not enjoy my walk, thanks to him. Try as I would, I could not put the encounter out of my mind. I took the road past the primary school but the building was locked up, the asphalt playground without life. Perhaps, I thought, the world had always been full of young men who spent their spare time in search of a mother, but I doubted it. There was a more explicit reason for his unexpected arrival, and it made me uneasy. Whoever he was, his last remarks made me fairly certain that he was really after the money in the suitcase, though how he could have known about it was beyond me. Perhaps he was an agent sent to spy on me, to find out what I was up to.

I followed the road as it curved round the foot of the hillside to rejoin the river. The children's playground had been deserted the last time I walked this way, but today everything was in motion: swings, roundabout, the seesaw. Small figures grubbed about in the sandpit and slithered down the slide. I stopped to watch, then sat down on an empty public bench at the edge of the playground.

The seesaw was close by. I watched two children going up and down. Shock alternated with pleasure, and one child's uplift was at the expense of the other, who had just come down with an uncomfortable bump. However, once down, the child with his feet on the ground was in control of the mechanism. 'Let me down,' shrieked the child in mid-air after dangling for a while. The child at the bottom decided to get off the seesaw and his playmate came down in an uncontrolled crash.

A young woman in a short coat, with a scarf tied under her chin, sat down on the bench beside me. She had been pushing a pram with one hand, and dragging a toddler with the other.

'Go on,' she said now, giving the small child a push. 'Go and play with the other children.' The child, apparently a girl, began to suck the ungloved fingers of one hand and developed such a rigid spine under the mother's hand that she seemed immovable. From the top of her furlined bonnet to the small shoes below the leggings her body formed a firm curve of resistance.

'What's the matter with you? Go and play.' The woman's voice sounded loud and cross now. 'Oh, they are a nuisance,' she confided to me. Her face looked tired under the brightly coloured scarf, and bluish with cold like her long exposed legs. Meanwhile the small child had developed a pout, her face flushed threateningly, and her lower lip began to quiver. She was obviously about to cry.

'Oh you are a ninny,' her mother said impatiently. 'What are you afraid of? Nobody is going to hurt you.'

Tears rolled down the child's cheeks, silently. She sniffed, but not hard enough. Her mother took out a handkerchief and wiped the runny nose.

'I don't know why I bother, really I don't.' She turned to me again. 'Would you mind keeping an eye on the baby while I push her on the swings? He's fast asleep, so he won't be any bother. And I'll be back in a minute.'

I sat with my hand on the bar of the pram. She was gone rather more than a minute. After a while I leaned forward to peer under the canvas hood to see what lay under the neat mound of blankets. A small head, almost bald, with eyes screwed up tight and a look of disgust on his features. He had burped up something sour, judging from the expression on his face and the damp patch near his mouth. It was not a promising face: disagreeable, if pugnacious. Now the egg-shaped head stirred slightly, frowning, as though annoying sensations, perhaps even a dream, had intruded on his wish to sleep on undisturbed. His mouth puckered into a grimace. I had noticed the network of tiny blue veins under the skin, now it darkened to an angry red. He snuffled once or twice, then began to bawl in a thin persistent whine. My attempts to rock him back into oblivion were to no avail. He refused to be content. Perhaps he was dimly aware that he was being fobbed off, and that the pram was not going anywhere. The whine gathered volume. If they say crying is good for the lungs, no doubt he was also exercising them for further demands in the future. There would be no stopping him.

The mother came back to the bench, pulling her small daughter, who was also crying. 'I told you not to get in the way, but you wouldn't listen, would you? Oh, they are a trial,' she said to me, shaking her head. 'Shut up,' she added, slapping her daughter on the hand. 'Now, what's the matter with his lordship?'

'I really don't know,' I said, with a hint of apology in my voice. 'I haven't touched him. I've tried rocking the pram, but he won't go back to sleep.'

'I expect it's wind,' she said, starting to pull back the layers of blankets, 'but you never know with him. You couldn't call him a good baby—I haven't had a good night's sleep since he was born. My mother warned me,' she went on, propping the bundle with the lolling head against her shoulder while she rubbed and patted his back, 'but I didn't listen—you never do listen, do you, not till it's too late?' She laid the bundle back in the pram and started to tuck him up. I could see his eyes, wide open now, gazing fixedly at her head above him. 'I always wanted a boy, but she said that boys are much more difficult than girls. Stop snivelling, Sarah.' The latter, subdued now but still tearful, was trying to shift her bottom on to the wooden seat, which was too high for her. She lowered her head, apparently in shame.

I tried saying a few encouraging words to her, but she only hung her head a little lower, now presumably also bashful.

'Answer the lady,' said her mother severely, giving her a prod. Conscious of having made things worse, I tried to think of some way in which I could help the child, but nothing occurred to me. To deflect attention from her I made some remark about the weather, but the mother was in no mood for a change of theme.

'Kids,' she began, on what was obviously going to be a monologue. 'Sometimes I wonder what it's all for. You try to bring them up proper, but it's an uphill job. I'll be glad when she's old enough to go to school, then at least I'll have one off my hands. As it is, I haven't got a minute to call my own. If it's not one thing it's another. There's no end to it.'

'There is,' I interposed, but she did not hear me. She was still talking, about the good old days, not that she didn't love them mind, but how she would give anything for a good night's sleep, a day to herself, a night out without a care in the world, just like the good old days, without a care in the world, not having to worry about teething, nappy rash, coughs and sneezes, the girl's delicate chest, and what had happened to her own figure since childbearing. It wasn't the same. She was afraid her husband would go off her, especially now they could not go out like before and she was always tired anyhow. 'It's a mug's game really, isn't it?' she said finally, looking at me as somebody who was likely to support her unorthodox opinion.

'Children do grow up,' I said soothingly. 'It's only a matter of time.'

She snorted. 'When I'm an old woman.' The hair visible under her scarf was dyed a crude henna red, the eyes in her unremarkable face already looked old. The rest, it was all too obvious, would soon follow, coarsen and fade. 'And anyhow, that's not what I had kids for. So they'd grow up. What's the point of that? Just look at those louts over there...'

She nodded towards a group of older boys at the far end of the playground who were hurling themselves about on chains attached to a central pole: they swung away from it, each time the chain swung them back they kicked themselves outward once more. It was an ugly, senseless game, but they put a lot of strenuous energy into it.

The baby had become restless once more. His mother tried rocking the pram, but the persistent whine did not stop. Finally she got up with a sigh. 'I'd better take him home. I expect he's dirty. Anyhow, his next feed is almost due.' She had already moved off several yards with the pram when something seemed to occur to her and she turned round.

'Sarah!'

Sarah was still sitting on the bench, as though she did not belong anywhere, forgetting and forgotten. Her small forefinger explored a thin crack in a wooden slat of the seat, up and down, up and down.

'Are you coming, or aren't you?'

Sarah did not move, absorbed in the crack of the wood, painted green. Her mother's voice took on a more threatening tone. 'Do I have to come and get you?'

Slowly, laboriously, Sarah's bottom shifted along the curve of the seat until she slid down and her feet touched the ground. She ran off to follow her mother.

15

I had a peculiarly restless night, disturbed by dreams of the railway station, which keep recurring. Last night I was conscious of wanting to get away, but each time I arrived on the empty platform with the dusk closing in, shaken and out of breath from running because I was so anxious not to miss the last train, I found myself alone in a bleak, dark silence, watching the last light fade on the far horizon where the track vanished.

I felt rather unwell when I woke up, so I decided to take things easy and have a leisurely breakfast served in my room. The maid who brought up the tray, and who has become quite chatty over the past few days, was quite excited on this occasion and could hardly wait to tell me the cause: apparently the local bank had been robbed. Nothing like it has happened in the town in years, since nothing much ever did happen. Thousands of pounds were missing. I hope, I said, that nobody has got hurt in the process. Oh no, she went on, it was an inside job. In fact they already knew who it was, a cashier who had vanished overnight, quite a young man, somebody local, the hotel manager had been to school with him and was very shocked when he heard.

'Of course it's his wife I feel sorry for,' she said in a tone of delight which suggested nothing of the sort. 'Apparently she had no idea what was going on—hasn't seen him. If she's got any sense she'll move out of the neighbourhood to get away from the gossip. Anyhow, I don't suppose she can afford to go on living in that house. Fancy him going off like that with all that money, leaving her without a penny. Or perhaps she's really in the know, and she's waiting to join him somewhere else when all the fuss has died down—what do you think?'

'How should I know? Your guess is as good as mine,' I answered listlessly, but somehow sure that the young woman would be waiting for a long time, to no purpose.

The maid closed the door behind her and I cracked the top of my boiled egg, reflecting as I did so that banks were not necessarily as safe as they were made out to be, in which case I ought to have left my money locked up in the wardrobe. On second thoughts I recalled the police inspector's remarks about insurance, which presumably took care of this sort of eventuality too. In any case, the bank manager could hardly say it was my particular notes which the clerk had stolen, even though I knew this to be the case. Poor young man, I thought, spooning out the last of the yolk and pouring out more tea, I wonder what he thinks he can do with the money? Perhaps, I speculated, it was cruel to lock a healthy young man up all day in a cage, counting banknotes. He was bound to get obsessive.

My lazy morning did not improve my general sense of discomfort. I continued to feel almost ill, though I could not have said how or why. If anything, it was as though something poisonous or highly disagreeable had been injected into me, and was now circulating round my body, so that everything felt uncomfortable, if not downright painful: digestion, limbs, head and muscles. I did not feel in the mood to do anything, and yet I was not sufficiently incapable to do nothing. I ate lunch, but did not enjoy it, I tried a little reading, but soon noticed that my mind was not taking in the words on the page.

Then I remembered that I had noticed a doctor's plate outside a nearby house on one of my walks. It seemed as good a way of passing the time as any, under the circumstances: at least it could do no harm, if I was duly cautious.

A middle-aged female receptionist was at first reluctant to allow me to see the doctor at all. She told me that they operated an appointments system, so that patients had to give notice of illness in advance or take the consequences. She became more amenable when I told her I did not wish to register, was simply passing through, staying at the Black Swan Hotel a few yards down the road. She said the doctor would see me right away.

He was a young man, fair-headed, clean-shaven, and almost painfully polite. He asked for my name and I watched his immaculate hand move across the paper on his desk as he noted the false name I had given him. Then he asked my age, and I made a rough guess, giving myself the benefit of the doubt by a year or two.

'What seems to be the trouble?'

He was looking at me now, and I looked back, somewhat at a loss. I had come with the notion that it was for him to tell me.

'I haven't been feeling myself lately,' I said rather lamely, and became conscious that this was more than a trite remark. It summed up the whole truth, but how was he to know that?

'I see,' he said slowly, and it was obvious that he saw nothing at all, except perhaps a middle-aged woman with too much time on her hands. Nevertheless his manner continued polite, almost kind. I tried to tell him about the aches and pains, the unpleasant sensations I had experienced during the day.

He nodded as I spoke, regarding me with his kind brown eyes. 'Perhaps I'd better examine you,' he said.

I lay down on his couch in my underwear, and he prodded my clumsy body, the falling unshapely flesh, looked into my eyes with one instrument, listened to my chest with another.

'Any serious illnesses?' he asked.

'Not that I can remember.' I was trying to be helpful, but it was the best I could do. He mentioned a number of complaints, but I shook my head. He wrapped some dark grey cloth round my arm, preparatory to taking my blood pressure, and began to pump.

'Family?' he asked, unwinding the cloth.

'I beg your pardon?'

'Any children?'

I hesitated, looking at him with increasing embarrassment. I realised we had come to the nub of the matter, the central question, and I had no idea how to go about extracting an answer.

'Can you tell?' I asked lightly, almost jokingly.

'What do you mean?'

'What I mean is, can you tell, from examining my body, whether I have had children or not?'

He looked annoyed, as though I might be wasting his time, or testing him unnecessarily when he had qualified as a practitioner several years ago.

'Well,' he began, 'there are of course physical indications of past childbirth. The breasts, for instance, and stretch-marks on the skin of the abdomen. However, in your case childbirth would have occurred some time back ...' He broke off, as though he had decided that he was under no obligation to prove his knowledge to someone like me. 'In fact, it's a routine question which really has no bearing on the complaints for which you have come to me.' He indicated that I could put my clothes back on, and walked back to his desk.

'I think you are probably run down. Perhaps also a mild virus. Very common at this time of year. Nothing to worry about.' I had dressed now, but came back to the chair alongside his desk feeling as though everything, blouse, skirt, stocking tights, were slightly askew. He had begun writing again. 'Take these three times a day after meals. I'm sure you'll feel better in a day or two.' He handed me the prescription. I could not read the cryptic scrawl.

'What are they?' I asked.

'Vitamins.'

He saw me to the door. The receptionist saw me out. In the street I crushed the piece of paper and dropped it in the gutter.

When I got back to the hotel I put the DO NOT DISTURB notice on my door and took to my bed for the rest of the day. I listened to the radio for a while, without hearing much. I made these notes. I spent a lot of time staring at the room and its contents, for no particular reason, except that a crack across the corner of the ceiling made an obsessive impression on me: my eyes kept being drawn back to it, though I could not say why. Once the telephone rang, reception calling to say that a gentleman had arrived to see me. I told the voice that I could see no one today, since I was feeling unwell. It was only afterwards that it occurred to me that I had not been given the caller's name, and that I had not asked for it. Not that it would mean much if I knew, judging by the past few days. No doubt somebody wanting something, yet again. I have already become thoroughly disenchanted with visitors.

16

The weather is getting milder. It feels almost kind on my face. Little bits of yellow are sprouting inexplicably from bare branches. I can also hear birdsong in the hollow sky, occasional but clear, on my solitary walks. Crocuses are shooting out of the earth in muddy patches of front garden like purple and yellow fireworks. A small but unmistakable celebration is taking place, though I am not sure why. I suppose it has to do with climate, the promise of the rich dark earth and of spring in the air, though this has little to do with me, being mainly confined to horticulture. However, the change has enabled me to go for walks without an overcoat.

Such small seasonal changes break up the growing tedium of my days. To distract my thoughts from the monotony of the same walks, and a more profound disturbance about my existence here, I pay particular attention to the minutiae of coming spring, and am conscious that my admiration of the trees now bursting out in a festal flutter of blossom, like youthful brides blushing and virginal once more, is also sharply jealous. Why should mere trees be allowed a fresh start year after year, when human beings only have one springtime?

I am getting bored with the hotel menu, with what has already become a routine existence. I tell myself it is time to make a decision, and shy away from making one on the grounds of my recurring nightmares of the railway station, which prevent me. And yet ... and yet ... I have to admit to a certain nameless excitement, a change in temperature in tune with the weather. It could almost be called a quickening in the blood. Quite literally, as though my blood circulation had speeded up, gathered momentum, to cause a tingling sensation through my body. I do not know what to do about it. Occasionally I feel I would like to dance, or burst into song, if I knew one, or had a voice, and if I were not stopped by the fear of drawing attention to myself, the possibility of becoming a foolish spectacle. So I have not done any such thing. But I do take longer walks, smile encouragingly at the small brave flowers, perhaps say a word or two when they shiver in the wind, having sprung from such cold damp earth, and have come to regard the blossoming trees with the affectionate complicity due to much younger sisters.

The river, also, appears to have changed pace. It runs clear and fast, spawning under the gleaming surface, moving, cloud-shadowed, half-revealing but secretive. Now one or two anglers occasionally sit on the grass verge.

As far as my own situation is concerned, I have decided that I must at least do something about the wardrobe with which I find myself lumbered. I could do with rather more variety: whoever started this whole thing off seems to have had little sense of style and an aversion to colour, and the clothes with which I am fitted out all seem to be in muted shades of grey, as though a person were trying to remain unseen, merge into the background and become invisible. Anyhow, the few clothes I have will soon be much too warm for this milder weather. I have already bought myself a pink silk blouse in the High Street. Wearing it makes me feel more cheerful although, studying the effect in the wardrobe mirror, in no way is it comparable to the flowering fruit trees.

Whilst I was drinking my coffee in the lounge after dinner tonight I was disturbed by a middle-aged man who came over and asked whether he might join me. Although I was a little annoyed I could hardly refuse. In any case, as I told him laughingly, there was no law to forbid him. He did not take the hint, and sat down.

The interruption seemed a little crude, since I had made

it patently obvious that I was studiously engrossed in my book. Also, he had looked in my direction once or twice earlier, when he caught me looking at him in the dining room, and forced me to look elsewhere and avoid his hard and steady gaze. This had been embarrassing, although it is natural to pay attention to a new guest. If nothing else, it distracts from the monotony and tedium of the hotel food, which has become familiar.

And then I had another reason for looking at him over dinner. He did not fit, somehow. He was obviously a professional businessman, but he was dining alone. Nor could he be off duty, simply relaxing, since his behaviour was not in the least relaxed. What, I asked myself more than once, was he doing here? Groomed, expensively dressed, with the heavy build of a man well into middle age, he combined a man-of-the-world assurance in handling waiters, knives and forks, and the ritual of ordering and testing a bottle of red wine with an underlying unease, a nervous tension quite at odds with his offhand authority. At times, when he thought no one was watching him, he looked almost shifty. He ate hurriedly, but left much of the food untouched, while he downed several glasses of wine in quick succession. He was, I decided, a man to avoid. Which was why I was displeased when he asked to join me, and why I had been so overtly engrossed in my library book when I saw him come in. Out of the corner of my eye I had seen him hesitating near the door before he came over.

'Do you mind if I join you?' he asked in a deep voice, leaning forward. A first class tailor had not done badly in making the most of his stocky figure. Any flab or past excesses were neatly concealed under the cunning cut of dark quality cloth.

'There's no law against it,' I said laughingly. But my voice was brittle, consciously, artfully so. 'It's a public room. The chair is unoccupied.' Impervious to irony, whether thick-skinned or simply unamused, he chose to sit down beside me.

I snapped my book shut and glanced pointedly round the room, which was half empty, with many unoccupied chairs. Having sat down, he appeared to have nothing to say, and a long silence followed. I watched him as he rubbed his hand over the lower half of his face several times, as though considering whether he should not, after all, have shaved before dinner. It was, at least in his mind, a debatable point.

'I expect the waiter will be along in a minute,' I remarked brightly, by way of an apology for pouring myself a second coffee whilst he had nothing. 'The service is very good here.'

He nodded absently, but the silence continued. I wondered whether it would be permissible to pick up my book and continue reading. Perhaps, after all, he had chosen this particular chair for reasons which had nothing to do with me, or for no reason, and not because he wanted to be sociable. I glanced uneasily from my book to his face, then across the room for some sign of the waiter. But the service seemed unusually slow tonight.

'Wilkinson.'

He said it so suddenly, that I was hardly sure if he had spoken and, if so, whether the utterance, which sounded so peculiar, was intended for me: he pronounced it like a challenge, as a dishonoured husband cracking a pistol into the slumber of a misty dawn, startling birds. Or it could have been a code word spoken at a pre-arranged spot by undercover agents who had not met before.

'I beg your pardon?'

'Wilkinson,' he repeated. 'My name is George Wilkinson. The name means nothing to you?'

'No,' I answered. 'I'm afraid it doesn't. Should it? You must forgive me, but my memory is terrible when it comes to names.'

'What about my face?' He leaned forward, his tone aggressive, challenging.

'What about it?' I felt helpless, at a loss for words, not knowing what he expected of me. 'I'm sure it's a very nice face ... I mean, as faces go. Should I know it—are you famous? Or have we met somewhere? I'm sorry, I'm just as bad about faces. And I'm afraid I don't watch television much.' I was floundering now, getting more and more embarrassed, and he made no attempt to help me out. It was as though he were putting either me or himself to some sort of test: I was not sure which of us it was, only that his self-image was at stake.

Luckily the waiter arrived. Mr Wilkinson ordered coffee and invited me to take a brandy with him. I accepted, we smiled at each other as the waiter left, and the situation was defused, at least temporarily. I noticed that he had quite a nice face when he smiled, attractive, almost handsome.

'Are you staying here long?' It was only one of those remarks one makes to fill the gap in hotel-lounge conversations, but he seemed to regard the question as the first move in an awkward interrogation for which he was already prepared. He shifted slightly in his seat, but tried to look frankly into my face, as though I could possibly be concerned, while he answered, with an odd tone of apology in his voice:

'We'll see. It depends how things go. I'm a very busy man, you understand. Lots of commitments. A heavy schedule. In my position so many people depend on me. It's hard to find time away from it all. You've no idea how much work I have to get through.'

'I'm sure you have,' I answered consolingly. 'You don't have to explain. I've heard how busy some of you men are. I was only asking. And perhaps you shouldn't say any more—I expect it's very important and confidential. And after all, it's no concern of mine. I wouldn't wish to pry into what is none of my business.'

He looked suspiciously at me, as though he was not sure whether I was poking fun at him, being sarcastic, or whether this was a new move in the interrogation. I cannot think why he should have thought his doings or life style should fascinate me, but he looked at me long and levelly from under his somewhat bushy eyebrows, reduced to silence. I drank the rest of my coffee, occasionally returned his gaze, and did not flinch. Finally he said, reverting to his earlier ploy, like a stuck gramophone needle:

'Are you sure the name Wilkinson means nothing to you?'

I felt like a backward schoolgirl. I pretended to rack my brains, but of course I knew it was useless. I tried to think whether I had seen the name on some commodity, the hood of a motor car, wrapped round a bar of soap or chocolate, perhaps it was a household word for a vacuum cleaner. Who knows, perhaps even this was doing him an injustice. I shook my head and answered, duly contrite:

'You must forgive me, but I know very little about the world of big business ... public affairs ... politics ...' Perhaps I would stumble on a clue, if I did not fall headlong in the process.

My half-hearted search for truth was cut short by the waiter, who came to our table and began to unload the paraphernalia of more coffee and two glasses of brandy on to its surface. Mr Wilkinson placed a note on the man's emptied tray and magnanimously told him to keep the change.

I cupped the glass in my hands and swirled the warm amber liquid round the bowl. 'Cheers,' I said, glad of a chance to drop the subject. 'Your very good health.'

He lifted his glass. 'And yours.' After we had both swallowed a few sips he suddenly added: 'How is it?'

'I beg your pardon?' The man's conversation had this tendency to take unexpected turns, full of odd questions. 'How is what?' Then it dawned on me. 'Oh, I see, you mean the brandy. It's very good. Though of course I'm no connoisseur.'

'No, no.' He sounded impatient. 'I mean—how is your health?'

This time I was truly astounded. 'Splendid,' I assured him. 'What made you ask? Do I look so unwell? It's hardly very flattering,' I added coquettishly, to make light of his oddly serious, almost intense manner. I at least succeeded in embarrassing him.

'Of course not. You do look splendid. A very handsome woman, if I may say so.' He did the gentlemanly thing in making the obligatory remark, paying the compliment now due. After a pause, during which he studied his brandy, he tried to explain himself. 'I somehow assumed you were staying in this place for your health. That perhaps you had been ill.'

'How odd,' I said brightly, now warmed by the brandy. 'I don't go round assuming that about people I see in the hotel.

When I saw you in the dining room, for instance, I didn't say to myself, now there's a man who has had an operation, or a mental breakdown, or even a bad bout of pneumonia. Do you think that was wrong of me?' He did not answer. 'No, no. I'm just having a break from my normal humdrum existence, a little holiday. One needs a break now and then, don't you think?'

Mr Wilkinson did not answer. The conversation, if it had been going anywhere, which was doubtful, died away. Frankly, I had found his behaviour distinctly odd from his first approach, which surprised me; now he became suddenly subdued and quiet. I felt quite sorry for the poor man, leaning forward with his elbows on his knees, head bowed, frowning into his brandy glass, which was empty anyhow.

'Drink your coffee,' I said, to bring him round. I was beginning to feel responsible for this stranger who, for all his display of aggressive self-assurance and worldly rank, was obviously human, with problems. In only a few days of my new life I have already become over-burdened with the agony of people unknown to me: each one ordinary, different, unique. It remains a mystery to me why I should inspire such a compulsion to confide.

I waited for Mr Wilkinson to begin, but he obviously had difficulty amounting to a blockage. I suspected that his worldly success and authority had a lot to do with it: that he found it hard to be humble now, having been in command of all situations for so long.

'Won't you drink your coffee?' I asked. 'It must be nearly cold.'

He was still frowning into his emptied brandy balloon, cupping it in both hands. Now he suddenly came out of his private reverie and looked up.

'I suppose you think this is all a huge joke.' His voice was accusing. 'You are laughing at me.'

He was so serious, and I was so taken aback by what he had just said, that I found it hard not to laugh.

'What an odd thing to say. Why should you think that?'

But I had difficulty in suppressing the giggle surging up in my throat. The man was too absurd, in spite of his good clothes, the almost handsome face, his starched white cuffs with the gold links, and strong masculine fingers curved round the empty glass. A pity. I had quite taken to his hands with their neatly trimmed nails.

'You coffee must be quite cold by now.' I persisted in trying to divert our conversation back to a mundane level. 'Why don't you order some more?'

I thought he had not even heard me, until he suddenly asked:

'Is it too late?'

'Oh no,' I said cheerfully, 'I'm sure it's not. They usually go on serving coffee until quite late.'

Mr Wilkinson stared at me like a man possessed, though certainly not in possession of his normal faculties. He looked like a haunted man.

'Coffee?' he asked. 'What has coffee got to do with it?'

I was now seriously alarmed. The man's behaviour was more than odd, he struck me as mentally disturbed.

'Are you feeling all right?' I asked anxiously.

He did not answer, but started rubbing the lower half of his face again. I watched him for a while, uneasily.

'Perhaps,' I suggested, 'you should go and lie down. You've probably been working too hard. All your commitments, and that heavy schedule.'

'You want to get rid of me,' he said lugubriously, giving me an accusing look. 'What,' he added, 'have I done wrong?'

He was waiting for an answer, leaning forward slightly, his forearms supporting his heavy weight. His eyes, under the bushy brows, held an expression of sorrow rather than anger.

'No, no, of course not,' I protested feebly. 'You really must not ... I assure you, Mr Wilkinson ...'

'Stop this farce,' he said abruptly, in the same dark tone. 'Call me George.'

'George.' I said, to humour him. I was struck by the odd sound of the word and had to suppress another giggle.

Without giving me a chance to refuse, he ordered two more brandies and began to confide in me. He was not, he assured me, ill, but the tension of the past week had begun to tell on him, he admitted that. If he had in any way given offence, he hoped I would make allowances, put it down to the strain he had been under. Not many people, he went on, downing his second brandy, appreciated what it meant to be successful at his age, the heavy responsibilities involved, the stress entailed, least of all women. He hoped I was not one of those.

I told him I would try to understand.

'Because I want us to be friends. I like you.'

I thanked him, and he urged me to finish my second brandy. I tried to demur as he signalled to the waiter.

'Two more brandies. Why not relax, eh?'

I assured him I was sufficiently relaxed already. In fact my head was swimming.

'I'm not perfect,' he confided, 'but then, who is? I've got my faults, same as the next man, I admit that. I've made mistakes, but then that's only human, wouldn't you agree? All I ask for is a little human understanding. Do you think that is too much to ask?'

'I suppose not.' I wondered dizzily what he was going on about. But I was beginning to warm to him: he was, as he admitted, human. And the brandy helped.

'It's difficult.' I noticed that my speech was slightly slurred.

'What is?'

'To understand human beings. Let alone men and women ... if you know what I mean.'

'There you go again,' he objected, pointing his finger at me. He was obviously nursing an old grievance. 'You women are all the same. What's so difficult about an ordinary chap like me? All I need is a bit of understanding. I've never yet met a woman who could understand that. So I get irritable, or drink too much or ... well, you know. I've got normal physical needs, I see no reason to be ashamed of that. In fact I could be bloody proud of it, a man of my age. But that's not it, it's emotions that count, what I need is a woman with a bit of understanding. Instead I keep getting impossible demands made on me, falling into a trap.'

'Oh dear.'

'You see the problem?'

'Oh I do, Mr Wilkinson.'

'George,' he insisted.

'Sorry ... George,' I obediently repeated after him.

In spite of the amber glow of brandy which had my ears ringing, eyes swimming, and filled my body with an expansive sense of wellbeing which overflowed to my immediate surroundings and those in it, I noticed with displeasure that George (daft name) Wilkinson had not taken the trouble to find out what my names were.

17

Mr Wilkinson has followed me round all day like a shadow.
I came down late for breakfast and the first person I saw when
I entered the dining room was him, sitting by himself with
a newspaper propped against his coffee pot, but watching the
door rather than reading. He half rose from his chair as I
entered, seemed uncertain whether to address me or simply
nod, and I had a distinct suspicion that he had been waiting
for me.

I must admit I felt a distinct flutter in my chest, less at the
possibility of an adventure, though the possibility could not be
wholly excluded, than as a result of my recurring anxiety about
the motives of those who pay me attention of any kind. Why
was he still here, this busy man of the world with all his commitments and such a heavy timetable? And what could he
possibly see in me? I tell myself that I cannot go through life,
which I have only now begun to live, doubting the motives
of all and sundry, but I am held by a deep-seated conviction
that my doubts are somehow justified. I still have a thirst for
adventure, and the tedium of my existence in this place
certainly has its drawbacks, yet I feel safer left to my own
devices, reading, walking, eating, calm and composed.

Mr Wilkinson rose from his chair with such alacrity that
he tipped over the pot of coffee, spilling a rapidly expanding
puddle on the white cloth. There was much commotion, a
waitress rushed over and attempted to staunch the flood with
a napkin, whilst Mr Wilkinson asked whether I would join him
for breakfast. I was forced to give in gracefully, and the

waitress took my order. I tried to find a dry patch of tablecloth for my library book. Mr Wilkinson watched my every move.

'I notice you read a lot,' he commented.

'So do you,' I answered. He looked baffled, so I tapped the top edge of his daily newspaper, now somewhat coffee-stained. He laughed.

'Oh, I wouldn't call that reading. It's not fun, you know, entertainment, escapism. In my job you have to be aware of trends, forestall the future, so to speak.'

I told him I usually heard the weather forecast on my bedroom radio, whereupon he explained rather condescendingly that he was talking about economic forecasts and share indexes. When I asked him how reliable he found them he looked embarrassed, and fell silent. I began to tuck into my breakfast with relish, savouring the strong hot coffee and my soft boiled egg.

'All right,' he conceded finally, 'perhaps the future is unpredictable. But one ought to know what happened yesterday.'

'I don't see why,' I said airily. 'Yesterday has gone for good. It's over, finished with. Who knows what tomorrow will bring?'

'So in your view the past doesn't matter—it doesn't add up to anything?' I felt he was quizzing me now, quite deliberately.

'Not necessarily. A lot of days don't necessarily add up to anything. And if they do, you are more likely to find the sum total in here—' I patted the cover of my book '—than in that ragbag of odds and ends,' and I pointed to his sodden newspaper.

Mr Wilkinson looked thoughtful. 'I understand,' he said finally. 'You're not interested in current affairs. But then there is the personal angle. Everybody holds on to their own past.'

'Not necessarily.' I poured myself a second cup of coffee.

'But,' he persisted, 'where would any of us be without a past?'

I shrugged. 'Who knows? Here perhaps.'

Mr Wilkinson leaned back in his chair with an expression of disbelief. He began to scrutinise my face, bit by bit, like the map of an alien country, as though he had not seen it till now. 'I don't believe it,' he murmured, 'I just don't believe it.' I sat there rather calmly, allowing him to study me, this curious animal. If anything I was quite flattered by his attention. 'What has happened to you, do you know? Can you tell me?'

I shrugged, smiled, and shook my head. 'I don't know,' I said truthfully.

He appeared bothered or bewitched by my inscrutable smile, so much so that he insisted on accompanying me on my morning walk. We had barely walked fifty yards when he suddenly stopped and said, quite crossly:

'I don't know what you see in this place.'

I was struck by his odd comment. 'I see what there is,' I said. 'What else is there to see?' He continued to stand on the same spot, like a sulky schoolboy. 'Anyhow, why have you come here? Presumably for pleasure, not a penance?'

He said nothing, but started to frown, and kicked a nearby gatepost quite viciously before following me on my way. Even after that I had a distinct impression that he was dragging his feet whilst I, meanwhile, was feeling more than usually energetic, full of the joys of spring. I could feel it in the air, inhale it, breathe it out like laughing gas. It would not have taken much more to make me laugh out loud, and the least thing could have provoked a smile.

'Look at the blossom,' I told him encouragingly, 'isn't it delicious?' The pink and white stuff was dropping into my hair, drifting on the ground like confetti. You could see where, in the dark tangle of branches, now garlanded and adorned, the fruit would eventually grow to term. But George W. saw nothing, appeared to be already sorry that he had wasted his valuable time in this place with such a companion. Instead he had viewed the buildings we passed on our way back to the river with contempt: the schoolyard, the old-fashioned locked chapel, the low functional frontage of the public library.

He trudged along beside me, apparently not even enjoying the exercise. 'I've got a car,' he muttered at one point. 'We could have taken the car.'

'In that case,' I pointed out, 'it would not have been a walk. Anyhow, it will do you good.'

We stopped down by the riverbank. The water was flowing fast today. It made me think of life, how it was suddenly shooting out of the dull heavy earth, sprouting on naked branches. It was exciting, hopeful, but not unmixed with panic. The water, I thought, was flowing so very fast, too fast. It would carry anybody away with it.

Mr Wilkinson started throwing stones into the water, viciously, as though it were an enemy. Each time a small spurt of water erupted momentarily on the flowing surface but the pebble was immediately swallowed up. Unconcerned, the river moved on and yet remained unchanged, unruffled; too deep, it could swallow anything, even the landscape of which it was a part.

'I used to be able to make them bounce four or five times along the surface,' Mr Wilkinson declared wistfully, 'but I'm out of practice.'

'The river always wins in the end,' I said. 'We're none of us getting any younger.'

'I'm just out of practice,' he insisted, frowning, and hurled a pebble hard at the surface of the water, where it sank without a trace.

We sat down on a bench overlooking the river. He was now breathing rather heavily, still scowling, as if he were angry, either with himself, or the river, or the stone which had refused to float. 'I do not know what I've done to deserve this,' I heard him mutter at one point, I think it was after I had tried to distract him from grieving over the loss of his youthful skills by asking him about his home background. Far from causing him to cheer up it seemed to deepen his mood of gloom and self-pity. He gave me a dark suspicious glance once, as though he thought I might be doing it on purpose.

'I am a man,' he said portentously, perhaps thinking I had not been aware of his sex. 'I am a man,' he repeated, this time looking me in the face with an expression of sincerity, 'more sinned against than sinning.'

I found it impossible to reply to this assertion, though I felt sure I had heard the words before. Perhaps if I had known when and where, I could have framed a suitable answer. There might be a formula. Conscious of my handicap, I patted him consolingly on the shoulder and pointed out a charming sight: two parent ducks calmly escorting a flotilla of small ducklings, paddling frantically to keep up. One was already straggling some way behind. But the sight failed to amuse or engage his attention: his boyish obsession with ducks and drakes must have been confined to throwing stones.

In spite of our unpropitious walk we did not separate on getting back to the hotel. Perhaps he had reasons of his own for cultivating my acquaintance, but Mr Wilkinson insisted that I should take a pre-lunch drink with him in such a way that I found it impossible to refuse. At the bar he suddenly became determinedly cheerful, almost too much so. He seemed to have decided to change his whole approach. He pressed several drinks on me, rubbed his hands, smiled a lot, put his arm round my shoulder, and took me in to lunch, where he ordered a bottle of wine and behaved as though something were being celebrated, or he had not eaten for a week.

After lunch, since the weather continued bright, George proposed that we should take a boat out on the river. Several are moored with a FOR HIRE notice on the other side of the bridge, where the bank is dark with overhanging trees. Gone was the moody silence, the brooding sulks of the morning: George had apparently decided to behave as if he were on holiday and galvanise both of us into enjoyable activity at all costs. It was not that I was against the idea, but I must say I was glad of the extra layer of woollies I had taken the precaution to put on before we set out. In spite of the crystal bright air, a cold wind blew across the water. I felt the first gust as George marched me purposefully across the bridge, holding on to my elbow and propelling me forward so that I was almost forced to run, to keep up with his brisk pace. We both got slightly breathless and laughed a lot. I was not sure if the cold air tingling on my face had sobered me up or gone to my head. I just hoped that George's large frame and habitual business drinking made him capable of controlling the situation, both me and the boat.

'Isn't it marvellous,' he said, rubbing his hands together, to warm them I suspect, rather than in gleeful expectation. 'Doesn't it take you back?'

I did not answer. I began to have misgivings, both about his motives in bringing me here, and the vessel we were supposed to float in for a whole hour. Instead of choosing one of the rowing boats, which looked relatively stable, George insisted on a punt which looked as though it had seen better days. What did he mean about taking me back? To where, or what? He gave me a helping hand as I gingerly stepped into the old wooden vessel, which moved precariously, and tried to settle comfortably, or at least look relaxed in the low seat. The surface of the water was too close, and looked decidedly cold.

George Wilkinson had obviously handled a punt pole before, though he fumbled alarmingly at first and took some time to get into his stride, particularly as he would keep looking down at me and grinning, instead of watching where we were supposed to be going and what he was doing. I smiled back, but my heart was not in it, and I knew it to be a frozen watery smile. An hour, I thought, I am stuck here for an hour.

I watched his large, bulky shape standing up at the end of the craft, trying to manoeuvre his pole and us against invisible obstacles and an unfamiliar riverbed, and the sight did not reassure me: he looked altogether too middle-aged, heavy and slow for an activity which called for nimble grace. But he tried hard, I give him that. Too hard. As he got the pole jammed in an unexpected morass of mud and weeds, almost losing his balance in his efforts to extricate it, I glumly envisaged being called upon to rescue him, either bodily from the cold and decidedly uninviting water, or simply the drenched remnants of his pride. But he pushed on, undeterred by such minor incidents as the submerged rock which scraped the wooden floor

149

of the punt with an ugly tearing sound but miraculously left it intact. I wrapped the edges of my coat round my freezing knees and hoped the punt was still watertight. At least for the rest of the hour.

Finally we got stuck on a marshy bank thick with reeds overhung by a clump of old trees, their gnarled roots reaching into the water. George had been unable to avoid the obstacle in time, and our vessel came to a halt in a swish of reeds. He had hit his head against an overhanging branch but showed no sign of being seriously hurt.

'Might as well stop here,' said George, hastily smoothing down his hair which was now in enough disarray to reveal a bald patch which had not been obvious before, 'and have a bit of a rest. It's a nice spot.'

I did not think so myself. It was chilly now, and the spot was gloomy; since the water was almost static here it smelt odd, almost foul, as though something was rotting in it. It was the sort of place where one was liable to be attacked by swarms of midges, but I supposed it was too early in the year for insects to be a serious hazard. Still, I kept a wary look out.

I glanced across at George, since there was nothing much else to look at, and found he was looking at me. We looked at each other for a bit, while I wondered what was supposed to come next. Somebody obviously had to say something, the difficulty was to know what, and how to begin.

'Well, old girl,' he suddenly said in a tone I had not heard before, relaxed, almost teasing, with a timbre of affection, which made me forgive the vulgar familiarity, 'well, what does it remind you of?'

I became wary: he was playing this curious game again, at least, I hoped it was a game.

'Midges?' I said guardedly. 'Swamps?' Perhaps it was some kind of word association game. Meanwhile I was playing for time. By the look of annoyance on his face I knew I had said the wrong thing. His bland expression had crumpled like a gust of cold wind on the surface of the water.

'What are you playing at?' he asked sharply.

'I'm not quite sure,' I admitted. 'I was hoping you would tell me.'

He hesitated, then leaned forward in the punt, so that his face was quite close to mine, and gazed into my eyes: 'Why are you so cold?'

'I'm not too bad,' I began, 'it's just the wind—'

'No, no,' he interrupted me in an angry voice, 'you know what I'm talking about. Are you totally devoid of sentiment, feelings?'

I thought about that, while he watched me. 'I don't know,' I said slowly. 'You'll have to try me.'

I could see that the answer embarrassed him, though I had answered frankly. Unexpectedly his face flushed darkly. He seemed to be considering something.

'Nelly . . .'

He got no further. I was struck by the fact that he had known my name, however false, all along. I suppose he must have looked up the hotel register.

Now he leaned forward and placed his broad hand on my knee, looking steadily into my face, as though for some response. 'We'll have to see about that,' he said heavily.

'Yes, I expect we will.'

It was a feeble answer, light, half playful, but I could think of nothing else to say. He now pushed my overcoat aside and tried to move his hand up my thigh, but he could not get very far without shifting his seat in the boat, which was fixed. Ignoring our situation, he half crawled, almost fell forward, re-distributing his weight in such a manner that we began to teeter dangerously in the shallow water. All this time he never took his eyes off my face, apparently oblivious of the fact that we were liable to tip ourselves overboard into the weedy water, which was cold, and stank.

'George,' I pleaded, one hand clutching at the edge of the craft in a helpless attempt to steady it, the other clutching at his exploring hand for the same reason. 'Don't rock the boat. Steady on.' I kept hold of his hand to indicate that nothing

151

personal was intended, though I did not want it to go any further. Not here and now, anyway.

George no longer met my eyes. He removed his hand and smoothed down his hair to make sure it covered the bald patch. As he shifted backwards in the rotten old craft I saw that his trousers were stained in several places from the dirty bilge water at the bottom of the boat.

'Shall we go back?' I suggested, to ease the situation. 'It is rather cold sitting out here, and I can think of better places to get to know each other. We are, after all, not children.'

George muttered something inaudible and stood upright to get a grip on the pole. He pushed with it against the crumbling earth of the bank with its exposed network of roots, which looked like an old gnarled hand clutching at less and less; but weeds and underwater mud held us back.

'Let me have a go,' I suggested. 'I think I can push us free from this end.'

George handed me the pole without looking at me. 'Do you have to be quite so matter of fact?' he asked, subdued but surly.

'I was only trying to be helpful,' I said gently. 'I wasn't trying to put you off. There's a time and place for everything. Besides, I think our hour is up.'

I could see that my own end of the punt was hopelessly jammed in spears of tough grass which interlocked under the surface of the water. With one hard push of the pole I set us both free. I could feel the wood move under my feet, and we began to float downstream with the current.

18

George Wilkinson has vanished overnight. He must have checked out of the hotel in the early hours of the morning, before I was awake. No note. Nothing. I suppose I ought to feel relief, but I must admit that I was a little hurt when I first found out, and disappointed. I had not expected him to be such a coward.

After all, it was not as though the episode in the punt put a frigid end to our relationship. I went out of my way to be nice to him afterwards, because I could see that his masculine pride had somehow taken a hard knock. And by now I found I rather liked him, perhaps because he was behaving like a small boy. He really was being too silly, I told him, and made a point of taking his arm on the way back. I could, I said, do with a drink, and shivered theatrically.

We had a good deal to drink last night, and at first I thought that this was why he had not come down for breakfast. It was only at midday, when there was still no sign of him, that it occurred to me to ask about him at the desk in the entrance hall. The clerk told me he had left.

I have no notion what, if anything, I did wrong. I coaxed and cajoled him back into a good humour last night, I even made a point of flirting with him, which seemed to please him. He certainly took the bait.

When the bar closed I decided to go upstairs, and he followed me. When we reached my door he put one arm round me, the other hand on my thigh, and pressed me so hard against the edge of the door that the handle dug uncomfortably into my back. Meanwhile his mouth was on mine, trying to force it open. I was unable to respond at first because he had knocked the breath out of me and I was trying to get it back. Also I had been somewhat overcome by the suddenness of his attack. His eyes tight shut, he kept pushing his head and body forward as though to stop me escaping from the doorway. In spite of the alcohol I had consumed and the fact that I was now slightly aroused I was sufficiently clear-headed to realise that the situation was somewhat ridiculous: somebody was liable to come along the corridor at any moment and see us, groping like a couple of children in an alleyway. So I managed to slip my hand behind me and press down the door handle. The door gave way and we both fell backwards into the room. I managed, I am not sure how, to stop George from falling headlong, taking me with him, since he was still determined to be an irresistible force meeting an immovable object, regardless of the fact that I would probably have been prepared to meet him halfway anyhow, and now, far from resisting, had allowed him in, if only to save us both from making public fools of ourselves.

George allowed me to shut the door before returning to the attack. His tongue explored my mouth while one hand searched for buttons and zip fasteners without making any significant headway. After a while he began to pull and tear in frustration and, since he seemed in danger of ruining them, I moved back slightly and began to take my clothes off alone. Finally I lay naked and exposed on the bed whilst Mr Wilkinson struggled out of his trousers, took off his socks and had difficulty with the knot of his tie. I saw he had hairy legs. I saw, but tried not to notice, how little appeared to be happening under his shirt-tails. He was decidedly a heavy man, and the bedsprings sank several degrees when he joined me.

He got on top of me right away, without more ado, letting his whole weight go, so that I found it hard to move or breathe at all. He grunted and groaned for a while, breathing heavily, rubbed the skin of my face raw with his stubble, and bit one nipple so savagely that I cried out in fright and startled pain.

He stopped biting after that, and I responded as well as I could but, pinned down as I was, I could do almost nothing which might have proved satisfactory for him, or me, or both of us.

After a time he stopped moving about on top of me, though I could still scarcely breathe. His penis, which had been getting progressively smaller and more limp as his motions became more furious, flopped damply between my legs and just lay there. He now let me stroke it for a bit, but it did no good. I would have preferred to masturbate to a climax, but I thought he might be offended, and it did not seem to occur to him to help me.

Suddenly he got up, put his clothes on, and left my room without saying a word. It occurred to me that we had not exchanged a single word since it started. I wonder why he behaved like that. I suppose I shall never understand now.

19

The young man who claimed a filial relationship to me some time ago has been back. He calls himself David. On this occasion he did not come alone, but was accompanied by a somewhat older man whom he introduced as a Mr White, a colleague of some sort with whom he occasionally played squash.

The presence of a third party excluded the possibility of any embarrassing reference to a prior physical relationship of an intimate sort, a fact of which David appeared quite aware: he made no attempt to launch on to the topic or mention his preposterous claim, indeed, he was pleasantly polite, with the good manners reserved for casual acquaintances.

We ordered tea, and conversation while we waited was decidedly tedious and rather halting. To break the silence I asked David why he played squash, whereupon he began giving me a lengthy description of its benefits, rules and advantages to which I soon stopped listening. Meanwhile I noticed that Mr White had almost nothing to say: his eyes did not light up at the description of the joys in which he was supposed to have participated recently, in fact he did not look like a sporty type. Nor did he look like a suitable companion for David, who was much younger and rather more facile. He had a guarded look, like a man with serious things to turn over in his mind. A man who was conscious of having a mind, and set himself apart.

I found him rather solemn, in marked contrast to David,

who appeared to have a whole list of badly rehearsed conversational trivia to which politeness forced me to respond while I poured out tea, mused on a striking passage in the book which I had lately put down, and noticed the comings and goings in the public lounge. Then I became aware that, far from being bored or preoccupied, Mr White was covertly watching me, noting my every move, any change of expression, the slightest flicker of an eyelid. He may not have heard the gist of David's tedious chatter, but he listened intently to those few comments I made, whether it was 'Indeed?' or 'Really?' or 'How interesting' when I had become thoroughly bored. I began to keep a suspicious eye on the curious Mr White, whilst endeavouring to be nice to David. Poor boy, I thought, he tries so hard. I told myself that it would not be kind to turn him away too rudely, and it was not his fault if I found him tediously ordinary.

Or was it? I began to wonder whether there was a purpose behind the presence of the unlikely Mr White with his taciturn watchfulness and the sheer inanity of David's casual remarks, apparently thrown out at random, and all requiring a response. Was I enjoying my stay? What did I think of the political situation? Did I like the neighbourhood? Who was staying in the hotel, and had I made any friends? Was the food good, and how did I pass the time? Did I plan to stay long? My answers became increasingly vague and monosyllabic, and I tried to hide behind the ritual of playing hostess and fussing over the tea tray. Would David like another slice of sponge cake? How about some more tea? As I replenished the teapot with hot water I watched David bite into the sponge cake with satisfaction: that would stop his mouth for a while. Meanwhile I was conscious of Mr White studying my every move, as though each gesture spoke a hidden language which was comprehensible only to him. I dropped a lump of sugar into a full cup with a skittish gesture, and from sufficient height to cause a tiny splash, and turned to Mr White.

'Well,' I said, 'what do you make of that?'

Mr White turned his head slowly to give me a long, challenging stare. 'What do I make of what, Mrs Dean?'

'The way I just dropped sugar into the tea. You seem to take an uncommon interest in everything I do. Or perhaps I'm flattering myself?'

Mr White was not put out. He answered slowly and deliberately, as though weighing each word: 'I am interested in human behaviour, that is all. Do you object to being watched, Mrs Dean?'

David's face froze anxiously, the smile died away, as his eyes flicked nervously between the two of us. I saw that he wanted to avoid a confrontation at all costs.

'Not normally,' I answered coolly. 'Is there any reason why I should?'

Mr White did not answer immediately. I waited. David looked somewhat panic-stricken.

'I mean,' I prompted, 'it rather depends on who is doing the watching, and why. For example, odd as it may sound, this place is crawling with police detectives in plain clothes. Did you know that?'

'No, I did not, Mrs Dean. And it sounds a little paranoid, if you don't mind my saying so. A quiet, respectable place like this.'

David tried to interrupt: 'Mr White is not a detective or a police officer, I assure you.'

'I never said he was.'

Mr White spoke in a tone of pontifical authority. 'People who believe they are being watched are either suffering from paranoid delusions, or they actually have something to hide. Have you, Mrs Dean?'

I did not like the way he kept calling me *Mrs Dean*, with a peculiar emphasis, as though he knew the name was assumed.

'And if I did, *Mr* White, is that a crime? Do I have to be an open book to all and sundry? I suspect you are something infinitely worse than a policeman, Mr White. They only want to know my movements, to control my body at worst. You want to own my soul.'

'I assure you, Mrs Dean...'

'As for paranoid delusions, there is a poor creature in this neighbourhood, name of Miss Wyckham, who at this moment is lying sedated in the local hospital after being bashed over the head. Why don't you go and diagnose her for paranoid delusions? Perhaps you might even persuade her that none of it ever happened. But if it's the truth you want, which I doubt, ask at the local police station for a detective inspector, name of Smith, unlikely as that may sound. He is the imaginary police officer I was telling you about.'

David tried to intervene once more. I think he was anxious in case someone overheard us. My voice had got rather loud as my diatribe gained impetus. I was conscious of a sense of outrage, sharpened to a knife-edge with scorn.

'Please, mother,' he pleaded, back to his obsession once more, so that I felt even more annoyed: 'He was only trying to be helpful. He's just a friend, that's all.'

'I don't want his help,' I said firmly.

'I didn't say you did. And it wasn't a conspiracy, I assure you. He just happened to come along. Like I said, we only dropped in because we were passing.' Poor David was floundering, hopelessly out of his depths. He knew that I knew he was lying, if only because he had been warned that I was predisposed to paranoia, and thus slightly less gullible.

'I see. In that case I'm sure he won't mind leaving now.'

David flushed a deep peony but Mr White got to his feet.

'It's all right,' he assured him, 'I'd better leave. Your mother is obviously deeply disturbed, and I think I can guess at some of the reasons for her irrational hostility. It lies at the root of all her problems, I'm afraid. I'll discuss it with you later.'

'No conspiracy,' I repeated sarcastically, 'no plot. But you'll talk about it later. It's a good definition of paranoia, Mr White. You must have a nice little set-up. I expect you are very rich? Or at least comfortable, as the saying goes. I congratulate you. Very clever.'

Mr White bowed slightly and murmured: 'We only try to help.' He nodded across to David, who was obviously at a loss for words, and unsure whether he should stay behind.

'Have you ever heard of freedom?' I asked him, as he was already turning to go. He gave no indication of having heard my question, so I added, much louder: 'Have you any idea what it means?' Mr White closed the door of the public room behind him. Several people stared across at me. David looked acutely embarrassed and shifted about in his seat. I tried to explain: 'There is a law about habeas corpus. But I think the mind is just as important, if not more so. Don't you?' The young man expressed no opinion. 'I wonder if one could get a writ of habeas mentem?' I mused.

There was an awkward silence, though not for me. I felt in charge of the situation.

'I'm sorry,' he said finally. 'I shouldn't have brought him. It was a mistake.'

'Never mind,' I said gently, as though speaking to a school-boy who had been found out. 'We'll say no more about it, shall we?' David looked incapable of saying any more about anything, so I added, to make him laugh: 'To tell you the truth, I don't think your Mr White is quite right in the head, poor fellow.'

Instead of laughing, David's expression became more serious. 'I can't make you out,' he said finally. 'You've changed. Beyond all recognition.'

'And yet you claim to recognise me.' I spoke very quietly, without looking at him, conscious of having won. David tried to brush aside this impeccable logic.

'But, mother—' he began. I interrupted him immediately, kind but very firm.

'Now look, young man. I've got nothing against you per-sonally. I'm sure you're very nice, and I have no objection to talking to you, provided we can both be civilised. But you really must stop making this absurd claim on me, or demanding a special relationship. I don't know who you are, or where you came from. In any event, whoever you may be, I really cannot be held responsible for you. I am sure any woman would tell you the same thing.'

I suppose it was a cruel thing to say, perhaps unnecessarily so. His face crumpled visibly, as though I had forgotten he was playing in a make-believe world in which he was supposed to be quite grown-up. He tried to remind me.

'I ... I ...' he stuttered finally, 'you don't understand. I feel responsible for you.'

I assured him he could put his mind at rest: I was not a child, nor destitute, nor suffering from a painful disease. I had to spell it out to him, since he found it so hard to understand.

'But you are not yourself,' he argued, after I had enumerated all these points in my favour. The boy seemed incapable of logical thought, as this last comment showed all too lamentably. I tried to show him the absurdity of his last statement, privately I thought that on the grounds of low intelligence any blood relationship was ruled out, and added:

'I am not who you think I am. But I have been trying to tell you that all along. You have obviously been living under some enormous misapprehension. If that worries you, I am sorry. But you really cannot expect me to try and fit in with your image, stop being me, and play some rôle you have assigned to me in your mind.'

Nothing could help him now, I could see that: neither his acceptable face, nor the good suit of impeccable cut which fitted him so well and placed him firmly on the ladder to an acceptable future. He had done it all for nothing, the polished shoes, starched cuffs, neat haircut and cleanly shaved jaws, if there was nobody standing by to watch him climb.

And then I made a tactical error, in a moment of weakness, because I felt sorry for him. I agreed to meet his wife. I allowed him to arrange to come back next weekend and drive me over to his house. Just for tea, he said, and he would drive me back afterwards. It sounds harmless enough, but I feel uneasy about it. As though I could be sucked into a whirlpool. I tell myself I am being stupid, but I cannot put it out of my mind. Once my underlying anxiety got the better of me, and I started to pack my things with the intention of going to the railway station yet again. I did not go, but only because I have tried unsuccessfully to go before, and not because I decided I was strong enough to stay and stick it out, cope with whatever is coming.

SECOND NOTEBOOK

I

My odd story, such as it is, begins one afternoon in May. It had been an unsettled day, mild, with low grey clouds hanging overhead and sudden flashes of sunlight which caught one unawares, so that one did not know what to do with them, being almost blinded by the sharp dazzle of brightness. But they did not last anyhow, the dull clouds would return, and with it my mood of depression.

I felt as unsettled as the weather, perhaps because of it. I cannot say for sure. I found myself pacing up and down, unable to sit for long, when I would open my handbag and go over the contents yet again to pass the time. Sometimes I would look out through the main door, watch for an approaching figure, or glance through the window at the river scene, with its pleasure boats, eddying grey water caught in sudden light. Most of the trees had begun leafing, thus proving they were not dead but had wintered it out, and all the shrubs were blossoming hard, making a brave display of colour.

I had made a brave display too, for the occasion, but I was uneasy. Several times I had gone back upstairs to my room, for no particular reason, or, if I had one, I had already forgotten it by the time I unlocked the door and stood in the middle of the floor, gazing vacantly round the four walls, anonymous furniture, the unrumpled bed already neat and blank for anyone with money to pay, the secret wardrobe.

Young David was due to arrive at any moment, to pick me up in his car.

I had been ill. I was told I had been very ill, though I had absolutely no memory of it. I suppose that was the extent of its severity, that I should have no recollection of it. I was conscious, however, on that fitful afternoon in May, of feeling somewhat weak, a little fragile. My hands trembled, my stomach felt queasy, and I was undeniably nervous of the ordeal which lay ahead. Indeed, the prospect of the coming confrontation had put me in such a stew for several days past that I once got as far as packing my belongings and staggered halfway to the local railway station before reason got the better of me, and I turned back. After all, I told myself, I had no notion where to go. Where, I asked myself, are you supposed to be heading? I put down the heavy suitcase and stood for a few moments, gasping for breath.

Now I waited in the entrance hall of the hotel where I had been staying, a prey to unknown fears and almost no hope at all. I could not put a name to these fears, except that they had driven me here in the first place, when I found this refuge. But then, I was not myself—David had reassured me of this more than once, not realising that this did not help, and only made the whole situation more confusing. I did not know what sort of person I was supposed to become, once my health returned, or if I wanted to be that person, though David seemed to have a clear image in his own mind of how she could be expected to behave.

Differently, obviously, though it was not clear to me whether this would be for better or worse.

I had by now been persuaded, though by no means convinced, that David was my son. I tried hard to adjust myself to the idea of this relationship, which had been foisted on me. I hoped I would learn to like him, and his family. The possible embarrassment which lay ahead made me most uneasy.

Nervous for days of the coming tea party, I had got myself a new outfit for the occasion. Somehow this spring suit of light blue wool with its smooth and shiny lining which rustled loudly each time I moved seemed not only suitable, but designed for the person I had been chosen to play. I was not comfortable in it, though at the time I bought it the costume seemed like a sensible choice, a little more gay and cheerful than the dreary wardrobe I had brought with me to the hotel, and in tune with the season.

Now I felt like a self-conscious guest at a wedding. Perhaps, I thought, glancing at my wrist watch, an unwanted one. When would the ceremonies begin? I decided that the new suit was a mistake, and I would probably never get used to it. To do so I would have to wear it again, possibly several times, and I could not see myself doing that. Anyhow, it was not entirely my fault: there had been remarkably little choice in such a small town.

I remembered standing in the only boutique the High Street had to offer, trying on a series of expensive garments brought by a tiresomely attentive shop assistant who fussed round me, called me madam, and burst into small fulsome eulogies on each change. The mirror called her a liar. With each change of costume I found myself facing a figure whom I did not like and refused to recognise, a reflection which, however alien, continued to look inescapably solid with each change of colour and cut: a hideous solidity which no shade could soften or shape transform.

Finally I bought this particular suit in pale blue wool, lightweight, because I thought it might at least serve as a kind of disguise. I could have been anybody in it. It was ordinary, but impeccably ordinary. No doubt, in a thousand similar places, thousands of identical women would be wearing this uniform, trying to conceal unsightly outlines under the cut of good cloth. On a clear day one might hope to merge with the blue of the sky and look invisible.

Then it occurred to me that a visit to the hairdresser a few shops down the High Street might be both therapeutic and suitable, to go with the new outfit. I was, in any case, having difficulty with my hair. I had once tried to wash it in my hotel washbasin, and it had been in a state of rebellion ever since. It refused to lie down, perk up, comfort my ears, flatter my face, or do any of the things I tried to coax it to do. When I caressed it with a brush and comb it sulked and went limp, looked suddenly dull and lifeless, as though pretending to be dead. Once out of doors, however, it got its revenge by going with the wind, quite wild, blowing all over the place, even, on occasion, into my eyes. If I suppressed it under a scarf it would get its revenge afterwards, by acting dead for the rest of the day. Once, in a rage, I even thought about getting rid of it and adopting a tame wig. Now it occurred to me to mollify the awful fibre by the attentions of a professional.

I also wanted to make a good impression on my unknown daughter-in-law. From my readings at the public library I have gathered the impression that ladies with straggly windblown wisps, particularly if they are greyish, are liable to be considered deranged, and I did not want the young woman's undoubted preconceptions to be confirmed on first sight.

However, I did not enjoy the session. It was not only that a long period of enforced immobility made me restless and irritable, though I knew this to be illogical, since I had no other engagements. No doubt this was a typical symptom of the convalescent. Or so I have been told. But once more I was required to confront the stranger, this alien and unlikely female, in the looking glass. Only this time it was worse, since on this occasion we were forced to look each other in the eyes at close range for an unusually long period. I could not really take to her, but now I came close to pity.

I tried not to show it, to control my facial muscles in a shield of rigid stoicism as I watched, helpless, the pathetic creature opposite robbed of the last vestige of dignity: her hair was pulled so hard that the head was tugged backwards as the comb got caught in the tangled mop. Scissors hacked at it. Then the tangled old mop was lathered and rinsed and came up from the basin looking as though it had been dipped in a bucket and wiped over some kitchen floor. She sat there shamefaced, wet strands clinging to her white scalp, now clearly visible. She could see, I saw, the final ridicule of becoming a bald old woman. I saw her wince, surreptitiously wipe a drop of liquid from the corner of her left eye—or was it her right? My heart bled for her, but there was nothing I could do.

The young man asked how madam wanted it, and when his

victim looked doubtful, proceeded to make several suggestions. Her eyes gazed back into mine, wide with alarm, appealing. Yes, I said, I thought that might do, and saw her look of relief. She smiled slightly, humbly. I got the impression she was the kind of woman who had always relied on other people to make decisions for her; as I watched her mutely being manhandled, I suspected that she had all her life known what she did not want, but had not dared to voice her objections for lack of an alternative. She did not, I saw, as the man patted and preened, twisted and twirled, want this any more than the rest. But it was too late now, so she submitted.

I supposed that I would have to defend her, become her unwilling ally. But I could feel something close to contempt rising up in me, and suspected that I would never grow to like her. But we were stuck with each other now, like two inseparable sisters. One timid, the other hard and rebellious.

'There!' the young man exclaimed triumphantly, brushing a non-existent hair from her shoulder and standing back to admire his handiwork.

I was speechless, dumbfounded. She slowly got up from the chair, a look of uncertainty reflected in her face. She rose with spine and head rigid, as though she had just emerged from a factory mould, and the entire edifice might topple to the floor. I could see her assessing the possibility of living under this odd and alien structure, and saw that she did not hold out much hope of coming to terms with what had just been imposed on her defeated head. She put up a timid hand, perhaps the left (or was it the right?) to touch the grey shell-shaped structure, and hastily withdrew it: the texture felt quite foreign, as though it did not belong to her. Wait till we get back to the hotel, I thought, it won't take long to undo, but I dared not say it out loud. Instead I smiled doubtfully, with an attempt at gratitude, like a mother who had sent an unruly brood to boarding school and was now rewarded by well-behaved, total strangers. The woman in the mirror continued to look stunned, as though her worst, unvoiced doubts about human progress had been confirmed.

It was as much as I could do to get her through the short walk back to the hotel. She was self-conscious in the High Street, even though there was nobody about, apart from a man in a brown overall unloading goods from a van, and he did not even turn his head to look at her. Once she thought she heard footsteps behind her and darted nervously into the doorway of a newsagent's shop. The blind of the glass door had been pulled down behind a sign saying CLOSED. She realised that nobody had been following her. The pavement was deserted.

My spirits lifted a little when we got to the bridge: a gust of wind caught the rigid structure, it lifted, began to give way. I took a deep breath of fresh air, leaned over the parapet to look down at the placidly flowing water, and saw six ducklings follow their mother upstream. Their downy feathers, still the colour of egg yolk, ruffled in the wind. The last duckling was always a little bit behind. He kept going off on forays of his own, afterwards hurrying to catch up with the rest of the group. I smiled. I could feel her begin to relax a bit now. Old leaves and new blossom. The chestnut branches overhanging the moored boats heavy with candelabra. A smell of pollen.

Once inside the hotel we sneaked upstairs past the desk clerk, happily absorbed in the contents of a lurid paperback, locked the bedroom door and took stock of the situation. She looked ridiculous, and I had to laugh at her woeful image in the glass. She had enough good sense to laugh with me. It was awful, but hardly irreparable. 'Admit it,' I said, attacking the structure with a brush and comb, 'you were a fool to let yourself be persuaded in the first place. Who cares what anybody thinks?' My trimmed, washed and newly docile offspring, having been pushed about in their old-fashioned school, kept springing back into the places they had been taught to keep. 'Relax,' I said. 'You're at home now.' Gradually they began to be more like themselves, though I must admit, with a touch of unaccustomed obedience I rather liked. My newfound companion, whose face at close quarters showed alternating emotions of doubt and disgust, was obviously annoyed with me. Why could I not make up my mind about anything? She was right to lose patience: I was annoyed with myself.

The trouble was that, since David's mother had first appeared on the scene, my time was no longer really my own, and I no longer felt the sense of freedom I had known, however briefly, before David introduced her. I tried to get to know her, to like her, but I found it hard going: had it not been for David's arrival at the hotel I doubt whether I should ever have found much in common with her. We would certainly not have become friends.

Put it this way: in some obscure way I did feel responsible for her. I knew it was expected of me, and I did not want to draw attention to myself by making a fuss, or starting unnecessary gossip. But she did make life very difficult for me. She was quite painfully self-conscious, to begin with, and tended to panic if anyone spoke to her. She kept herself to herself, and this made life decidedly dull for me. I felt duty bound to stick by her, and some of her inhibition rubbed off on me.

I hoped that the situation was temporary, and that the weekend invitation to David's home would put an end to our uneasy relationship. It would somehow be proved that it had all been a ghastly error, I would get rid of my dreary companion, and be free as before.

Meanwhile we spent an uneasy few days filling in time somehow. Perhaps because of her need to keep up appearances, her underlying anxiety, she decided that one ought to look at 'places of interest'. The desk clerk obliged with a leaflet about the area. She announced herself devoted to church architecture, and we duly looked over the local parish church, which had a Norman tower, foundations dating back to the twelfth century, and various bits from other periods of history. She was, she said, anxious to acquire a feeling for the past, and peered intently into the disused charnel house.

The churchyard was untidy and overgrown. Stones leaned wearily. She read the worn inscriptions and thought they had a sad poetry about them. After a while I found them monotonous. How comforting, she commented, that at least in death husbands could lie at peace with their wives. This woman, I thought, has a hidden side to her, but she betrayed nothing to suggest that her remark was anything but disingenuous, perhaps almost sentimental. Churchyards, she declared, made her intensely aware of the present moment, that she was alive. And would soon be dead, I thought wryly.

I wondered idly who the Normans were. They built solidly, anyhow.

Tired of the worn inscriptions, illegible, covered in lichen, I waded through the lush uncut grass to the porch, which contained a noticeboard. A whist drive, somebody would lecture on bird migration, the old folks' annual coach outing was coming up, and the Norman tower was in danger of collapse. Funds needed for necessary repairs.

David's mother insisted on putting money in the collection box for the restoration fund. Why? Because, she declared, it was a place of interest. Besides, one had a duty to keep up appearances, one had a duty not to allow monuments to the past, our heritage, to tumble to wrack and ruin. Why not? I asked. She was not sure why not, but she was nevertheless shocked by the question. It goes, she declared, without saying. Besides, she added, although not a believer in the accepted sense, she had a feeling for the beauty of all things artistic, particularly if the art was also religious.

So we admired the carving on the font, the rich embroidery of the altar cloth, and the old oak beams in the high roof. She was particularly taken with the richly coloured stained-glass window above the altar, until I read in the guide book that this only dated from the previous century, whereupon she decided, on second thoughts, that it was rather crude and vulgar.

2

So all in all I had spent several tedious and strained days since David had arranged to drive me to tea at his home. Perhaps it was for this reason that I had gone to such lengths to prepare for the event, and felt increasingly nervous as the day approached. Too much depended on it now, though I had asked myself more than once since his visit why I had agreed to go. I must have been out of my mind, I told myself, to allow myself to be imposed upon in this way. However, I realised that my initial reaction—to run away—was a foolish one, and might do incalculable harm of a dreadful and as yet unsuspected nature. No, the only thing to do was to pretend to go along with him, and extricate myself as best I could, when I could.

Meanwhile, the woman who had now appeared as David's mother did not need to be convinced, since she was quite incapable of flight, or anything requiring personal initiative. She admitted that she felt nothing for the young man who now claimed her as his mother, did not know the first thing about him, but was already afraid of him. She wrapped her terror in woolly feelings to make it less painful, and take the sharp edge off it.

Nor had she forgotten the young man's accomplice, Mr White, for whom she had an unholy and fearsome respect. I had managed to get rid of him unceremoniously once, but she felt sure that he was not to be so easily disposed of. A man like that, she thought, had not got where he had got without being able to cope with a few rude words from a rebellious woman. He would have powerful connections, know the right people. He had, she thought, only to make a telephone call, fill in the appropriate form, pull a switch, press a button, and hey presto! She had what amounted to a paranoid fear of such male professionalism, and this included her son. He was, she reminded me in an awesome whisper, already an executive.

David arrived, looking immaculate in what people of his type call casual wear. The formal suit had been replaced by a carefully tailored jacket which did not match, but toned in with the brown trousers, which in turn toned in with the checks of his informal shirt, which was unbuttoned at the neck. David apologised for being five minutes late (he was half an hour late) and steered me by the elbow to his parked car, upholstered and painted in muted tones of brown which tastefully matched his clothes.

I had scarcely buckled myself into the safety belt when he reversed and swung out of the drive like a man bent on retrieving minutes irretrievably lost, with such force and an uncomfortable forward impetus that I was thankful for the safety belt.

'A nice car,' I said nervously, for something to say, while he gave a vicious jerk at the gearbox and muttered curses at the vehicle in front.

'It does a hundred and fifty,' he informed me, swerving past the offending car and hooting his horn.

'Is that allowed?' I asked. He did not answer, perhaps deafened by the sound of his own engine but went on frowning even more fiercely through the windscreen at the road ahead.

I was slightly alarmed at his behaviour behind the wheel. I had not, during our prior encounters, found him an impressive young man, if anything, it would be true to say he had failed to make any impression on me, but I had thought him a harmless young man, civilised and well-mannered. I had understood from the beginning that this was a person determined to get ahead in the world, but I had not expected his competitive

174

nature to take such a dangerous form. He was obviously a potential murderer. Moreover, he appeared to have forgotten the purpose of his visit: he had hardly glanced at me, had not enquired after my health or wellbeing, nor had he seemed to notice the startling change in my appearance. It occurred to me that he could have picked up almost any woman in that hotel foyer, given a certain age and build, without looking at her too closely. He was not, I concluded, choosy about whom he picked up as a mother, so long as he had one. And he was not even going out of his way to be nice to me. I had a feeling that he considered his mission to all intents and purposes accomplished.

I began to see how David's mother could have become the sort of person I had found her to be, and sympathised with her fears. On the other hand I felt bound to ask myself how she could have nurtured such a monstrous being to her bosom: surely at some stage, when his backside was still tender, his tiny mind malleable, she might have made a different human being out of him?

We were now on a stretch of open road, along with double rows of more metal containers speeding in two directions. The sun was obscured by consistent cloud, so I had no notion whether we were going north or south, from east to west or west to east. Both ways, as far as the eye could see, stretched a vista of ugly buildings on the banks of this two-way concrete river.

But David sat back now, slightly more relaxed. He even had the trace of half a smile on the corner of his mouth visible from my side, as though he had given himself a fix of speed, and the needle on the dashboard dial measured his pulse rate, perhaps the high octane in his blood.

'That's better,' he muttered.

The main thoroughfare had narrowed into the high street of what might once have been a quiet and peaceful residential area. David had ignored the sign to go slow, and we were now approaching a pedestrian crossing, much too fast. A woman was pushing a pram between the kerb and the central island. We screeched to a sudden halt, and I saw the woman's head turn in sudden alarm as I was flung forward in my seat and restrained from serious injury by my seat belt. Now she stood staring at the car, our faces through the windscreen, as though immobilised by fright, her own face pale as chalk, her dark eyes wide open with shock.

'Well, go on then, move,' he muttered under his breath, glaring through the windscreen. 'Don't take all day.'

As David started the engine once more I watched the woman slowly wheel the pram with its hidden contents to the opposite kerb before she was lost out of the corner of my eye. Perhaps she was also nursing a time bomb.

'What did you want to be when you were a little boy?' I asked.

'Fighter pilot,' he laughed, watching the road. 'Very annoyed that I was born too late. Think I never forgave you.'

'You don't know how lucky you are,' I answered, as he swerved violently to overtake another car much too short. I breathed deeply to recover my calm. 'People get killed in wars.' And not only in wars, I thought edgily.

The speedometer needle had swerved upward on an open stretch of road. Trees, fences, a grazing horse whisked past before one could appreciate them. But David's frown had been replaced by that odd smile I had noticed before.

'I suppose I wanted to prove myself,' he mused. 'Don't all little boys? It's a whatnot complex, you know, having to show you're as good as your own father...' his voice suddenly trailed off, as though he had become aware too late of having broached a dangerous subject. I looked at him curiously, waiting, but a brooding silence came over him. He began chewing his lower lip, struck dumb by what might have been taken for a flushed embarrassment.

Ahead of us an old-fashioned small car was dawdling along, driven by an elderly gentleman who seemed totally unaware of the modern demands for speed. David was unable to overtake immediately, and gave a couple of impatient honks on his horn. The old gentleman glanced round once or twice and proceeded at exactly the same pace as before, quite unperturbed by what was going on around him.

'You said something about your father...' I began tentatively, probing.

At first I thought he had not heard. We were being overtaken by an enormous articulated lorry whose noise drowned out all other sounds. I hastily shut the window as heavy grey fumes with a noxious smell filled the surrounding atmosphere. But he had heard, after all. I saw him flush darkly as he turned the wheel to swing left into a side road.

'I'm sorry,' he said. 'I didn't mean to bring that up. It was a slip of the tongue. Let's forget about it.'

Since I did not remember anyhow, I was puzzled rather than reassured. Fancy telling a supposed amnesiac to forget something that so nearly concerned her. I sensed something not quite nice, by his standards, a family skeleton in his cupboard which he wanted kept shut. If David's mother was now disturbed and anxious, I could well understand it. Not for a moment did I think he was trying to spare her feelings; if anything, I thought, he wants somebody to place in front of the cupboard door, to help keep it shut.

Nevertheless, I could not but wonder: a recent widow, deranged by grief? Death was supposed to be an unmentionable subject, but David's mother had positively enjoyed her visit to the churchyard; she had relished the epitaphs of husbands laid beside beloved wives as though they were exquisite poems of irony or sentimentality, or both. Or perhaps he really had been shot down as a war pilot, lacked the comfort of a known grave, and she had tossed uneasily year in year out at the image of his bones cradled at the bottom of the rocking ocean? Could somebody go demented with grief after decades of disturbed dreams, a night tide eating at the cliff façade until it finally collapsed? Or would decades of ordinary days filled with mundane and ordinary things wipe the beach clean of yesterday, both castles and bones?

The cupboard, I decided, would have to be prised open, deftly and with cunning, when I could catch him unawares. I owed her that much.

Meanwhile David had been manoeuvring the car through a network of quiet streets lined with identical houses, small but immaculate, with newly pointed brickwork and regular windows painted an identical shade of white. Each doorway boasted its own classical façade, although small, a brass coach lamp, electric, and a short footpath to the private pavement between verges of neatly mown lawn. An eerie silence prevailed, as though nobody was at home in any of these small dream houses, newly conjured up from an architect's drawing board or a sketched advertisement glimpsed in a newspaper. As though it belonged to the mortgaged future.

David slowed the car down and came to a halt. 'Here we are,' he said, applying the handbrake with finality. I wondered how he could be so sure. It looked like all the other houses to me. Immaculate, uninhabited. Panes of glass which revealed nothing. No face at the window, no sounds from within. Nobody waiting on the doorstep. But the patch of grass in front was neatly cropped: perhaps the owner had, putting first things first, delayed his departure to trim the edges with the special shears before driving off to collect his mother. He liked to finish a job, and it showed.

David ushered me up the short garden path, having first double-checked to make sure that all the doors of the car were locked. We squeezed into the narrow entrance hall. 'Darling?' he called, dubiously, testing. The interior space was shadowy, small and enclosed, after the light outside. 'Hello,' he called with assumed jollity, 'is anybody at home? We've arrived.' We listened to the silence in the narrow passage. Beyond a door of frosted glass I heard brief childish laughter. The sound seemed to be coming from a great distance.

'They must be sitting out in the back garden,' David explained. 'I don't suppose they can hear us.'

He opened the door of frosted glass and I saw a glossy coloured photograph advertising garden furniture framed in an open french window. A woman, heavily pregnant, was sitting in a deck chair. Cups and plates stood on an aluminium collapsible table. A small child with wispy blonde hair was hopping out of an inflatable miniature pool made of plastic to swing on an aluminium swing, obviously a recent purchase too. The neatly cropped grass below the terrace was littered with more plastic toys, some inflated, in bright primary colours. Little of the grass or the lattice work fence beyond was visible.

'Why, hello,' said the heavily pregnant woman slowly, lazily, barely turning her head. 'We didn't hear you come.' She seemed anchored to her deck chair, as though her centre of gravity was too low for her to get up, ever again.

I smiled, nodded. David indicated one of several aluminium garden chairs scattered about the small terrace, overshadowed on both sides by neighbouring fences.

'Would you like some tea?' asked the heavily pregnant woman in a sleepy voice. 'I'm afraid this lot is cold.' She had ugly legs, perhaps because of the pregnancy, as though some of the amniotic fluid had sunk into her thighs, so that they looked unnaturally fat.

I would have liked some tea, but did not dare to say so. I was thirsty after the long unpleasant drive.

'Did you have a good journey?' she asked, as though reading my thoughts, but she had addressed herself to David, who proceeded to launch into a detailed and boring account of the route, time taken and possibly wasted owing to the volume of traffic, incompetence of some drivers, all partially compensated for by his own ingenuity in choosing route A rather than route B at the juncture with X and Y.

There was, he added, also something wrong with the car's performance, in spite of the enormous bill he had just paid the garage. The chap was obviously trying to hoodwink him.

Meanwhile the small child was still hopping and skipping from one large toy to another. Faced with such a variety of conspicuous choice, it seemed unable to concentrate on even one, and began to stare at the occupied chairs on the terrace, sucking two fingers.

'Hello poppet,' said her mother, 'how about another splash in the nice pool.'

The child gave a half-hearted kick at a large plastic ball

which happened to lie near her right foot.

David had taken off his jacket and hung it carefully across the back of a chair. He made relaxing gestures with his arms and shoulders and then heaved a sigh as though he had not breathed air for at least a week. He smiled at his daughter.

'Hello poppet,' he called, in the same coaxing tone. 'Come over and say hello. You remember granny.'

The small girl stood her ground, surrounded by her kingdom of toys. She sucked her fingers, stared suspiciously at each face in turn, and began to swing her body from side to side, feet rooted firmly to the ground, legs rigid. I clearly got the message that she, for one, did not remember granny, any more than I remembered her. I had one ally at least. She no more wanted an elderly relative foisted on her than I wanted to become one. The word 'granny' had come as a shock, and it was several seconds before I understood that he was referring to me. Not content with making a mother of me, he was now asking me to play grandmother too. It was asking too much of anybody. But I liked the child, and felt some sympathy for her.

'Hello,' I said, as kindly as I was able, squinting into the sunlight, and trying to make my voice sound normal. 'What's your name?'

She continued to stare at me suspiciously, and crammed a few more fingers into her mouth. Quite right, child, I thought, conscious of the fact that we had both been put in a false position, and that she was conscious of it too.

'Come on,' David spoke encouragingly, but with an edge of thunder in his voice: 'You know granny, and you know your name. Don't be silly. Tell granny your name.'

'Shan't,' said the small child defiantly, having withdrawn several wet fingers from her mouth for the purpose. She promptly put them back in.

David's tone became sterner. A small dark cloud no bigger than a man's fist momentarily blocked out the sunlight.

'Come on now, Amanda, don't be naughty. That's no way to behave, is it? It's hardly polite, is it?' A silence, during which the electric field of tension was palpable in the small area of garden. 'Do you want to be sent to bed?'

Amanda's face flushed. She looked ready to cry. But it was obvious that she was prepared to become a martyr for the cause, if necessary. I began to identify with the child. Perhaps we were related after all. Meanwhile I saw that a pulse had begun to beat in the father's jaw, which was set ominously rigid.

'Shall I tell you my name?' I said, to break the tension. 'It's Nelly.'

I was not sure how this remark would be received. I saw David glance at his wife but she had leaned her head back, her eyes closed against the sun. The child pulled wet fingers out of her mouth.

'That's a funny name,' she commented.

I laughed, a little anxiously though, because I expected David to become angry once more at a remark so lacking in polite response. To my surprise he beamed with pleasure, first at his daughter, then at me.

'She's a little imp, isn't she?' he said proudly. 'The things she comes out with!'

Amanda, conscious of having scored, stopped scowling and screeched with triumphant laughter. She kicked a ball towards her father's face, but it only bounced lamely and rolled against her mother's swollen outstretched legs. The woman opened her eyes and blinked in a sort of daze, then smiled wearily, with indulgence.

Her father leaned forward in his chair. 'Tell granny how old you are,' he coaxed, glancing across at me to make sure I was ready to enjoy the performance.

'Fwee.'

David beamed. I duly smiled.

'And when will you be four?' asked her mother, using a nursery brand of voice.

There was silence.

'Well?'

The child peered dubiously into the future. 'I dunno,' she said at last.

Her mother laughed. 'Soon, poppet. And then we'll buy you a baby brother at the baby shop. For you to play with.'

Amanda seemed uncertain whether to smile or resume her scowl. She compromised by letting out a screech of sadistic laughter. 'And I'll smack his bottom and make him behave.'

Everybody laughed. David, his face creased with tolerant amusement, looked round to verify whether my face reflected the right amount of admiring approval. I put a hand to my forehead, to suggest that the frown had been caused by too much sunlight, and tried to smile.

'Show granny how you can sing,' he coaxed Amanda, his voice honey-warm with pride, face bathed in sunshine. Amanda stood looking coy amidst her many possessions, like a child star used to the limelight, but felt in a mood to oblige now that she had gained the upper hand. I was not in the least interested in hearing the child sing, but had to sit patiently whilst she was prompted line by lisping line through 'Pat-a-cake', 'Little Bo-peep' and the authorised version of 'Jack and Jill'. Each time she got to the end of a nursery rhyme her performance was greeted with vociferous encouragement and much clapping of hands, all of which Amanda had obviously learned to take as no more than her due. She duly obliged with an encore on request, smiling with unabashed pride.

I realised I had been brought a very long way, kidnapped, one might almost say, simply to hear the child perform and confirm the parents' admiration of their product.

It was not the only possession I was called upon to admire. When David's wife finally heaved herself out of her deck chair to go indoors and put the kettle on for fresh tea I was shown a new automatic washing machine, several electric gadgets, and a new teaset. Whilst his wife was setting the latter out on a tray David called me aside to admire a reproduction antique bureau with a tooled leather top and a new bathroom shower.

He then announced that he had bought a new powered lawn mower. I followed him back down the narrow staircase and through a door which led into the garage. He had not asked whether I wanted to see it. I felt I had been brought here to wonder as much at his possessions, his machines, gadgets and awful reproduction furniture, as his ordinary small offspring.

'Susan showed you the new washing machine, did she?' he asked, to make sure. I presumed the heavily pregnant woman in the kitchen to be named Susan and said yes, she had.

'Good.' We were staring down at an elaborate machine which occupied much of the concrete floorspace inside the garage.

'It's a bit big, isn't it?' I asked dubiously, not knowing the first thing about machines. But it did look almost as large as the small plot of grass I had seen in the back garden.

David confided that they were planning to move to a larger house with more space. In fact they already had their eye on a house with two acres of ground. It was a bit remote perhaps, for Susan, but the children would have a chance to run about in real fields. Trouble was, the asking price was higher than they could afford to go. There was a pregnant pause, while he looked thoughtfully in my direction. I said nothing.

'Of course it's a good investment. It's bound to go up in value, but on my present salary—which will of course go up shortly—I'm fully stretched. I couldn't afford to take out a much bigger mortgage. It's a damned shame. I would hate to miss out on the chance of a lifetime. I'm hoping they'll bring down the price.'

'Perhaps they will,' I said.

'For the sake of a few thousand,' he muttered, frowning. Then, when I said nothing: 'For the sake of the children.' His tone had a suggestion of melodrama, as though both were in danger of suffocation.

'Isn't there a park where they could play?'

Susan had arrived with the tea tray resting on her bulge. We followed her out into the garden.

'Yes,' David admitted sulkily, 'but it's not the same thing.'

I supposed it was not, but was inclined to be philosophical about it. Susan was cutting heavy slabs of homemade fruit-cake.

'And I can't stand being overlooked by neighbours,' the young man added irritably, as though this last straw should clinch the argument and provide justification for a higher standard of life he could not afford.

I could not imagine what any neighbour could find of enough interest to watch, or why it should matter if they did. But David obviously felt sufficiently spied upon and peered at to have added several extra feet of fencing and trellis work to both sides of the small terrace.

'But surely,' I began, 'company for the children, and for Susan, come to that...'

'They're awful,' spat David.

'Dreadful,' drawled Susan. 'They are always complaining about something.'

'And the noise they make,' added David. 'I've asked them not to wake Amanda every Saturday night, but the music is just as loud.'

In small unspoken ways it became obvious that David regarded himself as forced to live in a neighbourhood which was somehow inferior, an inferiority which manifested itself in a thousand little ways which alone entitled him to move upward and out. He owed it to his children, I owed it to him. Hence his aggrieved tone at the missing money, the gap between entitlement and purchase. He had, he thought, found a dream house which would also prove a good investment, so his righteous aspirations were sensible. Had he found someone misguided enough to give him the extra money, he would have thought it no more than his due. Luckily, the world lacked fairy godmothers. I told him so.

'It is a mistake to invest your whole life in bricks and mortar,' I told him.

I saw him scowl slightly, and glance at his wife, who shrugged almost imperceptibly and then turned to me with offers of more tea and another slice of cake.

'I think I'd better be getting back,' I said.

'Oh, but you've only just come.' Susan's voice was effusive. 'Won't you stay to see Amanda have her bath?'

David's face had flushed darkly, and he was still scowling.

'Daddy's cross,' commented Amanda, between mouthfuls of

cake which crumbled down the front of her dress.

'Of course I'm not,' said her father, scowling more heavily than before. 'I'll drive you back then, shall I?'

'If you would.' I got up from my chair. 'It's a long way and I want to be back at the hotel in time for dinner.'

I kissed the child goodbye. She squirmed and giggled under my grasp, but kissed me back. Her flesh smelled sweet. The smell reminded me of something, though I did not know quite what.

3

I write now with hindsight, and it is therefore not easy to say just how accurate my description of that first afternoon spent with David really is, because the impression I had of him and his family has since been reinforced by a continuing if half-hearted acquaintance. Since that May afternoon I have, so to speak, been adopted by him, and it is quite possible that my account is coloured by what I have found out about him since.

Since that first appalling afternoon I have spent many similar hours in his company. It is the price I have had to pay for the tattered remnants of freedom, and I sometimes feel that I cannot go on meeting it, that it is altogether too high. On the other hand, I see no alternative. I am trapped by my unfortunate resemblance to a pathetic creature for whom I feel no affinity, only pity. I know that certain persons are capable of becoming quite ruthless towards this defenceless woman, and that a certain diplomacy is called for.

But even while my acquiescence is not unmixed with a certain calculating cunning, I cannot help asking myself—what made this poor woman so spineless in the first place? I have only to read the other notebook to understand that she undoubtedly was rather mixed up and confused. She seems to have been quite lost. I have now decided to try and impose some kind of narrative coherence on my life, or what is left of it. There must be some sense to it somewhere. Meanwhile, it is passing, and I cannot get a grasp on it. I can find no meaning in it. The whole thing slips through my fingers like water or sand.

I am also bored.

I do not know whether this is due to my recent illness, and how much of my restlessness and lack of any sense of direction is a direct result of the watershed in the course of my life. There must surely be something abnormal about a mind with such a conspicuous lack of retentive power, whether of purpose, emotion, or memory.

I write as a corrective to this defect, though I can never be sure to what extent I am falsifying. Everybody should have a story which is coherent, with a certain consistency. If I cannot vouch for its total accuracy, it does relieve my boredom and help to pass the time. And that, since I have been trapped in this house, is quite something.

I find it difficult to think back and understand just how I came to get myself inveigled into moving into this dreadful house. I find it hard to sort out my feelings and motives at the time and, under the stress of events, I stopped keeping a record during that period. I only know that on a certain overcast afternoon David drove me here in his car and deposited me on the doorstep. That I stood helpless and, as though waking up from, or going into a bizarre dream, found myself pushing a key which I held in my hand and which, miraculously, or disastrously, fitted into the lock and turned. The door opened, and closed behind me like a trap.

David had watched me from the other side of the garden gate. I think he had nodded and smiled once, when I turned round uncertainly before using the key he had handed me, but as soon as the door gave way I heard him start the car and drive off very fast. Possibly he was afraid I would change my mind if he gave me a chance to do so. He did not get in touch for several days after that.

I stood in the empty hallway and listened to the silence coming from the rooms above. It felt very large, this house, much too big for me. I was drowning in dusty furniture which should have been removed long ago but still stood in corners, along walls, where it had been abandoned by somebody. Then I remembered that the key in my hand had not turned in the lock at first, it was then that David had answered my doubtful look with an encouraging nod, and some instinct made me withdraw the key slightly before twisting it clockwise once more. This time it clicked, but how had I known? I heard the car zoom into life behind me, and the front door slammed shut, echoing into silence up the deserted staircase.

I stood in the empty hall breathing in an odour of must and decay, as though the windows had not been opened for months. There was dust on the small table on which the telephone stood. Mute, also rather dusty, with a message pad but no messages lying beside it. Behind it the staircase rose to the right of the hallway, the carpet worn thin on each tread. The paint on the banisters had once been white but had now yellowed down, and small chips showed the dark brown of a previous age. Someone had chosen floral wallpaper which now looked faded and slightly absurd, like bygone summers dried between the pages of an album. Above the radiator a column of circulated dust had discoloured the wall to a darker hue. Near it a mirror, looking blank. I have developed a dislike, almost amounting to horror, of mirrors since I have lived alone here. They are dangerous, and you never know what is going to come out of them next. I give them a wide berth, avoid looking into them.

At the far end of the hallway somebody had left the kitchen door ajar. Through it I could see light coming from a window looking on to the garden. A distant vista of green, a jumble of weeds and overgrown shrubs stirring in moving air, breathing.

I suppose I should have picked up the telephone receiver right away and dialled for a taxi to take me away. I certainly thought about it. But I decided to look round the place first, in spite of my initial aversion. It was no more than sensible to do that, give it a try, and my aversion was not unmixed with curiosity. I told myself I could leave any time. First I would take a look round. Perhaps I would learn something about myself as a person, or about David's mother. I have always been curious about other people's houses, have a sneaking desire to snoop in cupboards and drawers.

'You can always leave,' I said out loud to the empty hall, defying it. Since it did not immediately collapse on me in retaliation I gained enough courage to walk past the mirror, eyes carefully averted, and into the kitchen. A lot of empty milk bottles, glass fogged through the light, stood ranged on the window sill. One of them had a note stuck in its neck. I uncurled it. 'Owing to family circumstances...' it read, and went no further. Although the kitchen was dusty too someone had meticulously washed and cleared away any dirty dishes before leaving. The sink was empty, the draining boards bare.

Somebody had recently put a minimal stock of fresh food in the refrigerator: several eggs, a carton of milk, a pat of butter. I guessed it was David, his inducement to oblige me to stay. At least somebody did not want me to starve.

For some reason I decided to go upstairs next, leaving my suitcase still standing in the middle of the hall floor. On the first floor landing I found a door standing slightly ajar; above the lintel a crack ran up the wall to the ceiling, as though someone, once, long ago, had slammed the door in anger. Or perhaps the whole house had begun to subside on its inadequate foundations. Anyhow, the crack looked deep and old, as though successive layers of paint had failed to hide it.

The bedroom gave me a deep feeling of unease. Not that it was uncomfortable: on the contrary, the decorations and furniture were in good condition, the floor was covered with a soft fitted carpet of faded blue which muffled every footfall; it was light, clean, and reasonably spacious. The large double bed looked well sprung under its smooth unruffled cover. It reminded me a little of the bedroom in the hotel.

I sat down on the corner of the bed and looked round at the faint tracery of blue flowers running along white wallpaper, the large wardrobe along one wall, the dressing-table with its long mirror standing at an angle to reflect a little of everything, including a possible intruder, one of the blue curtains, part of the ceiling, the floor, the wardrobe, and a vacant portion of bed.

I now keep an old dressing-gown draped over the mirror. On further exploration of the house I was struck by the fact

189

that it had too many mirrors and too many clocks, all of which were found to be in working order though they had stopped dead on an unspecified date.

I sat for a while on the end of the bed, which resisted my weight and struck me as too large for one person and too small for two, its proportions designed for the maximum mutual discomfort and annoyance, or a sense of inadequate isolation: too much cold space. The air was musty and stale, as in the rest of the house, and I went over to open the window, which was stiff with disuse, the woodwork perhaps swollen with recent rains. Finally it gave way under both hands.

The sky was still overcast. It would rain again soon. There had been a sunny spell earlier on, but it had not lasted. The bedroom overlooked the back garden, which was quite pleasant. At the bottom fence trees, now in full leaf, breathed heavily, waiting for rain. In spite of, or because of the owner's absence several shrubs flowered wildly, sturdily, in small clusters of pink and yellow. Something delicate and faintly mauve was clinging tenaciously to part of the fence and had managed to reach the upper edge. Clumps of small blue flowers, like vestiges of morning mist, showed bravely amidst the encroaching grass and weeds. It looked inviting. I thought I would go down and breathe some air before it began to rain. Even from the window the earth smelled damp, with a scent of green leaves and raindrops.

But first I intended to take stock of my surroundings. I was determined to be methodical. I also had to find the lavatory.

It was just across the landing, next door to the bathroom, and smelled strongly of synthetic perfume, exuded from a mauve object, and presumably designed to disguise normal odours, which some might have thought preferable. Someone had left a very tattered copy of a book entitled *One Thousand Best Poems* on the small window ledge, and beneath it lay an equally dog-eared and outdated railway timetable. Either, I thought, the volumes are here for wiping one's arse in case of a paper shortage, or the most frequent occupant is a constipated commuter with a schoolboy taste for indigestible poetry.

A quick flick through the pages showed that nobody had been in the habit of tearing out pages, and a spare roll of paper stood ready to hand on the cistern.

I sat down to relieve my bladder in the mauve scented bowl and, being a bit of a compulsive reader myself, began to read the motto inscribed on each sheet of toilet paper, simply to pass the time. Imagine my surprise when, instead of finding a reassuring *Impregnated with Germicide* or *One Hundred Percent Proof* or even *Government Property*, which might have indicated a compulsive thief recently returned to the household from a public institution, I saw inscribed, clearly but delicately on the uppermost leaf, the message *I am leaving you*. It had been neatly written with a biro along the perforated edge of the paper, and at first I thought that my recent illness was having a curious effect on my vision. That I was, to put it bluntly, seeing things. I pulled at the roll of paper and the same message appeared on the next sheet, and the next, until half the roll lay unfurled on the floor at my feet, and I thought I might as well begin to roll the paper back. There was no doubt about it: the same message appeared with meticulous consistency along each perforation. I hardly liked to apply such a personal and perhaps venomous sheet to my dripping beard and damp private parts. So much effort had obviously gone into the work. But the alternative was a romantic lyric or part of a comprehensive train timetable, and I supposed they had involved as much individual effort on somebody's part.

For the first time I felt something sinister about this house, an aura of evil generated by hatred, small perhaps, but stored up over a long enough period of time to become potent.

Downstairs I found that the living room, which by now felt more like a mausoleum, had french windows which overlooked the garden. I forced them open to let in some fresh air, walked out on to the terrace and looked around. Daisies had begun to sprout rather charmingly in the unkempt grass, a dandelion competed brazenly with the broom now in yellow flower and the straggling remnants of civilised plants.

I walked down the gravel path to the side door of the garage, which I unbolted. The garage was empty, apart from a lawn mower in one corner and a few tools arranged along the side wall. Somebody had removed the escape car.

I pushed the rusty bolt home and studied the house from the back, the neat rectangles, a drainpipe under the bathroom window, the steeply sloping roof. The house was larger than I had at first thought, too large for anybody to occupy. The roof line was broken by two attic windows, denoting a further floor which I had not even investigated. No doubt, I thought, they would turn out as empty and useless as the rest. How many rooms did one woman need? It would only mean more furniture to dust.

So I told myself, standing on the footpath, and lit a cigarette. I never did go to the third floor, but since then I have heard noises late at night, creaking, as though somebody was creeping about. It scares me, but I suppose I may be imagining things: being on one's own in an empty house can make one nervous.

The trees behind me began to whisper as the wind freshened. Clouds moved overhead. Perhaps, I thought, a sunny interval is due. For a moment a glint of sun was reflected back from the dead windows, then faded. I pushed the naked wooden match into the heavy dark earth of the flowerbed with the toe of my shoe, until it was buried and invisible. Wild speedwells had invaded this cultivated patch, still green with hardy perennials, with the azure eyes of innocence.

Now I began to hear noises in the undergrowth on the far side of the fence, as though some bird or small mammal were tugging at twigs and foliage. First a hand, then a shapeless felt hat, followed by a wisp of grey hair and the top half of an old woman's face, appeared over the edge.

'A lot of weeds this year,' she said.

I did not know what to say. The head bobbed out of sight, then re-emerged as she propped herself up with both hands. Her head shook slightly. She gripped desperately at the wooden fence, as though afraid of drowning. But one hand was holding a clawlike cutting tool.

'It's the damp weather,' she added. 'They spread so, it's hard to keep up with them.' I still had not said anything. She peered down at my patch of ground. 'You'll need to get working on your place before they take over entirely. But I must say, I find it hard going since my husband died.'

There was a brief silence. Not knowing whether his demise was recent enough to warrant an expression of condolence, I said nothing. I continued to watch her as she watched me.

'The seasons,' she began with a new intake of breath, hitching herself up a further inch above the fence, 'have become very unreliable. You don't know where you are from one day to the next. Not like the old days. I think this new-fangled weather forecasting may have something to do with it.'

'In what way?' I asked.

She was silent. Her eyes wandered on some curious flight path of their own and finally focused on some abstract point in midspace. I do not know what she saw, but I could see nothing. Then I was forced to move by a host of midges which had begun to dance round my head and found myself stepping into her line of vision.

'Are you going to stay?' Her manner was direct.

I shrugged. 'I'm not sure. I've only just come.'

'It's none of my business,' she went on. 'I only asked because I don't like to see a place going to wrack and ruin. And your weeds are going to start spreading across to my garden. It's the wind you see. But it's entirely up to you. I can't stop you.'

'I don't know,' I told her frankly. 'I haven't decided.'

'That's quite usual,' she said, taking a snip at a leaf that happened to be near at hand. 'Nothing unusual about that.'

She released herself from the fence and bobbed out of sight. I heard the snip snip of her sharp instrument as she moved through the undergrowth on the other side. Her answer intrigued me. I was still trying to work out why it should have pleased me so much as I walked back and the shadow of the house engulfed me. On an impulse I turned back and peered over the fence. She was bent almost double over a shorn rosebush.

193

'Excuse me.' She slowly straightened, but only half way. I saw that her back was permanently crooked.

'I'm sorry to disturb you,' I said. 'I can see you're busy. But would you say that you know me?'

The odd question did not appear to surprise her. She looked at me shrewdly for a moment, as though considering a philosophical point.

'I do,' she said finally, 'and then again, I don't. I wouldn't claim to know anybody. But when you get to my age you do, if you see what I mean.'

I nodded. 'I understand. But would you say we had met before?'

She looked embarrassed.

'Then you don't remember me?'

Her head began to shake with a nervous tremor. Her right hand opened and shut the blades of the secateur, snipping at some invisible growth in the air. 'You must forgive me,' she murmured. 'My memory ... I'm very bad at placing people ... So many faces...' her voice trailed away into the damp air.

Then she saw me smile. As my smile broadened the frown on her dry forehead dissolved. She slowly smiled back.

'Thank you,' I said. 'Thank you very much.'

We smiled at each other. 'It's a pleasure,' she said, reassured, and her head stopped shaking. But I could see that the attempt to stand upright was straining her.

A small brown bird landed on the fence nearby, and began to twist its head jerkily in several directions, its beady eyes registering the universe. Then it took off and vanished into the dense branches of the trees at the bottom of our gardens.

4

After I had come in from the garden I spent a good deal of time rummaging in cupboards and drawers. In the kitchen I found an ugly set of cups and saucers, a complete range of cooking pans and utensils, and a drawer filled with bits of used string. I made myself a cup of coffee and nibbled on a stale biscuit. Afterwards I threw the ugly cup into the empty rubbish bin. It did not seem worth washing up.

Upstairs I found more cupboards, opened up all the drawers. The wardrobe was crammed with dresses, a couple of coats, shoes, all worn though not exactly shabby. I found that both the clothes and shoes fitted, but had no wish to wear them. They were all respectable but dowdy, as though the wearer had wanted to merge into the background and become invisible.

I opened the window wide and took a deep breath of fresh air, heavy with damp earth and a scent of lilac which came from old Sybil's garden. I could see her still pottering about amongst the flower beds. She was to become a familiar sight in the days ahead, moving slowly and with effort, stooping, tugging. She spent most of her days down there and it showed: her small patch of ground was lushly green, so much had matured under her bony fingers over several decades that plants were always in bloom round the impeccable lawn. Strong shrubs had taken root and flourished, but small flowers also found space to turn their faces to the sky along the borders. Once a week a man came to do the heavy work. I could hear the sound of his lawnmower under yesterday's clouds, mingling with bird calls, the distant cries of children, and a dog barking. But it was not enough.

A jewellery case in the top drawer of the dressing-table contained several heavy brooches and a gold wedding ring, engraved on the inside with the letter G. Also an amethyst necklace. I thought that several pieces would probably be valuable enough to flog, if necessary. If I had to make my escape.

In the rooms downstairs I found a sideboard containing several bottles of alcohol, which I finished within days, and stacks of plates in the same hideous design I had found in the kitchen.

In the living room I found several shelves of books, a small collection of records with a record player, and a television set. Over the days I found myself quite unable to concentrate enough to read. The silence was overbearing. Nor could I listen properly to any of the music, or watch television programmes.

I opened the french windows on to the terrace once more. The atmosphere had become stifling, the clouds darkened. My neighbour had gone indoors. Several fat drops of rain splashed on to the terrace. It was obvious that any moment the heavens would open, but I hesitated, breathing deeply, before going back indoors. Just as I was shutting the french windows I caught a glimpse of a young woman, no doubt my other neighbour, rushing out to rescue some washing from the line.

I saw her again on several occasions, during the following days, weeks, months. She had two small children, one still a baby in a pram. After the downpour had stopped I saw her come back into the garden to retrieve a few soaked toys. I followed her out, but she looked blank when I asked her the way to the railway station. I went back indoors.

I decided to go out into the street, and began walking up and down. I asked several people the way to the railway station. One or two shook their heads and hurried on; an elderly gentleman asked me which railway station I wanted and became visibly impatient when I was unable to be more specific. 'I'm a stranger here myself,' said one young man, whilst a dark-haired girl answered volubly in a foreign language. Finally a middle-aged woman of ample proportions, who did not seem to be in much of a hurry to get anywhere in particular, stopped when I spoke to her. She told me that the local railway station had been closed down a year ago.

'Nobody was using it,' she added, when she saw the bewildered expression on my face, 'at least, that's what they told us. It was making a loss, you see,' she endeavoured to explain, as I stood there, mute and frowning, 'and you mustn't annoy the taxpayers.'

She was smiling broadly, in an encouraging kind of way, waiting for a response, as though she did not mind if it took all day.

'Do you pay taxes?' I asked finally.

'Oh no,' she laughed, as though the idea was absurd, like asking her if she had ever climbed Everest because it was there. She added: 'But my husband does.'

I glanced back at the garage, which I knew to be empty, and stood absently, puzzling out a possible next move.

'Of course,' the woman went on amiably, 'my husband has the use of a company car. He needs it for his work. I missed it at first, not having the railway. It was handy. But I suppose beggars can't be choosers. You can't expect them to run trains for the likes of you and me.'

'I don't see why not.'

'It's not profitable,' she retorted in the tone of a woman who might not have had the benefit of a higher education but did listen to news broadcasts on occasion. 'If everything was run for the convenience of unimportant people like us, where would we all be?'

'Not here,' I said drily. I was beginning to find her self-deprecating acceptance rather irritating.

Her plump neck flushed a deep purplish red, reminding me of a turkey at Christmas. 'I've no patience with people like you,' she began, and seemed uncertain how to go on coherently. 'Some people don't know when they are well off ... it's people like you who ... who ...' She glanced round for inspiration and,

197

finding none, uttered a final explosive sound of exasperation consisting mainly of expelled air, and marched on with her shopping basket.

That was in the early days, most of it happened on the first day. At least, I think so. I find it difficult to keep track of time or the sequence of events during this period, when one day was so much like another. I was more conscious of the changing weather: showers, a thunderstorm, several hot days in a row when the sun blazed from dawn to sunset in a clear blue sky that became white hot and flushed a triumphant crimson towards dusk.

So I did not attempt to make for the railway station, since I had reason to believe in its non-existence. Instead I tried to settle down under the roof over my head. I explored the network of roads in the neighbourhood, and found it difficult to get back to my own front door. Rows of neat uniform houses, with small patches of front gardens, garages and gates. Just now the outlines were softened by a new growth of flowering shrubs, perfumed lilac, hanging wistaria and lush laburnum, but nothing could hide the constricted lay-out. And nothing could hide the concrete tangle of roadways, flyovers and footbridges near the old-fashioned shopping centre. It cut through the peaceful planning of a shoddy bygone age like a post-historic dinosaur, a stone monster impervious to heroics, and the people had to live with it. They were deafened by its noise as they purchased sugar and packets of tea, so that they could not hear each other speak; as they walked between shopfronts, chose ripe tomatoes, picked out a bunch of grapes, they breathed in the poisonous fumes. So far no Beowulf had come to their rescue, even though entire houses had been swallowed up by the rapacious monster, and inhabitants who could afford to do so had already fled. FOR SALE notices peppered the area, wired to gateposts like flags signalling desperately, but without hope, for help.

I bought a few provisions, but found it difficult to eat, alone in this oppressive house. I was plagued by a lack of appetite, at times amounting to nausea. I nibbled at snacks, watching the sky, the birds flitting from lawn to fence to the secrecy of leafy branches, observed my neighbours: the old woman tended her garden, the young woman her offspring, picking up a screaming toddler, hanging washing, strapping the baby into its pram.

David rang several times to make sure I had not disappeared, but did not come to see me. He was, he explained, as though to forestall my reproaches, up to his eyes in work at the office. I see, I said. I did not want him to visit me anyhow, but I nevertheless thought his behaviour odd. He had seemed so anxious to acquire a mother, it was difficult to understand why he had bothered. He promised to drive me over to see his family soon. The baby was doing fine and Amanda had nicknamed him Piggy. She really was cute, and could now count up to twenty. Piggy was crying rather a lot at night, so that Susan was tired.

I supposed it would help if I could invite somebody to the house to share a meal with me. But I knew nobody, and I was also conscious of having nothing to say.

Once my so-called daughter-in-law came round to show off her new baby, littered the entire house with nappies, feeding bottles, plastic toys and a portable cot. I did my best to make the appropriate cooing noises of admiration, without success. The baby screamed throughout the entire visit, its prune-wrinkled face screwed up with vehement disgust at the universe in general and its immediate surroundings in particular.

'Piggy is being naughty,' commented a rather silent and subdued Amanda contentedly.

I heaved a sigh of relief when I finally closed the front door after their departure. Not once, I noticed, had the proud and preoccupied mother asked how I was: whether I was well and happy.

5

I decided to make an effort, and invited old Sybil next door to have supper with me, but she forgot to come. We continued to exchange remarks about the weather over the garden fence but I did not want to embarrass her by alluding to the evening when she had failed to arrive, so I did not ask her a second time. I felt it was better not to remind her of her little lapse. That seemed to exhaust the range of my immediate acquaintances.

I rummaged about, found an address book with a list of names and telephone numbers in a drawer beneath the telephone, and rang a number at random. It turned out to be a firm of plumbers with an answering machine which invited me to leave a message as nobody was in. I hung up. I tried another number and found myself having an equivocal and slightly hostile conversation with a woman who, rightly, was not sure what I wanted. Since I had no idea who she was, and her tone of voice, far from suggesting intimacy, conveyed nothing but a tendency to become increasingly irritable, I hung up in a panic. I did not try using the telephone again after that.

But I felt imprisoned in that house, and for long hours I was desperate for the sound of a human voice. I found a portable radio, and for a day or two got in the habit of carrying it about the various rooms with me. One station in particular seemed to wage a desperate war on my behalf: a frenetically cheerful voice gabbled on hour after hour, persuading me to keep my spirits up, not to do anything foolish. But the voice itself sounded desperate, ran out of words, conscious of its own inadequacy, interlarded the idiotic gabble with thrumming music through which a few thin words sounded even more stupid: saccharine, a drug, nursery rhymes to rock a brain which had outgrown the cradle and needed, it seemed, to kill silence rather than find peace and quiet. After a few days I drowned the machine in the bath.

To avoid going upstairs to bed, I sat watching television hour after hour in the darkening room, as the sky faded beyond the window, deepened to a luminous blue beyond the black outline of trees, and the moon rose. Images flickered, but I found it hard to concentrate. Men shot at each other from doorways, smashed their homes, and posed for the cameras with pride during a pause, grinning, making gestures of ultimate victory before getting themselves killed. I saw the habits of crabs in colourful detail and remained mystified.

Upstairs in bed I had nightmares, tossing about in the dark, or found myself unable to sleep at all. Sometimes I had a distinct impression that I was not alone in the house: I would lie rigid in the dark, sure that I had heard footsteps on the stairs, the creak of a loose floorboard, a door being cautiously opened and closed. I was much too frightened to get out of bed and investigate, but my insomnia got worse. I would lie awake in the dark, listening for the sounds of an intruder. On one occasion I heard the lavatory being flushed, the furtive sound of somebody moving about in the bathroom.

Then I had a stroke of luck, at least, so I thought at the time. I met Miss Wyckham outside the newsagent's shop one afternoon, looking almost unchanged. A little older perhaps, certainly a little greyer, as though shrunk into herself, but that was hardly surprising.

'How are you?' I cried, startled but pleasantly surprised at the unexpected encounter. 'Are you quite recovered?'

She stared blankly at me for a moment.

'Yes, thank you,' she said slowly, after some hesitation. Her pale eyes, looking dubious, did an exploratory tour of my face.

'I'm so glad,' I exclaimed. 'You must come and see me.'

'Well...' she began.

'Come for supper. This week,' I insisted, not giving her time to refuse. She took down my address and duly arrived.

I had gone to some trouble to prepare an appetising three-course meal, and began by offering her a sherry. She sipped it cautiously, still watching me with the dubious expression I had seen outside the row of shops.

'I am so glad you are better,' I said. 'It must have been a very unpleasant experience for you. When did you get out of hospital?'

She frowned, as though trying to put a jigsaw puzzle together in her head. 'About three weeks ago,' she told me. Her eyes wandered round the room. 'This is a lovely house,' she said.

'Move in if you like,' I laughed gaily, sweeping my arm round the gloomy area. 'It's much too large for me. I don't know what to do with it.'

'Oh, I couldn't do that,' she said primly, then apparently decided that I had only been joking and forced a shrill, false little laugh, which she hastily stifled with the hand which was not holding the sherry.

'Look,' I said frankly, 'I must confess that the first time we met, I really had no recollection ... I mean, I was just being polite. I couldn't remember anything. About the past. You must excuse me. I've been ill. And I didn't want to offend you, at least, I hope I didn't. But I'm much better now, and I'm so glad we happened to bump into each other. What a coincidence! Because now I really would like to talk about the past.'

Miss Wyckham sat staring at me, her sherry forgotten, as though her bulbous eyes might pop out of her head like marbles.

'Remind me,' I coaxed, 'what were we like as girls? What did we do all day, what did we talk about? I mean, did we have dreams, aspirations, secret desires? Did we discuss them? Or did we just go along from day to day like everybody else?'

'I don't follow you.' Miss Wyckham's tone was suspicious. She had put down her glass and continued to give me that peculiar glassy stare, her pale eyes protruding dangerously.

'I mean,' I tried to explain, 'was this what we wanted?' My hand swept round the confined, rather dingy living room. 'Is this what we dreamed about from the start, or did we just allow ourselves to be carried along the conveyor belt, until it was too late and we found ourselves trapped? Did we even struggle, protest? I mean, can you remember clearly—did we even whisper rebellion amongst ourselves, in between lessons, the physical training, grammar lessons, religious instruction, and the rest of it?'

'I don't understand.' There was a note of alarm in Miss Wyckham's voice now. Her eyes had begun to wander round the room again, but this time they appeared to be searching for the door. 'I did very well at school. I got five passes,' she recalled with pride across the decades.

'That's very good,' I said, to mollify her, and began to shepherd her towards the dining room table, which had been carefully arranged, with glasses, flowers in a bowl, and folded napkins for each of the two place settings. 'Do sit down.' I pulled out one of the chairs.

Miss Wyckham spread the napkin on her lap.

'Passes to what?' I asked. She looked bewildered. 'I mean, you said you got five at school.' Miss Wyckham became inexplicably agitated.

'English, biology...' she began, then turned on me. 'Look, are you trying to upset me? I left. I had to earn a living. I've supported myself all my life. But I could have gone on.' The familiar scarlet flush appeared in her throat.

'Of course...' I began soothingly, 'I was only trying to ... Gone on to what?'

There was a short, embarrassed silence. I felt that I had somehow made matters worse.

'I hope you like avocado,' I said brightly, bringing two plates from the serving hatch to the kitchen. She nodded dumbly and ate her way stolidly through the green oval fruit. I poured her a glass of wine, which she left untouched.

'The weather has been nice lately,' I commented. 'I like these long evenings.' We both stared out at the garden, ghostly in the half-light. A shrub gleamed like a wraith, flowering white, its heavy perfume penetrated the room.

203

'That's jasmine, isn't it?' she said tentatively.

'Yes,' I said. 'It is.'

There was another short silence. I excused myself and went to the kitchen to take the casserole out of the oven. It tasted surprisingly good. She said it tasted nice, and wanted to know what the curious vegetables were called. I told her—'Aubergines'.

'Oh.' She apologised. 'I was never very good at names.'

There was another silence while we both ate. I searched for something to say, becoming increasingly conscious of both of us munching, chewing, manipulating our knives and forks, swallowing. I could think of nothing to say which was not liable to be misunderstood or start her off on another bout of inexplicable, flustered agitation. For her part, Miss Wyckham did not seem to have much to say. When she was not looking down at her plate she stared out of the window at the deepening dusk. The trees sighed in a gentle movement of air which wafted an even stronger scent of jasmine through the open window; beyond them the sky had taken on the intense pellucid blue of a stained glass window.

'It's a nice evening,' said Miss Wyckham, having swallowed her last mouthful and dabbed at her mouth with the napkin.

'Yes.'

'We've had quite a good summer this year,' she went on, gathering courage and momentum at the sound of her own words: 'So far. At least, compared to some years. We can't complain.'

'No,' I said. 'We can't. In any case, there is nobody to complain to. Except,' I added, 'to each other.'

Miss Wyckham looked alarmed. 'I was only speaking ... in a manner of speaking,' she tried to explain. 'I've never been one to complain.'

'No,' I said, 'I can see that. In fact I find it remarkable. If I were in your shoes I would find such composure very difficult to sustain.' Her calm and unexpected equanimity was such that I did rather wonder what the hospital had given her in the way of drugs. It was not merely in sharp contrast to her behaviour before, it was downright inhuman. 'But perhaps,' I suggested, 'you prefer to turn over a new leaf and forget all about it. I think that is probably very sensible.'

She stared at me, eyes bulging, mouth agape. 'I don't understand.' She seemed to find it difficult to get the words out.

'You know,' I said, beginning to feel embarrassed, thinking, oh lord, I have only succeeded in upsetting her yet again: 'I mean, your recent ... hmm ...'

'My recent what?' she insisted.

'Well,' I went on, trying to evade the issue but finding no obvious way out of an impasse, 'I meant your unfortunate experience ... the assault ... the police told me about it. They came to see me. That's how I first heard. Did they ever find the man responsible?'

Miss Wyckham had risen from her chair. The hot flush in her neck was back, a deeper crimson this time. I realised she was angry, not embarrassed.

'I've never been so assaulted in my life,' she protested. 'What do you take me for?'

I put out a hand to calm her, pull her back into the chair. I had spent more than an hour preparing a delicious pudding, and now she was threatening to spoil the occasion I had taken such trouble to prepare.

'Please sit down, Miss Wyckham,' I pleaded. 'I quite understand if you don't want to talk about it ...'

'What did you just call me?' She broke into my apologies.

'Miss Wyckham, of course. I only ...'

'I knew it,' she said triumphantly, pushing back her chair. She placed the napkin beside her empty plate. 'I don't know you. I thought I didn't know you all along. My name is not Miss Wyckham, and never has been. I've been puzzling all this time, only I didn't like to say. It would have seemed rude and, anyhow, a person can make a mistake. You've mistaken me for somebody else. My name is Cox, Brenda Cox, and I've got documents to prove it.' Her voice was becoming increasingly aggressive, dominant in tone. 'I've never seen you in my life before and I have certainly not been assaulted ... well, at least, not recently. Now I really must be going.'

She could hardly wait to get out of the front door. I ate the pudding alone, brooding on the fact that my first attempt at playing hostess had not been an unqualified success.

6

After this fiasco I became moody and dispirited. A sort of brooding lassitude came over me, which I knew to be unhealthy. At the same time it was hard to know what I could do to snap out of it. In my bored idleness I became convinced that I was the victim of a conspiracy, that somehow David had succeeded in kidnapping me, or at least had trapped me on false pretences. Perhaps he was not my son at all. But what could I do about it, to whom could I turn? The police would think I was mad. What possible motive could a man have for imprisoning a woman who was not his own mother on the pretext that she was? In any case, the doors were not locked and bolted: theoretically there was nothing to stop me leaving.

It would be no good telling anybody how futile such an attempt would be. That I had tried it once already, and been brought back. That they had closed down the railway station. That I did not know who I was, or where to head for if I did find the courage to go. I was conscious that my courage, like the rest of me, was at a low ebb.

I debated the possibility of consulting a lawyer, but decided that such a course would lead nowhere. Could I, I already heard his cool voice question me, prove that I was *not* his mother? Perhaps, on becoming of age, children are given retaliatory custodial rights over their parents, a law of which I had heard nothing because it was so rarely invoked. Did I want to be evicted for trespassing?

I realised that to many people my position must have seemed enviable. The demands made on me by my supposed family were hardly onerous, and in return I was living in considerable comfort. I found it hard to explain that I was not living at all, that my freedom to think and act had been taken from me as surely as if I had been put behind bars. More surely. Only by whom? Was David really to blame?

I turned these questions over in my mind as I watched the light fade and brighten, change with passing clouds, the trees sighing in the wind, old Sybil moving slowly and tenaciously amongst her plants, the young mother hang out a fresh load of washing on the line. I hardly went out of doors any more.

Meanwhile I became increasingly convinced that someone was creeping into the house after dark. Not every night, usually about twice a week. But the nights on which I heard nothing were probably as bad or worse than those when the dreaded noises became audible: sly treads creaking on the stairs, doors being cautiously opened and as carefully closed, the sound, like a breath or sigh, of a solid body moving noiselessly through interior space. It was more than I could bear. Now I really thought I was going out of my mind. I would lie tense under the bedclothes, ears straining for the telltale sounds. Sometimes I buried my head under the pillow and shook with sobs or curses.

I decided to take a grip on myself. I made enquiries and found out where the local public library was. I remembered that, ill or not, I had been deliriously happy during my stay at the Black Swan Hotel, in comparison to my present state of mind, and that much of my equilibrium had been due to steady reading, a constant appetite for books. I brought back as many books as the rules allowed.

But I found it difficult to take anything in. *He watched my hand moving across the page as I signed a false name and address* I read, and thought, how stupid of me, I must have had this book out before. Or perhaps I was simply reading the same pages a second time, because of my lack of concentration. I had failed to comprehend what it was all about, and could not make out the plot, even if I had read it before.

I knew my brain was becoming fuddled from lack of sound

sleep. I had thought about the police, or a lawyer. I knew I could not consult a member of the medical profession. I had a vivid recollection of the fate of Miss Wyckham, alias Brenda Cox. When I remembered the unfortunate incident with the latter, and I tried hard not to think about it, I did rather wonder why the hospital had discharged her. The poor woman seemed slightly deranged.

I know it was cowardly of me not to wait up and challenge the intruder, but my spirit was at a low ebb. On several occasions I did stand on the dark landing, sometimes for an hour or more, listening for the sound of a key in the lock in the hall-way below, but it was always on nights when I heard nothing. Frankly, I am not certain what I would have done if I had heard sounds of the secret intruder on the nights when I stood waiting in my nightgown on the dark landing, listening, hardly daring to breathe: quite probably I would have retreated to my bedroom anyhow, out of sheer cowardice, rather than face up to the situation. After all, I argued, he had never come into my room or tried to harm me in any way, and it would be foolish to provoke him. But all I heard on those nights was the sound of a mouse scuttling under the floorboards, and the occasional creak of timber as the house subsided in on itself.

Again, I considered going to the police, and dismissed the idea. It occurred to me that I had no proof that my own stay in the house was lawful. If I did not know who I was, I could not be sure who would be regarded as the intruder, myself or this phantom of my disturbed nights.

The monotony of this negative and rather dreadful existence was broken only once. No, twice.

On the first occasion the sound of the doorbell startled me, it was so unexpected, and for a few long minutes I was unsure whether to answer it, stunned rigid by a mixture of caution and disbelief. When I did open the door I was agreeably surprised to find the brush salesman from the crossroads standing on the step. It was obvious that he had not called especially to see me, nor did he recognise me now. No doubt he was making routine calls from door to door in the neighbourhood. But I clearly recalled his not unpleasant features, the gingery hair and freckled skin, and the timbre of his voice as he had asked me the way to Maiden Lane in that town to which we were both strangers.

He took it as no more than his due that I should invite him in. I smiled broadly, and his manner was one of friendly diffidence, without being in the least humble. He produced some samples from his case, spreading them out on the hall floor. I was struck by the fact that he looked remarkably prosperous for such an old-fashioned trade, tidy, well-groomed, with an air of self-assurance and a pleasing voice. He spoke well. I bought several brushes from him as a gesture of friendship, and asked him to stay for tea. To my surprise he accepted. There was something unhurried about him, as though he had all day, which was unusual in somebody dependent on salesmanship for a livelihood. We began to chat in an off-hand way. Several times he smiled straight into my eyes, but without showing any sign of recognition. Perhaps it did not matter to him, one way or the other.

I noticed him looking through the books piled up on the sideboard as I moved between the kitchen and dining room, setting out cups, bringing in a plate of biscuits to the sound of the kettle humming gently as it came to the boil.

'Ah,' he said in a pleased voice, as I brought in the teapot and placed it on the table. 'You like poetry too.' He opened a collection of verse at random and read out, quite expressively:

> '*At the round earths imagin'd corners, blow*
> *Your trumpets, Angells, and arise, arise*
> *From death, you numberless infinities*'

I heard my own voice asking him whether he was the angel of death, shivered as a sudden gust of wind hit me at the crossroads, while I stood uncertainly glancing from the funeral parlour to the railway forecourt and he walked towards me with his heavy case.

'That's wonderful, don't you think?' he said, putting the book down. 'People don't write like that any more.'

'No, they don't,' I agreed. 'Do have a biscuit.'

He drank two cups of tea, ate three biscuits, and told me that he had to be moving on. He had a lot more calls to make before nightfall.

The second time it was the telephone which rang. This was a rare event, and I expected to hear David's voice, calling me mother and demanding to be heard. I braced myself for a full half hour devoted to his problems and achievements, during which time I would also be answerable for my own behaviour since I had last seen him. But the voice, which sounded distant, perhaps owing to a faulty line, was a woman's.

'Eleanor?' the voice asked, as though doubtful about the identity of the person who had answered. I found myself suddenly shaking, my heart thudding uncomfortably. I could not think of anything to say, or whether to utter any words at all. Speechless, I clutched the receiver in my hand.

'Hello, Eleanor?' The voice sounded worried now. 'Is that you?'

'Yes,' I croaked. I felt it was imperative to say something.

'You sound very odd,' the voice went on. 'Are you sure you're all right? Has anything happened?'

'No,' I said heavily, after an awkward pause. 'I'm all right. Nothing has happened.' I was conscious of a crack in my voice, but apparently this was not audible through the line.

'Oh good,' the voice said cheerfully, expressive of relief. It now began to speak rather hurriedly. 'Listen, I can't stop now. I'll tell you all the news when I see you. My plane only landed two hours ago and I still don't know whether I'm coming or going. I don't feel I'm really here yet—you know what I mean. I just wanted to make sure you were all right.'

'Yes,' I said lamely. 'Yes. Did you have a good time?'

'Marvellous,' she enthused. 'Absolutely marvellous. I can't begin to tell you. Well, I must go. Give my love to the children, won't you.'

The word came as a shock. *Children.* How many were there, I thought in bewildered alarm, and what had become of them?

'Yes, of course,' I said quietly, trying to keep my voice level. 'Any special messages?'

'No, no . . .'

'When do I see you?' I broke in, conscious that I was not far from pleading to somebody I did not even know, and that I was determined not to let her hang up without a promise from this unknown woman.

'Well,' she said, a little vaguer now but just as vivacious, 'I can't say at the moment. There's so much to get through after all this time. You can imagine. There was so much post that I could hardly get through the door. I haven't opened half of it yet. And I've got umpteen business appointments . . . but I'll ring you just as soon as things settle down a bit and I get back to normal. Then we must meet.'

'Yes,' I said dully, 'we must.' I was uncertain how to conclude. 'Well,' I remarked rather lamely, 'it was nice of you to call.'

'Eleanor,' the voice at the far end of the line sounded puzzled. I had heard a small intake of breath before she spoke. 'Are you sure you are all right?'

'Yes,' I said defensively. 'Why shouldn't I be?'

'I don't know. No reason. But you sound odd. As though you were holding something back. You're not, are you?'

I had begun to shake again. 'I don't think so,' I told the voice. 'Not that I'm aware of.'

'Oh well, I expect it's just silly old me. Like I said, I'm suffering from time lag, or whatever they call it. I'm not sure whether I'm really here yet. And then again, I'm not sure that I've ever been away. You know the feeling.' She laughed happily.

'I know the feeling,' I answered miserably.

'Well, see you soon.'

She had hung up. The receiver purred in my hand like a satisfied cat assured of a plentiful supply of cream.

7

Meanwhile I had become increasingly convinced that my phantom intruder was no phantom. I found two soiled shirts, by no means cheap ones, in the laundry basket. Business letters, none of them addressed to me, which had been left in the hall, mysteriously disappeared from time to time. Finally common sense prevailed over cowardice and I braced myself to search the attic rooms, which I had so far not investigated, since I had no need of the space. I had several times heard noises overhead as I lay quaking in the dark. Now I found, in an attic room overlooking the garden, an entire wardrobe of men's clothes: suits, several pairs of shoes, underwear and shirts, even a dressing-gown hanging on the back of the door. The room contained a narrow bed which had obviously been slept in and left unmade, the blankets rumpled and sheets creased.

I looked for clues, though I do not know what I was looking for: I searched through pockets, examined labels, but they told me nothing and all the pockets were empty. A small chest of drawers contained some handkerchiefs and several pairs of socks, but no papers, no letters, not even a diary. I felt a sudden desire to tear the shirts, soil and rip the suits, then throw the whole lot out of the window. I was seized by a sudden rage, as it suddenly dawned on me that I was being used as a victim in an organised plot. But I resisted the temptation to do anything foolish. I knew at once that I would have to be as cunning as my adversary. Nor could I confide in David. No doubt he was not my son at all, and he had simply chosen a gullible and respectable female as a cover for some nefarious doings which centred on this house. That was why he had brought me here. It was also why he had suggested, however indirectly, that I was not quite right in the head. No doubt if I had told him about the curious noises in the night he would have suggested I was imagining things, and it was all due to my nerves.

I could not help laughing, somewhat bitterly, at the way I had been taken in. The tone of concern, but the underlying threat of Mr White. Perhaps he was not a psychiatrist at all, and I had simply allowed myself to feel threatened. I was a sitting duck during my days at that hotel. It had occurred to me that I might be part of a conspiracy, but that I might merely become an unknowing victim had never entered my head. I had been on my guard during those days, but my guarded behaviour was only the result of my underlying uncertainty.

What I did not know, and could not know, was whether I had simply been unlucky, chosen at random so to speak, or whether the whole thing had been pre-arranged. Had I been chosen long before I arrived at the Black Swan Hotel without a memory and signed myself into the register as Nelly Dean? Had I, like poor Miss Wyckham, been brain-washed in some hospital ward and then set free, apparently free, to wander the face of the earth, but really programmed in advance to do just what I had gone on to do? This, however horrifying, would have accounted for the uneasy sense I so often had, of waiting to participate in some pre-arranged plan.

What to do? That was the next question. If I had wanted to get rid of the mouse under the floorboards I would have put down poisoned traps at strategic points. But this method was out as far as the nocturnal intruder was concerned. First of all, he never ate in the house, so far as I could judge from examining the kitchen for telltale signs. Any other form of murder would be difficult, since my adversary was male and probably stronger than me physically. Besides, I would have had the problem of disposing of the body afterwards, and I did not relish any of the ingenious methods I had read about. I am squeamish about such things.

After days of careful consideration I decided that there was only one solution: to smoke him out. I had already decided that attempts to change the locks would either prove fruitless or lead to worse if unimaginable consequences for me, since I did not know my own standing in law and could not go to the police. The scheme I devised had several advantages, besides being associated in my mind with the extermination of pests and vermin, which I liked. Firstly, it could be made to look like an accident. Secondly, and perhaps more important, the action was irreversible and I would not be able, through cowardice, to change my mind at the last moment. Lastly, the intruder would stand exposed: with luck his behaviour under fire would tell me more than either a corpse or a barricaded door could ever do. If he did not make a run for it, if he was not overcome by fumes, there would have to be a showdown of some sort, and I might actually learn what all this had been about. It only needed a little silent cunning.

I forced myself to stay awake for several nights in a row, but heard nothing. I began to think that I really had been imagining things. I found it difficult to stay awake for long stretches of time, and sometimes I dozed off, in spite of all my efforts, in the small hours. However, an inspection of the attic room during the day that followed confirmed that nothing had escaped me, that nothing had been moved or disturbed, and everything was just as it had been left the day before.

I got into the habit of sleeping during the day and staying awake all night. I would doze off at dawn and become alert and wide awake by dusk. My ears became sensitive to the least sound, my eyes accustomed to the dark, like some nocturnal creature. I found those night hours oddly soothing, and I was not in the least afraid. It was as though I had finally shed any attempt to make something of my life by following a routine, abandoned all hope of a clockwork existence, ordinary or not. I waited quite calmly, sitting in the dark, listening to the sounds of nightlife in the garden and beyond. I could have sat like that, in the cupboard under the stairs with door slightly ajar, until doomsday.

But it was not necessary. After about a week I heard a key turn quietly in the lock of the front door. It must have been about four in the morning, because a summer dawn was already outlining the silhouette of the man's head as he came through the door. I could hear the dawn chorus in the trees at the foot of the garden, as I had heard them each morning. I quietly drew back into the cupboard as the intruder shut the door. I heard his footsteps creak above my head, cross the landing, then fade away up the second flight.

I waited for almost an hour, then crept up to the first floor landing. I listened for a while, but heard nothing. In my bedroom I put a match to the wastepaper basket I had carefully prepared beforehand, after lighting a cigarette from the packet in my dressing-gown pocket. Then I went back downstairs and let myself out of the back door into the garden.

I stood under the trees, looking back at the dark outline of the house, as the blue-grey sky above it began to fade to a dirty white. The birds had stopped singing. Somewhere in the distance the engine of a car broke the silence, in a nearby house a baby began to cry but stopped after a few minutes. I trod the stub of the cigarette into the ground and lit a second one, because I was nervous, and I was inwardly willing the fire to take hold. I thought that by smoking I could control myself and the situation. And all the time I was watching the dark and silent house, one of a row, heavy bastions against the dawn. Sloping roofs and lifeless windows.

Suddenly the early morning silence was broken by the jangling sound of an alarm bell. It grew louder, closer, and ceased on the far side of the dark façade. There were other sounds, men calling to each other, the squeak of rotating metal, thumps and thuds, the sound of a sash window being lifted. Several yellow lights appeared in nearby houses as neighbours had been aroused, but no light appeared in the high attic window I had been watching.

I walked back to the house and let myself in through the french window, which I had left unlocked. In the hall I found a helmeted fireman holding the nozzle of a hose. It had been unrolled down the garden path, where several more firemen stood around in groups near two massive red engines. I could smell smoke, but the house looked remarkably dry and untouched. Not so much as a drop of water dripped from the end of the fireman's hose.

I stood in the background unnoticed. The fireman was speaking to a man standing at the foot of the staircase in striped pyjamas. As I heard his voice, studied his appearance, I began to feel a tight sensation in my chest. Any words were drowned by the drumming pulse in my ears, followed by a high-pitched ringing sound. I had seen the man who stood there, in pyjamas, before. Definitely. It was my inept seducer at the hotel: George Wilkinson. The man who had vanished as suddenly as he had come.

Now he turned round and smiled at me, as though he had known all along that I was standing in the background. My flesh turned cold. I was stunned, frozen to the spot.

'It's quite all right, officer,' he was now saying in his most worldly and assured voice. 'I'm afraid my wife is very careless about smoking in bed. I've warned her about it so many times. She's an insomniac, you know. But I managed to put it out before you got here.'

The fireman noticed my figure standing in the shadows for the first time.

'I'll have to check,' he said doubtfully, and tramped up the staircase.

George and I stared at each other, without saying a word. The fireman came lumbering back down and withdrew through the front door, taking the hose with him. 'Okay chaps,' he shouted, and pulled the door shut behind him.

George turned to me again, and shook his head more in sorrow than anger.

'My dear Nelly,' he said, both condescending and reproachful. 'We nearly had a serious accident. You really must learn to control yourself and be more careful. The neighbours will start to talk.'

* * *

I am at present convalescing in a very nice place, an old house which stands in its own grounds. Lawns slope away to mature old trees, including a cedar and some very fine copper beeches. The service here is very good, if the choice of menu is somewhat limited. Still, it is a pleasure not to eat alone day after day. Everybody is very kind, and I recognise a few old faces from the past. Sybil is staying here, and still talks about her son, who has apparently been made chairman of a very important organisation.

So far I have not been troubled by visitors, for which I am thankful. I do not wish to get involved in any more plots, and I have become doubly suspicious of the motives of so-called well-wishers.

I do not read much now, and rarely watch television. Instead I spend many hours sitting in a chair on the lawn, watching nature: the changing shapes of moving clouds, leaves stirring, a wasp crawling drunkenly into one more open bloom. It has been a fine summer, but now the days are drawing in and the leaves will soon turn russet and fall. Soon it will be too chilly to sit out of doors.

Meanwhile people come to chat to me from time to time. A bank clerk tells me he was wrongly dismissed for taking some cash, that he was the victim of a plot hatched by jealous colleagues. A retired police officer tells me that the world is full of murderers. Miss Wyckham wanders for hours among the trees, and talks to nobody.

This place encourages a strange lethargy which is new to me. I sit in the garden day after day. There is an interesting variety of insects for my amusement: ants, black beetles, a curious creature with green transparent wings, the occasional butterfly. But they are getting fewer in number, and I have watched flocks of birds calling and gathering to migrate. The flowers, too, are getting fewer in number, heavier, in sombre russet shades. It gets dark early now, and the shadows lengthen across the lawn by mid-afternoon, even before I have had my tea. Dark evenings lie ahead, and the long cold nights. I do not know where I shall go from here.

ABOUT THE AUTHOR

Eva Figes was born in Berlin, moved to England with her family in 1939, and has lived there ever since. She is the author of *Patriarchal Attitudes*, an important early work in the women's movement, as well as the highly praised novels, *Waking, Light, Ghosts,* and *The Seven Ages.*

PANTHEON MODERN WRITERS ORIGINALS

THE VICE-CONSUL

by Marguerite Duras, translated from the French by Eileen Ellenbogen

The first American edition ever of the novel Marguerite Duras considers her best—a tale of passion and desperation set in India and Southeast Asia.

"A masterful novel."—*The Chicago Tribune*

0-394-55898-7 cloth, $10.95   0-394-75026-8 paper, $6.95

MAPS

by Nuruddin Farah

The unforgettable story of one man's coming of age in the turmoil of modern Africa.

"A true and rich work of art...[by] one of the finest contemporary African writers."
—Salman Rushdie

0-394-56325-5 cloth, $11.95   0-394-75548-0 paper, $7.95

DREAMING JUNGLES

by Michel Rio, translated from the French by William Carlson

A hypnotic novel about an elegant French scientist and his shattering confrontation in turn-of-the-century Africa with the jungle, passion, and at last, himself.

"A subtle philosophical excursion embodied in a story of travel and adventure....It suceeds extremely well."   —*The New York Times Book Review*

0-394-55661-5 cloth, $10.95   0-394-75035-7 paper, $6.95

BURNING PATIENCE

by Antonio Skármeta, translated from the Spanish by Katherine Silver

A charming story about the friendship that develops between Pablo Neruda, Latin America's greatest poet, and the postman who stops to receive his advice about love.

"The mix of the fictional and the real is masterful, and...gives the book its special appeal and brilliance."   —*Christian Science Monitor*

0-394-55576-7 cloth, $10.95   0-394-75033-0 paper, $6.95

YOU CAN'T GET LOST IN CAPE TOWN

by Zoë Wicomb

Nine stories powerfully evoke a young black woman's upbringing in South Africa.

"A superb first collection."—*The New York Times Book Review*

0-394-56030-2 cloth, $10.95   0-394-75309-7 paper, $6.95

THE SHOOTING GALLERY

by Yūko Tsushima, compiled and translated from the Japanese by Geraldine Harcourt

Eight stories about modern Japanese women by one of Japan's finest contemporary writers.

"Tsushima is a subtle, surprising, elegant writer who courageously tells unexpected truths."   —Margaret Drabble

0-394-75743-2 paper, $7.95

ALSO FROM THE PANTHEON MODERN WRITERS SERIES

L'AMANTE ANGLAISE

by Marguerite Duras, translated from the French by Barbara Bray

A gripping novel about a savage murder in small-town France.

"Astonishing...a small gem."—Lynne Sharon Schwartz
0-394-55897-5 cloth, $10.95   0-394-75022-5 paper, $6.95

THE RAVISHING OF LOL STEIN

by Marguerite Duras, translated from the French by Richard Seaver

"Brilliant...shoots vertical shafts down into the dark morass of human love."
—*The New York Times Book Review*
0-394-74304-0 paper, $6.95

THE SAILOR FROM GIBRALTAR

by Marguerite Duras, translated from the French by Barbara Bray

By the author of *The Lover,* "a haunting tale of strange and random passion."
—*The New York Times Book Review*
0-394-74451-9 paper, $8.95

THE WAR: A MEMOIR

by Marguerite Duras, translated from the French by Barbara Bray

"Autobiographical narrative of the highest order."—Philip Roth

"This meditation on the horrors of World War II [is] a complex and extraordinary
book."   —Francine du Plessix Gray, *The New York Times Book Review*
0-394-75039-X paper, $6.95

ALL FIRES THE FIRE AND OTHER STORIES

by Julio Cortázar, translated from the Spanish by Suzanne Jill Levine

"One of the most adventurous and rewarding collections since the publication of
Cortázar's own *Blow-Up.*"   —*Los Angeles Times*
0-394-75358-5 paper, $7.95

BLOW-UP AND OTHER STORIES

by Julio Cortázar, translated from the Spanish by Paul Blackburn

A celebrated masterpiece: fifteen eerie and brilliant short stories.

"A splendid collection."—*The New Yorker*
0-394-72881-5 paper, $6.95

HOPSCOTCH

by Julio Cortázar, translated from the Spanish by Gregory Rabassa

The legendary novel of bohemian life in Paris and Buenos Aires.

"The most magnificent novel I have ever read."
—C.D.B. Bryan, *The New York Times Book Review*
0-394-75284-8 paper, $8.95

THE WINNERS

by Julio Cortázar, translated from the Spanish by Elaine Kerrigan

Julio Cortázar's superb first novel about a South American luxury cruise.

"Irresistibly readable...introduces a dazzling writer."
—*The New York Times Book Review*
0-394-72301-5 paper, $8.95

THE LEOPARD

by Giuseppe di Lampedusa, translated from the Italian by Archibald Colquhoun

The world-renowned novel of a Sicilian prince in the turbulent Italy of the 1860s.

"The genius of its author and the thrill it gives the reader are probably for all time."
—*The New York Times Book Review*
0-394-74949-9 paper, $7.95

YOUNG TÖRLESS

*by Robert Musil, translated from the German
by Eithne Williams and Ernst Kaiser*

A classic novel by the author of *The Man Without Qualities*, about students at an Austrian military academy and their brutality to one another.

"An illumination of the dark places of the heart."—*The Washington Post*
0-394-71015-0 paper, $6.95

ADIEUX: A FAREWELL TO SARTRE

by Simone de Beauvoir, translated from the French by Patrick O'Brian

Simone de Beauvoir's moving farewell to Jean-Paul Sartre: "an intimate, personal, and honest portrait of a relationship unlike any other in literary history."
—Deirdre Bair

0-394-72898-X paper, $8.95

THE BLOOD OF OTHERS

*by Simone de Beauvoir,
translated from the French by Roger Senhouse and Yvonne Moyse*

A brilliant existentialist novel about the French resistance, "with a remarkably sustained note of suspense and mounting excitement."—*Saturday Review*
0-394-72411-9 paper, $7.95

A VERY EASY DEATH

by Simone de Beauvoir, translated from the French by Patrick O'Brian

The profoundly moving, day-by-day account of the death of the author's mother.

"A beautiful book, sincere and sensitive."—Pierre-Henri Simon
0-394-72899-8 paper, $4.95

WHEN THINGS OF THE SPIRIT COME FIRST:
FIVE EARLY TALES

by Simone de Beauvoir, translated from the French by Patrick O'Brian

The first paperback edition of the marvelous early fiction of Simone de Beauvoir.

"An event for celebration."—*The New York Times Book Review*
0-394-72235-3 paper, $6.95

THE WOMAN DESTROYED

by Simone de Beauvoir, translated from the French by Patrick O'Brian

Three powerful stories of women in crisis by the legendary novelist and feminist.

"Immensely intelligent stories about the decay of passion."

—The [London] *Sunday Times*

0-394-71103-3 paper, $7.95

THE ASSAULT

by Harry Mulisch, translated from the Dutch by Claire Nicolas White

The story of a Nazi atrocity in Occupied Holland and its impact on the life of one survivor.

"Brilliant...stunningly rendered."—John Updike

0-394-74420-9 paper, 6.95

THE WALL JUMPER

by Peter Schneider, translated from the German by Leigh Hafrey

A powerful, witty novel of life in modern Berlin.

"Marvelous...creates, in very few words, the unreal reality of Berlin."

—Salman Rushdie, *The New York Times Book Review*

0-394-72882-3 paper, $6.95

FRIDAY

by Michel Tournier, translated from the French by Norman Denny

A sly retelling of the story of Robinson Crusoe.

"A fascinating, unusual novel."—*The New York Times Book Review*

0-394-72880-7 paper, $7.95

THE OGRE

by Michel Tournier, translated from the French by Barbara Bray

The story of a gentle giant's extraordinary experiences in World War II.

"Quite simply, a great novel."—*The New Yorker*

0-394-72407-0 paper, $8.95

NAPLES '44

by Norman Lewis

A young British intelligence officer's journal of his year in Allied-occupied Naples.

"An immensely gripping experience...a marvelous book."—S.J. Perelman

0-394-72300-7 paper, $7.95

THE WAR DIARIES: NOVEMBER 1939–MARCH 1940

by Jean-Paul Sartre, translated from the French by Quintin Hoare

Sartre's only surviving diaries: an intimate look at his life and thought at the beginning of World War II.

"An extraordinary book."—Alfred Kazin, *The Philadelphia Inquirer*

0-394-74422-5 paper, $10.95

Ask at your local bookstore for other Pantheon Modern Writers titles.